THE FATE OF LENN

DYLAN MADELEY

Cover art by Jenn St-Onge.

Cover art by Jenn St-Onge

❀ Created with Vellum

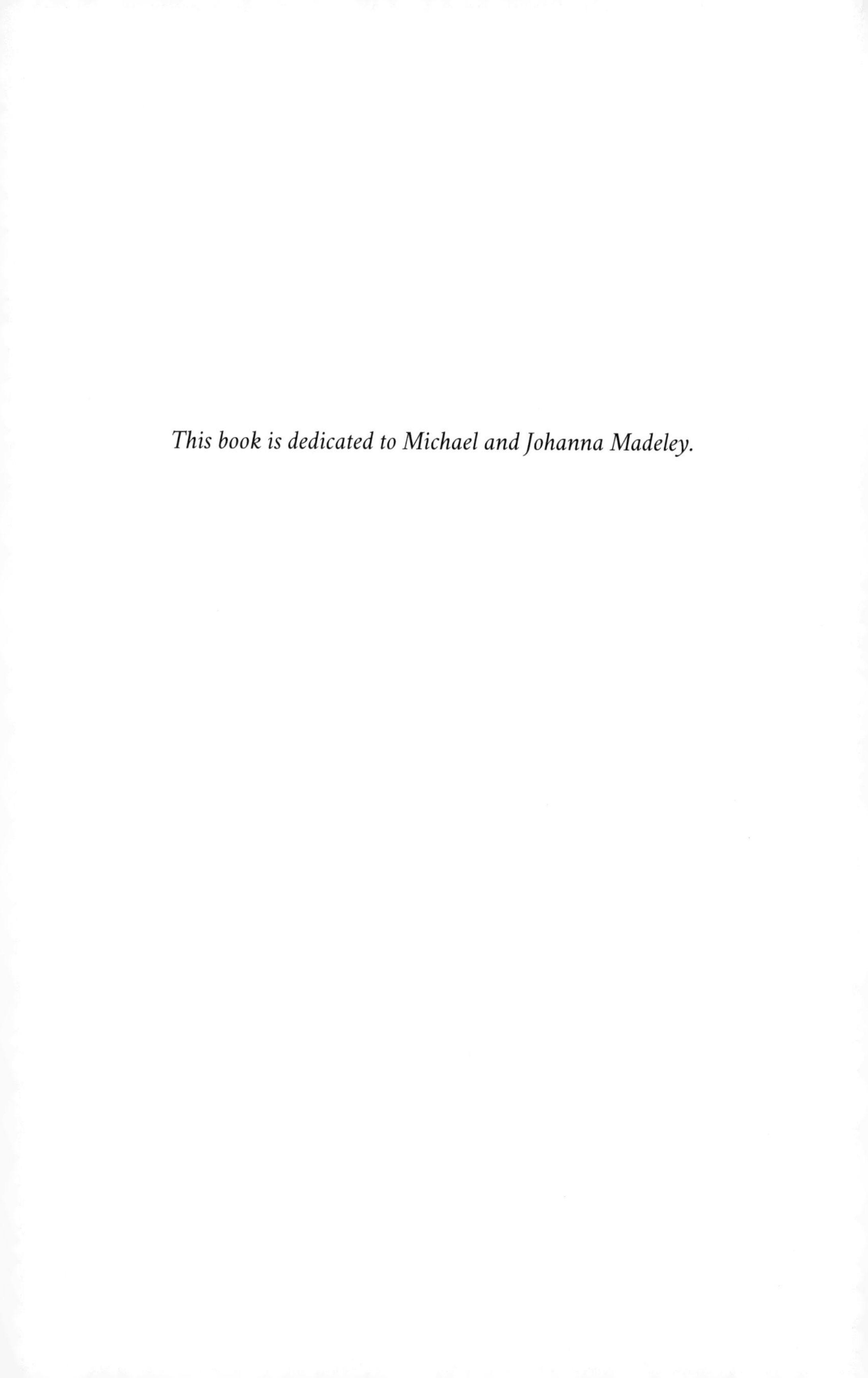

This book is dedicated to Michael and Johanna Madeley.

PROLOGUE - MEMORIES LIKE CLOUDS

Life begins with fragments of memories. Faces in broad daylight, the sound of familiar voices, and the texture he feels when quickly brushing his fingers over exquisite embroidery on his mother's dress or the engraving on a leather saddle while he runs past in play. The smell of rich earth when it's sowing time versus the sweetly fragrant fruits of the harvest. These memories are vibrant, pure, new, as a child would experience them, like the way a vigorous breeze would refresh his cheeks on warmer days.

Lenn Wancyek experiences their dulled facsimile every year as a grown man. He lives in countryside that appears little different from the front door of a Duke's manor. He sees the plains as far as any eye can, from a slight rocky hill on which that manor was built.

He knows the surrounds are kept the same by constant efforts, but they will never seem as bright as they once did.

Not without those he lost. He can only know this land as a duke with solemn responsibilities.

He remembers when his father Victor brought him to the widest fallow field, to lay on their backs and look at the clouds. There does not seem to be anybody else around. They put their cloaks down for blankets. Then they take off their shirts, lay down, and let the sun warm them.

"What are clouds, father?" Lenn asks.

Victor seems to have a perpetual subtle smile, or perhaps Lenn chooses to remember him happy.

"Great castles in the sky, cities out of reach. Not for us to know, but for our ancestors to uphold, for them to build and to display. Only breezy souls are light enough to live in them. If you were to climb the highest mountain to set foot in such a palace, you would fall."

Lenn frowns. "But what can be lighter than the winds? Even little raindrops fall down."

His father points to a hawk that drifts far above.

"Have you ever seen a falconer hold a bird? The falconer doesn't suddenly rise in the air. Some things are intimate with the winds and are upheld by them. Sometimes the winds uphold the water and other times they lend us some. They let the hawks up some of the way, but almost certainly not as high as the uppermost clouds. Everything is in its natural place up there."

"How can the winds be up there, and down here? I can feel them..." Lenn puzzles.

"Well, there are as many of them as everything has had ancestors. And they always want us to know that even though there is such a great world for them, they will never forget us. They have never fully left us behind. And one day, we all join them."

He pauses, but not long enough to give Lenn time to ask another question.

Then he adds: "But for you, that day is too far away to think about. You're young. Just stay grounded, where we live our lives, and don't get carried away."

LENN DOES NOT KNOW how much of that is memory, or how much is narrative that seems to fit, for he dwells much in his own mind. He knows that he learned about the ancestral winds from someone, likely his father. He remembers some of the questions, some of the answers. In all his travels, he has never found a field quite like that one. He often questions whether he dreamed it.

But some memories are all too real.

LENN IS SEVEN YEARS OLD. He has two uncles. One of them is King Julian, but he isn't the one standing at the dining room table, both palms pressed on its surface, while Victor sits bearing a furrowed brow. This visitor wears war leathers: panels of compressed and hardened and lacquered animal hide linked together to cover wide areas of shoulders, upper arms, abdomen and elsewhere, while a smoothly compressed gambeson reveals itself wherever the leather does not cover. Victor wears a long-sleeved thin cotton shirt and striped trousers common to other men of his Dukedom, yet understated for a man of his station.

Victor wears the same slight grin as always, but he wears it like a stoic who is at peace when faced with his duties. Victor's brother explains what exactly that is.

"Brother, we have to reinforce them now. Once that wall fort is complete, the frontier watch can take care of themselves, but they're even more vulnerable with that exposed foundation and no finished defenses," says the man to Lenn's father.

"First, remove your palms from my table. I will not have you tip everything over," Victor says with barely contained frustration.

The man blinks and acquiesces. As insistent as he might be, he stands in someone else's home.

After witnessing this humble acquiescence, Victor continues: "We've already given you a lot and asked for nothing in return. If you require such immediate further assistance, can you guarantee that the bandits haven't already toppled your defenses, or that they will not have done so by the time we assemble and ride?"

Lenn nudges the door a bit to get a wider view of the room, and the hinges of the door give a terrific groan. There was a practical reason nobody ever kept it perfectly oiled.

The guest hears this. "Who—"

"I know that's you, Lenn. Go back to bed."

Lenn quickly shuts the door and scampers away. He will

hear about this in the morning, but a quietly stern lecture is the only consequence. He cannot fully understand the context or implications of what he heard.

LENN IS CONFUSED when the victory parade brings tearful mourners. His mother Silvia holds him so tight that the thread work of her dark dress might be imprinted in his cheek, but he struggles to get away, asking again and again where his father is. Exhausted from grief, she finally lets him free. He goes on a half-stumble, half-run through the manor until he bursts through the front doorway and comes to such a clumsy stop that he nearly trips over his own feet.

Outside he sees his non-regal uncle, and several similarly dressed others, their war leathers in varying degrees of ruin, missing lamellar panels, fleece poking out of torn gambesons, some warriors nursing injuries. Another boy, slightly older and heavier set, is quickly at his side to ensure he keeps his balance.

"If you're Lenn, and I'm guessing you are, I'm Jarek. We're cousins. Well, you keep some nice gardens on these grounds, quite pleasant..." Jarek glances around.

Lenn cannot at first think clearly enough to ask why everyone, even strangers, have come to his house except for his father. By the time things fall into place, he no longer needs to ask.

A brisk wind pushes at the tears that run down Lenn's cheeks from his brownish amber eyes. Lenn reaches out wide with his arms, wishing to grab hold of that wind and not let it escape.

Jarek fills Lenn's grasp before the younger boy can fall to his knees. Lenn can hear footsteps behind; his mother followed him, but she did not run. She could never run in such a dress, even if there had been a purpose in doing so.

"You won't catch him. He's already gone." Jarek says.

"But why?" Lenn weeps.

Lenn looks away from the sombre men and sees his mother, one forearm leaned on the doorway to the manor. She isn't crying behind her veil, for she already has, she most likely will again, and no one has enough tears to shed constantly. Her mournful face holds the same answer.

"I'm sorry you lost your father. We're going to finish the Frontier Wall, now. Thanks to him, many more children will not have to feel how you must..." Jarek explains.

Lenn hears his uncle's voice: "Jarek, let the poor boy go. You're not helping. Run back to your mother, nephew; she needs you now more than ever."

Silvia opens her embrace just as Lenn runs back into it. She lifts him up, not the easiest thing to do at his age, and carries him back inside, away from the mourners and the weary soldiers.

"He did what he must, Lenn; what they needed him to do," she explains softly.

Lenn weeps incoherently. The same one-word question repeats itself in his mind, but he knows they have already answered it. No matter how many times he could ask it, the answer will not change.

Silvia gently places him feet-first back on the floor and

shuts the door behind them. Then she stoops a little to wipe his eyes and nose with a handkerchief. He no longer wishes to run outside. He feels much worse knowing the truth. But even if he hadn't run, the truth would have come knocking.

"They mean everything they say, but they can't understand how much this hurts. They will never feel his loss as deeply as us. Tell me everything you feel. I'll be strong for you now. I'm always here for you, Lenn."

LENN FELT no relief from the view he had out the manor's front door, or the sight of great hazy spirit manors drifting in the sky. He wished that fateful day were the last he ever saw of Jarek. He retreated into his library, with its walls completely covered by floor-to-ceiling maple shelves, each shelf packed with acquisitions that were sectioned by country of origin, each section arranged alphabetically by author if their name was known. He would appreciate these surrounds while he could.

He had been invited to the capital of his homeland Wancyrik for a diplomatic banquet. He initially expected it was like any other common excuse to throw a drunken social. He had to pack light and pretend to be friendly and sociable while people drank his uncle's mead and banged the rhythm to songs on royal banquet tables.

Yet his kingly uncle had invited Kensrikans into the castle: a knight who was hand-picked by Kensrik's regent, and the governing lord of Kensrik's nearest territory. A territory once occupied by Wancyrik, no less, that Kensrik took by force over the longest lifetime ago. It seemed bold and shocking that his uncle invited the kind of people who waited until their enemies were drunk after a harvest festival and had gone to their barracks to sleep, sealed their enemies into said barracks, lit the buildings on fire, and trained their spring-bows on the windows as panicked soldiers tried to escape. The territory's valley capital was dubbed Garnecht after the king who ordered this, as if such acts were something to be proud of.

But King Julian must have decided that in the many decades since an incident prior to his birth, something had changed. Something to warrant befriending these people. Lenn couldn't imagine what that might be.

Though the shock wore off, Lenn remained troubled. None of this changed his responsibilities. If Lenn kept his kingly uncle happy, this Dukedom would continue to benefit from trade and protection. And Lenn could safely read in his personal library without so much as needing a guard to watch the manor, so peaceful was his countryside. He supposed that some inconvenient task was necessary in exchange for such luxury. His family had made many deeper sacrifices than this.

1

DUKE'S MANOR

The duke's manor featured two levels above ground, a rare design in the region. Whether interior or exterior, most walls were exposed stone and mortar. Some of the comfier rooms were lined with oak panels for a warmer feel, but there were no tapestries. Lenn kept a bust of his father on a pedestal in the same sitting room that held the fireplace, which was surrounded by grey stone. A painted and framed portrait of his mother rested on the wall opposite the fireplace. When Lenn needed to work, he used the same table as he would for dining. He most often dined alone.

The manor was kept clean by a large fellow named Piotr, an outcast who had been without family or an occupation before Lenn took him in. Piotr's daily indoor tasks included dusting all the shelves and furniture, eliminating cobwebs and moving the evicted spiders outdoors, and making sure everything was arranged exactly the way that Lenn's mother had left it.

On Lenn's shelves were histories of kingdoms, cultures, wars; there were one or two works of narrative fabrication that he procured for the novelty, but he rarely had taste for them. Lenn could read and speak three languages with ease: Kensrikan, Etroukan, and his own. He knew some of the common terms spoken by people to the north-east, neighbours of his cousin, but had no practical use for speaking these languages fluently. Jarek might, but Jarek's forces were too busy waging constant war on those people to learn anything from them.

Lenn shook his head. He wasn't sure what book he was in the mood for, if any.

Piotr entered the room holding a cloth. "'Scuse me sir, here to dust the books again. Wasn't expecting you in this early."

"Nothing has had time to settle on the books. You don't have to dust them." Lenn replied softly.

Piotr fidgeted with his hands. Lenn noticed and understood.

"I realize it's important to you, but I need more alone time than usual. "

"Did something awful happen? Need me to listen?" Piotr briefly looked Lenn in the eyes after he asked, which was unusual for him.

"It's the banquet I mentioned. Every capital visit taxes my feelings, and I must prepare for it. If you can do things differently today, I'll reward you for the trouble. You can go straight to gardening. Once you are finished with that, go to the village with your better clothes and boots and buy a nice big dinner. I'll prepare a stamped letter for you." Lenn gestured toward the door.

Piotr blinked as he contemplated the correct order of activities for following these instructions. Then he smiled, showing that he understood.

"Right. Thank you, sir."

As Piotr went to do just that, Lenn got out a small clean piece of cloth, some wax to heat by the fire, and a large sealing ring which bore his family crest. The resulting stamped wax on cloth was the duke's permission for the outcast's travel. Villagers had difficulty accepting Piotr, but their Duke knew Piotr was at least as trustworthy as any of them.

It was the surest sign of status not only to grow many flowers but to have someone spend time and effort out of their day to maintain blooms meant for mostly aesthetic purpose, and to trim ornamental bushes. The manor grounds held a garden for nasturtiums, sweet violets, marigolds, and rose bushes, but it was modest compared to the herb and vegetable garden familiar to farmers. Some blooms were edible; sweet violets, for one, could find their way into a well served dinner. Victor Wancyek had the grounds arranged under Silvia's direction: subtly luxurious, understated. Lenn changed nothing about it once he took over, since he agreed with the values behind it.

The manor and its occupant family were already known, distinguished, and respected; going any further to flaunt their wealth, as they might afford to, could seem overly condescending and even insecure. It was enough that they lived in just such a manor on such grounds without constantly needing more; better to keep the duke's purse ready for petitions and settlements, sudden local crises, and abrupt new demands of taxation from the capital. The rare time there was too tempting a surplus in that purse, Lenn could always finance grand outdoor banquets or festivals, something everyone could enjoy, but he only let himself do this if he kept enough aside to prepare for sudden crises and new taxes.

And it was not just the people's duty to love their Duke. He loved them. Their ways were imperfect, sometimes stubbornly ignorant as their attitude toward Piotr would suggest, but Lenn understood that everybody had something to work on about themselves. Lenn knew that about himself.

Lenn stirred from his contemplation as he noticed Piotr returned.

The groundskeeper now wore clean striped pants and a plain cotton shirt with loose-fit sleeves, a less embellished version of what local men would wear. Piotr accepted the stamped cloth, though he still wore a slight frown at not having been allowed to dust the books. Lenn took no offense. In fact, during Piotr's tenure, Lenn had become grateful for Piotr's inability to mask his emotions. In the past, clever lower nobles had vexed Lenn by deftly misrepresenting themselves to get whatever they wanted. Piotr's manner took getting used to, but this honesty made many things simpler.

"Please be patient with others. If you have any problems, remember that all the villagers answer to me, and let me take care of it."

"I know." Piotr said abruptly, then mindfully corrected his tone. "Thank you, sir."

Lenn gestured that Piotr was free to go. Now alone, the duke rubbed his temples. Perhaps he would turn in early, because it would require more energy from him to be social at the upcoming banquet. Besides, it was never too early to sleep.

2

THE BIG JOB

Wancyrik was a land of three provinces. Two of them, to the north and to the west, were ruled by Dukes Jarek and Lenn respectively. The capital was governed directly by King Julian the Fifth.

Proximity to power made the capital province a strange and interesting place to live. Jarek's northern province revolved around barely organized expansions and the defense and reestablishment of settlements; Lenn's western province was set to farm and build surplus goods for the entire country; by the time of Julian's reign, the capital province had become a place for partying elites and their families.

Thus, whenever musicians managed to outgrow kitchen or village festivals, or began to believe that their hands should be reserved for their instruments instead of sharing time with farming implements and other tools of trade, that person went to the capital. Dreams were made or broken by the moods of rich drunkards and the tavern keepers who served them. Outsiders viewed Wancyrik as a martial land devoted to farming, war and craftsmanship, but over a long enough period of time some upper class had managed to grow.

The trouble was the lower nobles were arranged into a handful of cliques that often informed each other. If one disliked you, the others would usually join in the jeering fun. And when they disagreed, it was best to flee before you got caught up in the ensuing duel, unless you were into that sort of thing.

"You understand what's at risk, here, why I would be this careful."

Samuel felt awkward sounding so businesslike, or even remotely practical. He was a man who made his living tuning, plucking, and strumming strings, and the length of his workday was a laugh compared to western farmers; it was more like a work evening, albeit an intense one. Having gained renown for his abilities, he enjoyed a degree of leisure normally only known by noblemen.

Well, noblemen had better beds to sleep in. Samuel had long thought of himself as one tier up from a village fool in the social hierarchy. He enjoyed the best leisure that shallow pockets could afford. His plain cotton shirt and faded striped trousers and road-worn boots, contrasting with his finely embroidered round leather cap on his short-cropped black hair and his tidy walnut brown vest with indigo trim and bright embroidery, testified to both aspects of his situation. He enjoyed great pay at random intervals, the fruits of which had to be stretched over dry spells of unpredictable length.

But here, leisure and pleasure were business at all income levels. In Bayrock, a wealthier kingdom's heart, there was material trade from every known port in the world for the wealthy to spend on. But in this smaller capital, a wealthy person had fewer options. Entertainers lived on the whims of restless and demanding rich folks and people one tier below them who pretended at heavier purses than they truly carried. Both types of patrons openly wished they were in Bayrock. It was an achievement for Samuel to live on his craft for so long in such a place.

"I understand you have a pretty good thing going. Made me curious about why you would want to change anything," said Adina, the interviewee.

Samuel took a long drink. Now was the point where he had to question how much he trusted this woman. She was much talked about in the capital, for good and for bad. There was critical acclaim, but also bitter accusations from rivals that her true talent had more to do with the fit of her corset, the unique scoop of her dress' neckline, and luxurious well-kept blond hair than her singing voice. He was willing to dismiss such criticism as jealousy.

He sought a unique, powerful, and unforgettable singer. The beauty of this singer was a minor consideration for the job. After all, King Julian had his Queen, and Julian was known to be true. When Julian summoned entertainment, he was only interested in the best music. Stories had gone around by other performing artists about their embarrassment after trying anything different. Tasteful, chaste, reverent, solemn; Julian's requirements were contrary to what got you ahead anywhere else in the capital province.

"It's an important job. Well, that's an understatement, but hopefully you understand. Words are more your strength than mine. Actually, that's a part of the reason."

Adina smiled. "You landed something in the castle. That's got to be it. Only way a fellow with such courage gets to look like such a nervous wreck."

"Not so loud." Samuel quickly looked left and right. His musical career had been brutally competitive, and he knew what jealous rivals were capable of. If she had avoided experiencing that side of the life to such an intense degree, then he was the jealous one.

"I don't think we have to worry about secrecy for the King's sake. Everyone loves him." Adina replied, albeit in the requested hushed tone.

"But we might have to worry about ourselves, hmm?" Samuel said.

Adina nodded thoughtfully. "But if you're so careful, why would you change anything about what you do? We've never played together. Will we have much time to rehearse?"

"Well, an act that works great for the merchants, the lower tier of nobility... it's not necessarily the right level for the big job. One man on a stage, alone, plucking the strings? Even if he's great at it, that's not so fancy. That sounds like a show which will only happen once, and I prefer to think longer term. What might the King want to keep near him? It has to be special..." Samuel paused.

Adina nodded again as she quickly read his hazel eyes. "Indeed. Not just one man by himself."

The drink had not dulled his recognition of tone and nuance, so Samuel understood that Adina had just focused on the real problem. Fortunately, this was an opportunity for a show of faith.

"When you've gone up on stage long enough, you realize that fright doesn't necessarily go away. You learn to work around it. But this is a big job, the greatest in all the land."

"And you really don't want to go up there alone." Adina said. "Nothing wrong with that. I always say, courage isn't lack of fear, it's what you're willing to do despite such strong feelings. And that only makes you one of the bravest men, especially since you're willing to admit it."

Samuel nodded and took another big drink, emptying his cup. He was glad he hadn't misplaced his trust, at least in the short term, but his stage fright extended to any conversation where someone had the power to deny him.

"Well, have we passed each other's trials?" She asked.

"I understand that you work in a duo?" Samuel changed the subject, but it was necessary.

"You understand correctly. Judit plays a sort of brass reed thing, of their own making. It's very unique, nothing quite like it. Unique in the best way, of course."

"And is there a particular reason they're not with us this moment?"

Generally, when an interviewee didn't show up for a social trial, their application was forfeit. It was quite different to have someone apply on condition that they didn't have to show up. Did Samuel even know this Judit was a real person? Against his usual procedures, he had agreed to the condition. Adina had come well recommended by others; he was too busy doing his own work to watch every tavern all the time, so he relied on such advice.

Adina adjusted her posture ever so slightly. "Judit has an even greater fright than," she avoided saying *you,* "most anybody. But when they meditate on it, save up their energy, it drives their best performance. Even to be here and see you judging them with your eyes, however unintentionally or gently, would be an exertion. We're already preparing for the next show, you understand."

Samuel blinked and let the decision simmer on the cooking fires of his mind. Then he looked Adina in the eyes in a most direct and challenging way.

"I like you, and I want to trust you. So, you work great as a pair; you know how I work solo. Tell me now whether you believe, whether you can even imagine, the three of us bringing our methods together to make music fit for this opportunity."

"Can you?" She redirected.

"I can go so far as to say we two could do something, but we need that third. Since Judit can't be here, I need your absolute confidence. I need to be sure you believe this can work, not just once, but perhaps many times, because I'm not interested in having a poor outing, even if it's well-compensated."

Adina thought on this for a long moment. "I think we both need another drink. I'll pay for it."

Samuel raised his eyebrows. "Take your time. And sorry for putting you out with big questions, but you know how important this is. You understand that, right?"

Adina was dissatisfied with the way the conversation was beginning to circle, and Samuel didn't appear as if he would add anything new to change that. It was up to her to take the reins.

"Well, how urgent is it that we answer your questions? You haven't seen us perform together. Might you be able to attend that Market Square show I mentioned?"

Samuel drummed the table with his fingers briefly before suppressing the nervous habit.

"How soon is that? Because I can bring any band to the royal court that I want, but as you earlier and correctly guessed, we only have so much time to rehearse."

She reached across the short width of the table and gently patted his right hand. Her palm felt so soft that he wondered if those hands had ever seen a day of hard labour; perhaps calluses were more common in the western dukedom he once called home. From the contrast between the light beige of her hand and his brown skin, he wondered if she saw much daylight, either.

He reasoned that her voice did all the hardest work and accomplished enough for her these days. She might also come from money, but nothing was wrong with that; it happened often in the capital.

Two things mattered most. First, she was kind and considerate. Second, if the critical acclaim was accurate, then she embraced the necessary and difficult work that earned it.

That made all the difference. He believed they would have to work hard, and he expected they would test each other's patience while doing so.

"The show is tomorrow night, actually. That's lucky for us, isn't it?"

He smiled at her gesture as she withdrew her hand. He

interpreted the pat as a friendly action taken in the hopes of calming him down; some people were just very physical. She hadn't been talking like it meant anything else. Samuel was not the kind of man to reach for other interpretations, nor was he after such experiences with women.

He let out a quick chuckle. "The job is many days hence. I may live from day to day most often, but I plan better than that when it counts! We should have enough time." Admittedly it was less than he would like, but he kept that to himself; he preferred that she treat the upcoming show as an audition. "Provided it all works out well, yes. When did you put the word out? I must have been too absorbed with deliberations. I always hear about your work; I just tend to have jobs of my own keeping me out of the audience."

"But you *are* free, yes?"

"I have no other commitments. I made sure my evenings would be clear in advance of the big job knowing this will pay off either way, but not wanting to do other shows while preparing for this one."

Adina smiled sweetly. Samuel the fleet-fingered, a much talked about musician, there specifically to watch her and Judit? A modest but notable accomplishment.

"It will pay off. And please don't worry; it'll be the best thing anyone has ever seen."

"Will it be unique in the best way?" Samuel grinned; he appreciated her enthusiasm.

She laughed and leaned back a bit. "Just watch our show. And at the end of it, tell me what you imagine we could accomplish. I'll trust your judgement."

"So, how will rehearsal work with Judit, provided we do

work together?" Samuel thought that was the one biggest question he couldn't answer by watching the duo.

Adina understood. "In a private setting, just the three of us? No problem. But never forget that the only person who gets to carry Judit's instrument is Judit. Don't take a polishing rag to it, don't touch it, don't even propose to hand it to them. It's sacred. They'll almost certainly work with anybody who can respect *that* rule."

Samuel nodded as he watched someone bring them their drinks.

"Well, if nothing else, this should be an adventure," he said.

3
THE GOVERNOR'S DAUGHTER

Willem den Holt, Lord Governor of West Kensrik, wondered if his daughter Zinnia felt uncomfortable dressing this formal. He would love her no matter what, but given the nature of their imminent visitors, he was quietly thankful to see her rising to the challenge. Her impeccable white high waisted dress with a light purple stripe banding it like a belt would have distinguished her from the labourers by itself.

Indeed, that was not all she did to look like a lady. The elegant yet confusing mass of braids and coils into which her black hair was pinned and tied would be considered too time consuming to be practical for a worker. Of course, it was quite a lot for this particular lady; she would usually keep it in a simple ponytail if it needed tying at all. The healthy shimmer of the hair from regular honey treatments would have stood out by itself.

On top of all that, she was trying to paint her cheeks and

lips with bright Kensrikan pigment powders. Sitting in her study, she had made repeat attempts with a warrior's determination and a master painter's subtlety. She no longer seemed to mind if he stood at the entry of the room and watched this latest iteration with a slight smile of understated pride and curiosity.

"It makes no difference," he said as he watched.

"No difference to whom?" Zinnia asked.

At her age, she was beginning to sound like her mother had back when den Holt was first installed as lord governor. Zinnia's mother had served his late predecessor, and it made sense to keep such an adept person in the manor instead of training someone new. Den Holt could thank that woman for too many things to recall, and he adopted her daughter to ensure Zinnia would be raised as a noblewoman.

But he suspected if Zinnia knew anything about their visitor, she would relax her efforts. He would let their guest represent himself when the time came.

"Well, if I remember correctly, Sir Wolter could buy us a second city with the gold baubles dangling from his jacket; can we expect him to be impressed by any effort we make?" Den Holt asked.

Zinnia winked each eye at her reflection as she tried to determine how well she had done with her eyelids. She expected her father to be too kind if she asked, yet no one else was around.

"'We must make an effort, lest he fail to tell us apart from anybody else on the streets of our city.' That's what you told me. But really, this is fun. There's never a reason to try on the pigments you gifted me, and I may as well practice. I think I managed to make this work for me. Do you?"

He took a closer look. He realized that she managed to blend the powders well, given how the pigments were formulated. He couldn't imagine anyone else would do better in a mere day's efforts, however intense.

"You look like the finest oil painting."

"I look *oily*?" She asked with feigned indignance, knowing what he meant.

"Please don't try so hard for Sir Wolter. I would hate for him to ask for your hand."

Zinnia groaned and looked for a cloth in case she needed to dab or smooth anything. He had unintentionally put the possibility of excess in her head.

"They do go for the heavily made look in the Kenderley palace, but again, the last thing you want to be is married to Sir Wolter. You can and should do better," he said.

"So, it looks caked on? I thought I blended it better than that."

Den Holt patted her shoulders. "Don't touch it. It's great, actually, and it would be a shame to ruin it."

She paused for a slow breath. Whether he was too kind or completely accurate, she was running out of time. "The way you carry on about this Wolter, I have to wonder why you would invite him here. Surely a more pleasant person could represent the House of Lords."

"All business, all trade, my dear. He has been to our destination before without us and established the very rapport that got us invited there. He must be quite useful in the highest of courts, or else someone would have plucked his feathers by now."

Lord den Holt stopped at the sound of signaling horns from the front entrance.

"Well, at least one eye matches the other," Zinnia mumbled.

"Take your time. We can make him wait."

"I don't wish to wait."

Zinnia turned away from the glass mirror backed with gold leaf and peered at her father. His attire mimicked local wear, but the white robes that went down to his sandals were embroidered with a stripe of intertwined gold and purple thread in a manner that locals would never do. His hair was shoulder length. A governing lord's medallion dangled over his chest from a thick gold chain around his neck.

In brief, he wore what he usually would. She was unsurprised and slightly jealous.

"What are you impatient for? What do you find so exciting about our rustic northern neighbours? It's not even time for one of their seasonal festivals. My offer to send you to Bayrock still stands. There's much more to see. You would love it."

"We already agreed I'll go there for my studies. Once I do, it could be years before I'm free to visit anywhere else. Wancyrik is much nearer, quicker to visit, quicker to return home. You know I want to see the other side of those mountains. And now that we're welcome..."

Zinnia smiled and hugged her father.

"And are you in such a hurry to send me away, when we could make this journey together?"

His heart softened to be held by this woman whom he had raised with the sincerest of fatherly love. He loved her as he loved the people of this land.

"I will protect you, as long as you need me." He replied.

It was something he had promised her when she was young and frightened by shadows or bad dreams. He would protect her from dragons, from sea monsters, and from Sir Wolter.

Not that he expected she would need much help with the latter.

BY HER FATHER'S DESCRIPTION, Zinnia expected a silk-feather rooster to strut out the door of the ornate enclosed carriage. This was not the case, though Sir Wolter's attire bore some slight resemblance in its accents of fur trim and other decorations. He wore a brown tricorn hat with a bauble of gems and small feathers dangling from the rearmost two points. Peacock feathers pointed upward from a rear fold where they had been affixed, and they bobbed a bit as he turned his head to look around. His jacket's base colour was hunter green, but this was overwhelmed by a combination of bright shimmering threads and furs, such that the furs looked like they were fighting to burst out from a fisherman's net of thick woven threads. Behind him flowed a blue cape with gold trim and sequins. His feet were clad with wooden soled boots that looked like they were recently painted with a cloudless sky.

"Luttwig, get the brushes out," he called to a page, "I know I'll get dusty just standing around in such a place. Dry season, indeed!" He brought out a finely embroidered handkerchief and sneezed into it.

"Sir Wolter, welcome to Garnecht, the City in the Valley." Lord den Holt gave a respectful nod; it was an odd situation where the lord outranked the knight, yet the knight was closer to the seat of highest privilege.

After glancing with a frown at the freshly soiled handkerchief, folding it up and pocketing it, the knight cast a circumspect glance at the surrounding buildings, and once again at the governor's manor. "Well, it's an interesting use of stone. I know we would protect our own; are all these surrounding buildings fortifications, though?"

"Homes and other necessary buildings for the populace." Lord den Holt explained. "The lumber around here is slim and knotty, and it would take quite a lot to build a manor. I believe in offering them something sturdy, and establishing a durable presence for our empire as well."

Wolter gave a disapproving sniff. "And when in your letters you mention the fresh air of your province, have you always referred to the stench of freshly laid dung?"

"We can rest inside for a time; we'll burn some herbs in a dish, if you like." Invited the lord.

Zinnia suppressed her gut-crawling disapproval of the visitor. Their streets were tidy for they knew exactly what to do with waste, or they would have died of disease long before the misfortune of being occupied. For the spirits they burned traditional fragrances that were rich and earthy and beautiful. She was torn between being brutally offended and laughing at his ridiculousness.

"Yes, I should like to stretch my legs, and my back. Travelling over such a rough road can jostle one so!" Sir Wolter said.

"Here," the knight offered his cape to Zinnia as he passed, "I grant you the privilege of holding this cloak, probably worth more than everything you own."

"No, I don't believe that I will." She replied with feigned calm.

Wolter was taken aback; den Holt suspected no one typically dared to address him like that.

"This is my daughter, Zinnia." Lord den Holt said.

The knight rapidly blinked a few times. "Yes, the one you adopted. My apologies, and may I say, miss Zinnia, your command of our fair imperial tongue is uncanny. Almost like a proper lady."

"Almost?" She asked.

Lord den Holt quickly gestured for a servant to take Wolter's cloak, distracting the knight before the conversation could escalate. The servant then led the lord and the knight toward the door. "Now, Sir Wolter, you can't assume anything about different people. What if I told you, they built everything you see? Once they were shown the tools, they took to stone masonry with great aptitude."

"Well that just cannot be," argued the knight as they entered the building that served as both the Lord's Manor and the seat of regional governance.

"How do you think it is that the South came to be civilized first, if the locals are so adept?" Wolter asked.

Zinnia shook her head slowly as she watched them walk ahead. She once thought her father had descended into hyperbole when warning her about Sir Wolter, but Willem den Holt had once again been too kind. She didn't think her father was capable of accurately describing the man she had just met without several terms considered too crude for noble parlance. Was this the kind of person Bayrock tended to produce? If so, it was better to avoid the place.

Den Holt gestured with his palms turned up in front of him as if offering an invisible gift. "How easy is it to build one's world up when others constantly knock it down?"

"Oh, that old line. Listen, Willem..."

Now Zinnia was concerned that her father was serious when he warned about Sir Wolter pursuing her for marriage; she had the legal right to decline, but her father would face social repercussions for that. Then again, Wolter's biting disdain was not the attitude she expected anyone to show to the person they wished to marry. Perhaps his prejudice would spare her from his pursuit.

She briefly reconsidered the notion of travelling with such a man; trapped in a carriage together for an unfamiliar length of time?

But there was more to her desire to visit Wancyrik. Lord den Holt was not the only one with business to conduct. It was for his good, as well as her own, that everyone believed her purpose was recreational.

ZINNIA LEFT her father to entertain Sir Wolter at the suggestion of the knight, who seemed increasingly uncomfortable with her presence. She was glad not to have to hear that infuriating conversation any longer.

She gave a cursory nod to the guard at the entrance who was supposed to alert her father if anything unusual was going on, like Zinnia leaving home at strange times. There was no guard, nor any person in all West Kensrik, who would have complied with keeping Lord den Holt informed. Their loyalties were to Zinnia and her cohorts who met under cover of darkness. Telling the truth to a pawn of House Kenderley would set no one free.

Let no one think that Zinnia did not love her father.

She loved him and had no complaint about his fatherly duties, nor did her true people have much to say against his style of governance; if they did not love him as she did, they found him soft and easy to forgive. Amidst the gradual material abandonment of House Kenderley, he looked to the local populace for all the labour required to build their city. He trained them to be guards so that he could send the scowling Kensrikan bowmen home and afford to pay everyone, to start the local economy going albeit at a trickle. He cracked no whip nor forced excessive work time on any labourer. He took care of them, taught them, looked out for their safety, much as he had done for Zinnia.

The problem was not his style of governance, but the fact that he governed at all, and on whose behalf he performed this task. He was the friendly middleman between Zinnia's people and the strong-armed empire that invaded this land with alarming brutality. Nobody had thought they would miss being ruled by Wancyeks until King Garnecht Kenderley rode in with his banner a lifetime ago.

But this was not about whether they preferred to be ruled by brutal Kenderleys or indifferent Wancyeks. Nor was it about choosing which imperial agent one preferred, between the ignorant Sir Wolters or the caring Willem den Holts, for they were at bottom two faces of the same creature.

The dusty streets were quiet at night, and there was not a cloud to be spared to cover the bright moon. She had no trouble navigating to the Council Round.

THE COUNCIL ROUND was a circular stone structure built around the ash circle where clan business was traditionally discussed. Given that other, taller buildings had since been built as multi-family housing, the Council Round was perfectly unassuming. Lord den Holt could easily mistake it for a granary, or some other mundane thing.

Inside the Round, the dimly lit gathering of people broke flatbread and passed around severely bitter herbs meant to purify the mouth prior to speech. Stone workers, farmers, and matriarchal leaders of extended families linked elbows for a soft recitation of a traditional prayer to the Hands of the Creator after having prepared their mouths to speak sacred words. It took intimate social familiarity to understand who the leaders were by sight alone, for most wore similarly styled kaftans and cloaks; not all of these were the same colour, but they were tinged with the same street dust.

And now, to business.

"Our grain stores have never been greater." Said the overseer of the granary, the full supply not truthfully reported to Lord den Holt.

Added the livestock counter, "Great rain brought plenty of

grass. It would have been hard to hide so many head of cattle from plain sight; thankfully, the lord appointed me to the task for a reason."

Roc, a tall younger adult of the council, rubbed his hands together. "So, it sounds like we can feed ourselves without having to beg or trade. Well, what are we waiting for, then? I propose that we take these imperial minions hostage and send our independence declaration immediately."

"You've proposed such hasty actions ever since we first convened!" Zinnia retorted. "It's almost as if you look forward to some sort of bloodshed, as opposed to our much better plan."

"Well, you're soft on your old man. Practically half Kensrikan..." Roc countered.

"Now, we've discussed and settled the matter of Zinnia's privilege," said Glyn, elder matriarch, with reserved sternness; she knew the sorcery of making sure everyone listened to her words without ever having to be the loudest in the room.

Glyn continued: "Nothing has changed in our plan, nothing is known that would make us reconsider it, and it seems nothing changes the impatience of younger men. Zinnia, feel free to remind us of why taking the knight hostage, however enticing, would disrupt our plan. He seems to have forgotten."

"I need to accompany him to visit Wancyrik and see what they might be plotting." Zinnia said.

"We shouldn't have to worry about them," said Helynn, a bald man older than Roc but younger than Glyn. "Don't they send wave after wave of riders past their own defenses, into the north? They raise warriors only to throw them at a never-ending failed conquest, they've done it for years. If that had ceased, people would be talking. I've heard no such whispers. And if they tried to send a suitably sized army past Etrouk, well, the Etroukans would have something to say about that."

Zinnia saw no threat in this added questioning. She knew Helynn wanted to understand any reasoning with which he hoped to agree. That was always his way, to phrase and ask the simple questions that might be on everybody's mind. Others valued having an established and respected voice ask those questions.

Zinnia explained: "We have a representative of the Kenderleys, on a formal diplomatic mission to their rivals the Wancyeks. The lord mentioned to me that Sir Wolter had even been to Wancyrik before, that he has a rapport; such cordial relations between them developing in a short time suggests something suspicious to me."

"That does beg investigation," Helynn concurred.

No one asked what the Etroukans would do. Both Wancyrik and Etrouk boasted massive walls which had never been breached. The difference was that the Wancyeks kept riding past their wall, and they suffered for their efforts to hold what lay beyond. Etroukans let their wall do its job, because history taught them that however formidable their soldiers and cavalry might be, they were vulnerable when they rode out. Whether that made Wancyeks bold or foolish by comparison depended on who made the argument. Some would call them the world's boldest fools.

"What would they be plotting to do?" Asked Roc. "It must not involve us. They have no knowledge of our plans. We're a peaceful flock of sheep to Kensrikan eyes."

Zinnia paused to blink, then leaned slightly toward the council fire, as if being more visible would lend more force to her argument.

"What if the Kensrikans planned to send most of their forces far enough away that they couldn't handle any disruption here? Through reading the lord's messages, I understand that Kensrikans have for years been anticipating an attack from kingdoms on the opposite side of the empire from us. They consider it a matter of time and some of them are even impatient to strike first. And suppose House Kenderley wants to ensure their old enemies wouldn't invade during that time; not only that, perhaps they would even pay them to watch us, if they suspect our plans. I should learn as much as I can."

"Once again, the Wancyeks aren't going anywhere south of their border without alarming the Etroukans. I see no need to take hostages, frankly, but I have yet to hear why we should worry enough about this to investigate," Helynn reiterated.

"But it would be great to confirm if the Kensrikans are actually turning their attention far away, would it not?" Glyn interrupted. "And while we speculate, it's strange to think that Wancyeks would ever help Kenderleys; on the other hand, what Zinnia learns could put this speculation to rest so we can agree on a path forward. Would the Wancyeks support our independence in order to sting their old foes without lifting a finger? There is much to be learned, and possibly gained, by this trip."

"I would approach that last idea with caution. We don't want to trade one occupier for another." Zinnia said. "But I think we should discover what they're up to, and what Sir Wolter might be plotting with them."

"You're right. And you are already set to do this; it would arouse your father's suspicion if you suddenly asked to remain at home." Glyn supposed. "Are there any relevant objections to letting Zinnia continue on her scheduled mission?"

Roc's glare at Zinnia wasn't formally considered objecting, so there were none.

"Then, Zinnia, run back home, before the lord notices you are gone. We have no further matter for discussion directly concerning you."

4

TRAVELLING COMPANION

Duke Lenn owned no carriage. Instead, he rode Slugger, a horse bred for combat, strong enough to bear armour with ease but fast enough without it. This horse earned his unusual name from the rough treatment afforded the first person who attempted to train him. Lenn had been the first to successfully ride him, starting the rumour that the horse could instinctively determine the noble character of a person. Lenn doubted that was the case, believing noble folk to be better dressed but not always better-read versions of commoners.

The choice of name respected the horse's fierce will. To do otherwise was demonstrably perilous, even for Lenn. He was certain that a lack of respect from the first trainer had caused the regrettable incident that earned Slugger his name.

As was common for a western rider, even a duke, the horse was packed light with durable fabrics and leather. Fine and bright embroidery was the traditional decoration. While some dwellers in the capital preferred decorative accents of gold and gems in recent years, Lenn would rather honour tradition. If he needed Slugger to sprint away from trouble, packing light could make all the difference.

"It must be an odd life for you, Slug." Lenn said, using the nickname he had privately adopted for the horse. He dismounted and led the horse to a lush clump of grass.

"Some part of you must expect to ride into certain peril at any moment. Yet here you are, ferrying me to the capital at a canter. Life is strange."

The horse grunted a bit and flicked his tail before he began to graze.

Lenn patted Slugger. "Just enjoy it. Believe me."

Years ago, Jarek taught Lenn all about the difference between nobility and goodness. He did this by example.

RAIN HAD BEEN A GREATER foe to that journey than any bandit. The paths Lenn's riders could traverse were dotted with patches of muck deep enough to get a horse stuck, but outside these uncertain patches and ruts were murky flood-paths of indeterminate depth.

The group rode through it, anyway, expecting firmer earth by the time they reached the village that had purportedly become a bandit camp. In fact, the conditions were one reason they expected no ambushes. Warriors on foot should have as rough a time navigating the muck and would not be upon anyone quickly.

Lenn coaxed a priceless and beautiful horse through these

grim surrounds. Eugen had been even-tempered and easy to train, a dependable mount with which Lenn was most familiar. While that seemed like a great rationale at the time, the creeping sense of dread that made Lenn grip the reins ever so tightly also made him reconsider his choice.

This was his first outing beyond the Frontier Wall. As a duke in his prime, Lenn was invited by Jarek to witness first-hand the kingdom's expansion. Lenn knew the invite was a family obligation in disguise; the King wanted Lenn to visit his cousin and to help the effort while he was there.

Lenn knew that seeing the wall which Victor had died to protect would stir long-buried sadness within him. He failed to consider that the farther past the wall he went, the more vulnerable he would feel. At least he didn't have to do it alone.

They neared the village, which became more and more visible despite the mist of the constant light rain. Lenn frowned with disbelief at neat rows of enemies already kneeling with hands behind their heads. The bare stick-and-straw structures that could have been houses remained intact, but the bandits appeared subdued, while an advance party of Jarek's foot soldiers stood with readied weapons.

"We are one sword!" Duke Jarek saluted from standing.

"Cousin." Lenn returned the salute, and observed, "I thought you wanted my help, but it seems you've gone ahead and won without me."

Jarek's dark brown hair must have been slicked back with oil under his helmet so that not a lock of it would get in his eyes. Any polished sheen to his cavalry helmet was dulled and tarnished; any colour to the threads and tooling of his battle leathers had long been made filthy with blood, muck, and who knows what else. Everything immediately past the wall seemed to get that way, and it would take more than a constant light rain to clean.

Lenn hadn't seen this cousin of his since Jarek had told him of Victor's death. With age, his childhood bulk appeared to have reshaped into muscle. Something about his eyes looked more threatening, as if they too were weapons, especially now. The falling buffe of his helmet was at its lowest leaving his sly grin uncovered and his ability to shout orders unencumbered.

"Well, you took some time to get here, and we found so few of them. We took the initiative."

After this explanation, Jarek reached to Lenn's saddle-belt and grabbed a helmet-cracker, a sturdy metal club about two hands in length designed to wreck armour.

"And now for your contribution to the victory."

"Jarek—"

Before Lenn could ask why his cousin had stolen his weapon, Jarek split the unprotected skull of one of the kneeling hostages in a single downward blow.

"There, cousin, your first kill!" Jarek struck another. "And your second. Here, now that I've demonstrated how easy it is, you can do the rest. I insist the remaining blows must be yours."

Jarek crossed back toward the speechless Lenn, who remained on horseback and couldn't determine how to phrase several questions about the brutality he witnessed.

Then a stone loudly glanced off Jarek's helmet. Lenn instinctively turned his horse around and drew his sword, looking for the source of the projectile.

Several bandits on either end of the path through the village, heads topped with grass piles, faces smeared with muck, had risen out of murky waters for an ambush once they were sure somebody important had arrived. They bore slings and reached down into the water for further stones. Lenn had no idea how they weren't sinking into that soft earth, let alone the projectiles they retrieved, but there was no time to find out.

The foot soldiers keeping watch over the hostages rushed to the shallows, leather-braced left arms protecting their heads from a pelting of stones, right arms wielding swords. The soft muck inhibited their rush to hack down the ambush party. As soon as the soldiers were halfway to the slingers, every hostage stood and rushed into different thatched huts nearby.

Lenn quickly raised the buffe of his helmet just enough to protect his mouth while leaving a broad slot through which to see. He drew his sword and eased forward slowly while the half-unit of elite riders who had escorted him formed a corridor around Jarek to protect him from stones. It was not long before the former hostages emerged from the hut with worn-looking swords and clubs.

After seeing two hostages struck down without provocation, Lenn had wished they would flee, evidently to no avail. While the first few rushed toward him from the huts, the other riders staggered their formation and made sure Lenn's flank was as well protected as Jarek. More attackers were on the way from outside the village. It was uncertain how many more.

Every nobleman was taught how to fight, but Lenn was

about to find out whether those lessons worked on the field. He had no more time to wonder.

The first few came at him with a fanatic's vigour. Lenn cleaved one; decapitated another; struck a third from the right shoulder clean through to the spine, then planted one boot on the body and desperately tried to kick his sword out from it. His motions and responses deeply ingrained, he only acted, for stopping to think would be fatal.

Lenn just barely freed his blade in time to skewer the fourth attacker in the throat and take another mighty hack to finish the kill. He could feel the blood churning within him. Let it churn, provided it would not escape. Not like that which left his attackers.

No other attacker made it past the staggered gauntlet of cavalry.

Now Lenn had time to think if he dared. He drew down the buffe of his helmet to let his hot breath escape easier. He saw the last few slingers hewn, their bodies dropping into what was now red water, while Jarek's soldiers taunted their victims and joked like this was a night at the tavern. He had time to observe how much cunning these fanatics were willing to put into a doomed ambush. It was as if his mind wanted to lead him away from slaughter and toward problem solving.

The only problem he solved was to distract and calm his hard throbbing heart.

Jarek emerged unharmed from his spot amidst the rider formation; his helmet was dented, but not to a concerning degree. "You'd best return on the path from whence you came.

They may have further traps set up ahead. If there are archers..."

Lenn hastily wiped his sword before sheathing it. If only he could wipe away the stain on his mind.

He thought, briefly, about Victor. But now was not the time for his father's kind smile.

"I'll gladly ride out of here, cousin, and never come back. Is this war, now? Is this butchery how Wancyeks fight today?"

Jarek laughed. "If that's your attitude, it's good for both of us that you go. They all wanted a piece of you, and I must say those four you did were expert kills. So a couple fewer had the chance to grab weapons before you killed them; what's the difference? Would you rather have given them a trial?"

Jarek casually strutted up to Lenn and offered the helmet-cracker back to him.

Lenn snatched the club. His full lips tightly pursed in rage, he glanced thoughtfully at the dent in Jarek's helmet. He pictured making an even deeper dent of his own, but this act would help nothing even if Lenn had it in him to try. He threw the helmet-cracker into a reddened filthy mud puddle.

"Let it sink. And same to you, for all I care." Lenn spat into the puddle where the club rested.

Jarek let out an incredulous laugh. "Do you know who those prisoners were, cousin? Do you know what happened to settlers, caught unawares in their homes? I think if you did, you'd not show such softness for them. You'd not hesitate to dispatch them in just such a way."

"Yet you hesitated, Jarek: you waited for me when you could have just killed them before, if they were so dangerous. When uncle tasked me with joining you here—"

"That same uncle tasked me with making sure you went home safely. I agree with him, your life is too important to sacrifice to these bandits, but what did he expect me to do?" Jarek gestured at Lenn. "Look how you react to a minor skirmish."

Lenn could not help but glare with moral indignation, even if it was wasted on Jarek; his words boiled like his furious blood. "Remember when you told me my father perished so that many others could be spared? How many are saved by that frontier wall when you constantly venture beyond it, and with such carelessness?"

Jarek sighed and waved dismissively. "It's back to him, again, is it? As if he was the first and last person who ever needed to make a sacrifice in this world. You're just an overgrown boy weeping for your father. Maybe you'll never be anything else. Well, go back to your gardens that we warriors make real sacrifices to protect. Thank you so very much for your help!"

Lenn sat for a moment on his horse, appalled by the flippant attitude displayed toward the death of such an important person, and toward so many other lives. He had witnessed nothing that protected his home or his people in any meaningful way. If he was angry enough before to imagine provocative things, he was too angry to picture anything clearly now.

Eventually, after a long deep breath came and went, Lenn's words came out cold. It was not like his anger meant anything to Jarek.

"Then tell our uncle about the four I slew in my own defense. They fought an honest fight and died clean. No games, just like how we ought to do battle. Everything you did with that helmet-cracker is on you. And if you set foot anywhere near my garden, I'll duel you."

"I wouldn't worry about that." Jarek cracked. "Your province is for farmers and basket-weavers; mine is for proper Wancyek men."

Lenn stared into the hollow where Jarek's soul should have been.

"There's nothing proper about you anymore. You've been fighting bandit kings so long, maybe you'll lose your mind like old Garnecht."

Lenn turned his horse, sparing no further glance at his cousin. He had seen enough.

Jarek bristled at being compared to a Kensrikan, and such an infamous one at that, but he held his tongue. He turned to organize his men as Lenn's riders escorted their Duke away.

After the incident in the north-east, Duke Lenn rode to the capital without further detour. He wanted to make it to his uncle's throne room before any human messenger, though he knew he could not likely outpace a messenger bird. His companion riders offered to escort him, but he dismissed them to their homes, to recover from the skirmish. He told them that he felt he was responsible for making this journey alone.

In fact, he wanted to be away from other people. The only dark side to persons that he wanted to see was the matter of his own thoughts. At least he knew himself well enough, and he could see his own good intentions. It was difficult to say the same for Duke Jarek.

"Eugen, I'm going to retire you..." He mumbled to his

horse, after the silence away from other human voices had made his dark thoughts grow deafening.

"You've seen enough. You've gone through enough. I have my duties. But you're a show horse, or perhaps a farmer's horse. Graze on green pastures and be patted on the nose by children. I shall find myself a war horse. I'm sorry, you were never bred to go through that."

The horse whinnied nervously as the main road of the capital province widened and became the main street of the capital itself. Here were people pausing their daily tasks to wave at him; here were the busy sounds of barter in the markets, and the laughter of children. Things which he felt should make him happy, but today they only made him guiltier for his inability to feel better. He hoped this would pass.

He slowed the horse to a trot.

"It's the good Duke from the west, come to visit," he overheard from the villagers outside the privileged inner city.

Now he felt like the timid Duke; he wished he had dueled Jarek. King Julian would never have forgiven it, and there was no standing law allowing Lenn to kill Jarek out of a general dispute, but somehow the law of the land didn't feel good enough.

But the law's potential to serve what was right had not yet run dry, he hoped.

The gate through the inner city's wall was open and barely guarded. The moat-like canal had only a stagnant ankle-deep collection of water left over from the previous night's rain; there were mechanisms to fill it on shorter notice if necessary. The drawbridge could theoretically be lifted, if it had not become stuck in the down position over years of not being used; the portcullis, at least, had been seen working sometime within the past year.

He rode past the finest dressed people in Wancyrik, many dressed finer than the duke himself; after all, he had not changed clothes since the skirmish, merely letting a light rain wash off what it would. They regarded him with amusement. Given that no one else in the west had nearly his status these days, it was easy to guess who he was. Oh, the agrarian west, so rustic that even their Duke looks it! Ladies in their finely embroidered wrap-around skirts curtsied for him. They hoped, seemingly in vain, that he would take an interest; they imagined him in the better clothes that they could likely afford to buy for him right that moment without even the windfall of marrying a Duke.

Meanwhile, he barely had the presence of mind to make sure Eugen didn't kick anybody. His square jaw clenched as he considered what to say to his uncle.

The servants at the stables were wide eyed at his unexpected arrival.

"It's the good D—"

"I request that Eugen be put to pasture, to stud, some sort of peaceful retirement." Lenn interrupted. "And I would like a new horse, bred for combat."

The stable master blinked. "Very well, I can pass your request along to King—"

"If you need his assent then I'll ask him myself. I'm going to see him now. Rest assured he will approve, just see to my request immediately."

The servants looked to each other, wondering why Lenn seemed so abrupt.

"Excellent." The stable master nodded. "Would you like anything else? Perhaps you would like someone to clean your riding jacket, or get you a new one...?"

"No thank you."

He wanted to wear his feelings, so that he would need fewer words to describe them for King Julian.

Once inside the castle, he made his brisk way down the hall, looking through doorways, until a servant began following him.

"Excuse me, greetings Duke Lenn... is there something I can help you with?" The lady called after him.

"I seek my uncle."

She continued to follow him, since he did not stop. "Oh, the Great King is in the smaller dining hall with our lovely Queen. It might be prudent if you waited for them to finish their dinner. Perhaps a bath can be arranged while—"

"I shan't be long. Go back to whatever you were doing. It's not like you can stop me." Lenn was glad he had been heading in the right direction and did not have to alter his route much.

She stared at him for a moment, appalled at his tone and condition. But there was nothing else she could do except return to her duties.

As Lenn approached the family dining hall, which was the more private and less banquet-oriented dining hall, he saw the guards at the door and understood the servant to have been correct. He mentally rehearsed what he would say again and again as he approached the door.

He looked, just *looked*, the guard away from the door. Lenn was at once too trusted yet too menacing to be stopped. To be fair, Lenn had not been seen with such a grim disposition, combined with such aggression, since he was a child. Servants and guards alike were speechless. Nobody knew how to react. Knowing Lenn's reputation, they couldn't imagine his anger would be directed at the regent.

"Uncle, we have things to discuss." Lenn said as he trotted into the dining hall.

King Julian was startled enough to spill mead on to his meat, not that the meat hadn't already been cooked in a glaze of mead to begin with.

"Nephew. I'm glad to see you return, but it's no cause to barge in here like that..."

Lenn did not reply. Knowing his uncle's gradually failing eyesight, he just continued to approach the dining table, and gradually slowed to a stop at a distance where he thought Julian could better make out the details of his nephew's appearance.

Monika, whose eyesight remained much better than her husband's, stood before Lenn came to a full stop.

"Oh, by the winds, by the storms!" She rushed over and hugged her nephew, caring nothing for what might rub from his battle leathers and jacket to her exquisite dinner gown.

"What happened, nephew? Forget that. I'm just glad to see you alive..." She said.

King Julian remained seated. "Well, I see now you likely have a story to tell, perhaps worth the suspension of manners. Monika, you're excused, you'll not likely enjoy what our nephew has to say."

Monika broke the embrace and glared at her husband.

"I'll judge that for myself," she said.

Julian raised his eyebrows, looked down at the table and nodded. "Yes, I suppose you will."

He gestured to the table and returned his gaze to his newest guest.

"Well, both of you should sit, then. The food's still warm; I'll summon more mead." He gave a resounding double clap in the direction of the kitchen hallway entry.

While they waited for the mead, Lenn recounted the unfortunate incident with Jarek in not particularly graphic detail, preferring the tone of his words to say what was left implied.

Julian listened attentively and took a thoughtful sip of freshly poured mead after it arrived.

"Young man, did I ever tell you the story of why I only have nine fingers?" He asked.

Lenn nodded. "Many a time; you were a young man yourself, during the Uphill Battle..."

"The last time we fought the Etroukans before the Settlement of Borders. If I hadn't stumbled back, I would have lost my head. 'Twas a grim day; streams ran red to the nearest village, they said, though the constant flow of water cleans itself in time. As will the constant flow of time cleanse your thoughts; it cleansed mine," Julian smiled kindly.

"Yet did not all who fought at the Uphill Battle, fight evenly armed and in equal exchange? And those many who died, can you deny that they did so honorably?" Lenn asked.

"I always knew you to be a sensitive boy, nephew. Don't

think I was about to throw you into an experience like my own." Julian said.

Monika brought her cup from her lips to a hard stop against the table. She let out a heavy breath that said well enough what she thought of this revelation. Then, she stormed out of the room; she had stomached Lenn's tale bravely enough, but not her husband's apparent complicity.

Julian's gaze followed his departing wife, though Lenn's eyes remained locked on Julian.

"It's strange how much she worried about your safety, only to become cross with me for doing my best to guarantee it," Julian muttered once she was out of earshot.

Lenn narrowed his eyes. "So Jarek was right about that. You knew. And you also knew he would have no qualms about it."

"I didn't hatch this plan," Julian raised his hands defensively. "I knew Jarek well enough to trust him to think of something. I can tell you right now that I deeply regret how things have gone."

Lenn stood. "You know who he is—*what* he is—and you let him remain a Duke?"

Julian stood and took Lenn gently by the shoulders.

"Men like him have their uses, nephew. They stop at nothing to win wars. They lead armies, and they become broken in battle and perish. And good men like you get to take the throne, in due course."

Julian let Lenn shrug off the feeble grip. The nephew judged his uncle with a fierce stare.

"And what would you leave me to rule, in due course? A

kingdom of muck and bodies, and beasts donning the battle leathers of men?"

"I wish you the world, nephew. I hope you understand that."

Lenn departed toward the stables, without having eaten a bite or drank a sip, shaking his head with bitterness. This time, he was the one without a reply.

Julian returned to his seat. Seeing that his cup was empty, he saw that Monika left half a cup and Lenn had not touched his. He finished theirs.

MANY YEARS PASSED until the first time in living memory that House Kenderley would send representatives to Wancyrik. The dukes of the realm were invited to greet and dine with the visitors.

King Julian was known as a quiet and prudent monarch. His servants considered him firm but fair, and they had no complaints about being able to live in their own separately built wing of the castle in return for their best efforts. Living within those walls was a status symbol among the working class.

"Here we have a matter of balance," he instructed to a servant who had a small cart full of shallow charcoal-lined dishes and a bag of frankincense.

He continued: "We are about to have guests who are obsessed with an otherworldly cleanliness, gilding everywhere... we can't change who we are, and we shouldn't, but we can show them a version of ourselves which they find more relatable. Your task, fortunately, is for aromas rather than scrubbing. So, you want to foster a noticeable but light aroma in every single hall of the castle. If you make the scent too pungent, too overpowering, you've made our castle dirty to them. But if you don't mask some of the damp, again, they will consider it dirty."

"No doubt, Great King," the servant replied, slightly confused.

"What we might normally burn in a dish for a festival, put only half that, this time. Once at dawn, and again at dusk; this spreads out the fragrance, makes things more even. It's a lot of running around, but they will only be here for parts of three days; two dusks, including the first where they will only have arrived."

"It's never too much running around for you, Great King." The servant bowed. "Do you, perhaps, intend for me to begin at dawn, on the day when we expect them to arrive closer to dusk?"

"Yes, my thoughts exactly. Otherwise, if they arrive before dusk, they arrive before the start of your task, and that leaves us exposed."

He left the servant to the task and continued his once-around-the-halls, walking past the scrubbers who removed soot stains, and the carpet cleaners, and those who swapped rug furs for fresh ones. This was a pleasant surprise for the servants, as this overseeing was typically done by Queen Monika. However, she knew about private matters of which King Julian's subjects and servants were altogether ignorant, and her absence was meant as subtle disapproval of the guests. With his poor eyesight, he was a less demanding master.

Julian let his countenance be pleasant, not needing the servants to whisper among themselves. As he returned to his study and bedroom, he would not be able to keep the ruse up around Monika.

He made sure the guard shut the thick door of ancient wood behind him before he turned to face her scrutiny. His sight could not make out the finer details, but she wore a simple light-yellow gown with a high neckline.

"Ah, my Monika. Are you feeling well today? Anyway, thank you for making sure I got my daily exercise with added purpose. I'm not sure why that was necessary." He forced a smile.

"Are the servants well into their tasks? Good. Let's not hide the proper value of this castle before you sell it to the Kenderleys," she replied, her tone not nearly as sharp as her words.

He found a chair and sat down before this familiar conversation could take the legs from under him.

"What would you prefer that I do? Any fresh ideas, perhaps, since the other twenty times we've tread this same ground?"

"Ah," she paused as if mentally counting every instance for herself and preparing to correct him, then retorted: "What is it that you told me those other twenty times? It must not have been particularly memorable."

"Well, I'm not going into it again. If your memory's beginning to fail you, I can always send for a doctor."

She knew full well what he planned, and his rationale.

House Kenderley had been behaving more aggressive of late, showing off their armies and newly crafted weapons, and building up their fleet to the point of harassing and boarding the occasional merchant ship. The belligerent King Jonnecht looked to expand, and there were a few directions he might consider. He could look to the east, which was likely, since the Eastern Kingdoms were no doubt staring right back at Kensrik and clamoring for a fight. But he could look to the north if he were so ambitious. King Julian wanted to appear as friendly and accommodating, yet also as well-prepared as he could to discourage Kensrik from attacking him.

"I remember. I just wanted to look into your eyes as you went over your plan and see if you still believe your own absurdities."

"And all the while, not offering the slightest practical revision or better idea."

"Is it wrong to have feelings and to trust them? To be in touch with intuition? Nothing good can come of this, Julian. This concern you have about the Kenderleys smacks of fear. We can't govern based on what frightens us. Your people need courage."

His tired mirthful grin returned. "Tell me where courage comes into play."

"Ignore the Kenderleys. Let their aggressive attitude lead them into something foolish and humbling. If they really dare to strike us, be ready to teach them a lesson they'll never forget. Don't do anything that might make us another one of their provinces."

"But I'm doing no such thing!" He whined. "Let them have no real case to make for coming here. The Eastern Kingdoms will most likely make war. No matter who wins, it should cost both sides greatly enough that they will need more than a lifetime to rebuild. We can maintain peace and stability here for our people."

"Of course. And Lenn can read his books, Jarek can play his war games... what if the Eastern Kingdoms are all bluster, Julian? What if Kensrik overruns them? Where do you think they'll look next; Etrouk, then us?"

Julian grinned sardonically. "What if the winds fall silent, and no longer bear the contents of the sky, such that the sun falls to the land and scorches away all life? Who knows what tomorrow brings?"

Monika looked down and sighed.

"Does my wife hate me?" He asked.

She went to him and brushed a lock of his long grey hair away from his face and looked into his eyes.

"I love you, Julian. I can't deny my feelings. For the same reason, I can't deny how wrong your course of action feels or hide my disapproval. I'm sorry if that hurts, but I will not be silent, either."

He leaned his forehead into hers and shut his eyes.

"And your feelings mean so much to me. If there was good cause to die for you, I would," he moved back and looked into her eyes once again.

"I'm not asking you to die, Julian."

"But good cause is exactly my point. I can't govern solely from feelings. Sometimes we must do things which don't feel entirely comfortable, but in hindsight we're grateful for them. Are you going to abandon me, Monika?"

"Never. But neither will I be false with you. I married a fool."

He nodded. "And you'll never let him forget it."

"Never."

WHEN LENN ARRIVED, far in advance of the diplomatic banquet with Kensrikans, Julian stopped what he was doing and warmly greeted his nephew, as he had made a point of doing every time since their years-past memorable argument about Jarek.

"Welcome, nephew. So good to see you again. I had the private library restocked..."

And ever since that unforgettable argument, every time Lenn saw his uncle, he saw the questionable future promised by an untrustworthy man.

5

A SHOW IN THE MARKET SQUARE

Samuel was concerned that his presence in the crowd would upstage the duo of Adina and Judit. He supposed this would be an important test: if the duo couldn't get more attention on stage than an audience member, however well known he might be, then the three of them wouldn't make a balanced trio. He didn't want to take the stage as *Samuel and his backing band*. Everybody performing for the King and Queen needed to be relevant or, he reasoned to himself, they shouldn't be there.

There were tables and seats available in this venue, not all of them particularly clean or in the best repair, but serviceable for the drunks. Samuel chose to stand; he didn't want to feel trapped between tables and chairs in case he needed to get away.

His instincts were validated by the one who found him; an old flame, his biggest fan...

"Hey, Sam's here," said Maryana, a shorter woman with a fox pelt draped over one shoulder of an impeccably kept traditional dress: a white long-sleeved blouse with a high neckline, a red full skirt down to the ankles embroidered with a floral pattern, a black vest bursting with vibrant embroidery and beads.

They had a history, indeed; only people who knew him well got to call him Sam, though he wished she wouldn't. He thought he had been clear that he didn't want anything to do with her, but like many in a particular generation of lower nobles, she took his denial for a challenge. It was a disturbingly common attitude to encounter, from what he witnessed and heard, yet Samuel had the good fortune to avoid it with this one exception.

Perhaps Maryana told the others she had already claimed him...

"You playing tonight, Sam? 'Cause that wasn't what got announced. I would so love a surprise performance. " Her rings tapped lightly against the half-empty cup as she adjusted her grip.

He didn't make eye contact, but he had to respond. The last time he had tried flat-out ignoring her, he eventually felt that fox fur tickling the back of his neck. That guaranteed his attention and a shudder that rippled the length of his spine.

But what could he do? She once boasted that her father was part owner of the venue, and not just this one. Samuel might be famous enough to get away with telling off any other patron in the city who caused him stress, but she was a troublesome exception.

"No. I'm not. And please call me Samuel." He replied with a perfunctory smile as he finally dared look at her.

There was nothing wrong with how she looked. Her red hair was intricately braided, and the braids were held up into a tremendous bun with many silver pins. Her eyes always looked wide and expressive, with the help of a generous application of makeup. Her lips were fine, likely kept in excellent shape with a common beeswax balm. Her complexion would be alabaster even if she didn't powder her face for good measure.

He imagined she could make someone happy, if only she had not become obsessed with him.

"Well, but that's even better! Then you're here for fun." She drew close to him.

His insincere smile made for an ineffective shield, but he would not let it down. "Might I introduce you to the concept of personal space?"

She gave a soft laugh. "It sounds dull, and a lot like you playing hard to get. I know you've kept your fingers nimble, *Sam*. We can make a duet later, hmm?"

"I'm here for business, actually. Someone recommended these performers to me, and I need to listen for myself. Mind leaving me be?" He gently replied.

She drew away from him, but gave one last look up and down while fingering the pendant of her necklace. "All right then. Your loss."

He nodded in a gesture of frank gratitude for the reprieve. She walked away like she wanted his eyes to follow her. They didn't. He knew from experience that this invited her return.

He supposed it could be worse. He didn't owe her any money. Owing people, from his observations, could be a dangerous thing to do. Provided he made enough money, he never let himself want more, never let himself get indebted and never let himself become the captive of anyone's plans.

The freedom to pursue life on his terms was priceless. It could not be borrowed or paid back. If he were ever to compromise that, it must only be for the biggest job he could imagine.

He could think of one. Fortunately, she had no part in it.

Temporarily spared, he looked around to see who else he might recognize. There were a good number of other party-goers, since life in the capital province was one long series of parties for restless privileged folks and the grown-up heirs to whom they gave money. However, Samuel was rather old to the eyes of most of them; they knew who he was but had little interest in him. He kept a quiet count of the attendance, a task which was never complete, nor would it bother him to lose count; this kept his nervous mind busy.

THE MARKET SQUARE was a venue right next to the actual market square, neither of which were particularly square except by a loose definition of the shape. No one got confused by the shared name, because colloquial speech differentiated the market where one bought and bartered from the square where performances and other festivities occurred.

The venue was oblong, and the narrower space was the stage and what lay behind it. There, Adina was bickering with a couple of brush and powder wielding people about what shade went with what, what was too much, what was too little, and who shouldn't interrupt the diva during her vocal warmup if they didn't want to compromise the performance. For the duo, this job was made most important by the possibility of landing the biggest one. Adina would let nothing slide.

Judit took a different approach. Their hair only needed to be brushed, and their light olive complexion was miraculously even to begin with. They wore a simple white gown with an understated traditional wraparound skirt, all of which was intended to be easily overlooked. Showing off was for Adina, who respected Judit's needs.

But this quieter half of the duo showed no stress before the show. Here was a sort of brass and wood and reed device they had invented, inspired by instruments from a distantly remembered homeland, and here were the keys to turn, the bolts to tighten or loosen for tuning, and while they were intensely aware of the instrument and what it needed, the anxiousness they felt about imminently being watched and judged by a crowd could wait as if suspended for a time. The task at hand was comfortably all-encompassing.

When the maintenance was complete, they interrupted the powder-and-colour argument.

"Adina."

Adina put her palms against the mouths of the others and gave Judit her undivided attention.

"Give me a low."

Adina sang the lowest note in her register. Judit internalized it and nodded. The others left to take care of other matters.

"Give me a middle."

The singer presented a standard note from the middle, a tone that felt like one of her most common.

"And a high."

Judit listened to each note, got their bearings, and adjusted the tuning of their instrument accordingly. There was no standard tuning in Wancyrik; if you were a vocalist with an instrument, you tuned it to yourself. A duo learned to tune with each other. Judit had no problem inviting Adina into their world because Judit didn't have much of a vocal range, and Adina's voice went well with the instrument. More to the point, Judit made sure the instrument went well with Adina's voice.

Then Judit went through a couple of different scales, while Adina listened intently.

"Sounds good to my ears. We ready?" Asked Adina.

Judit smiled. They could not be readier.

"GEN-TLE-FOLK!" Bellowed the announcer, which brought the crowd to near silence.

Samuel shifted his weight from one leg to another. Finally, the moment of truth.

"The Market Square is proud to present the duo you've all gathered to hear and see, The Famous Songbirds."

Before the audience had any chance to cheer or clap, Samuel began to hear sounds of a most unusual texture. He had travelled around every dukedom of Wancyrik and heard many traditional instruments, but what he heard seemed entirely new; ethereal, otherworldly. The smaller person whom he deduced was Judit commanded this instrument, the sight of which confused him; was it more like a large flute with a bell at the end, or a long-bodied trumpet with innumerable keys and attachments? He knew no direct analogue.

Samuel had no time to process whether this new sound was good or bad before Adina followed in with vocals powerful and resounding and pleasing to the ear. The music went beyond commanding his attention, transporting him into the melody and the words, such that his usual hyperawareness of the surrounding crowd was gone. There was, for a time, neither others nor self, only a landscape of sound with no audible percussion, just an implied rhythm. Their set was undoubtedly of a top tier act's expected length, but it seemed to end so soon, as if they had determined the precise moment they could finish to leave the audience wanting more.

Now he knew why this duo came so well recommended.

SAMUEL'S MIND wound out of a euphoric daze as he made his way toward the backstage entrance. It took some presence of mind not to strut in there like it was his show; sure, everybody recognized him, and they might just let him in, but he needed to be polite so as not to walk in on performers changing out of costumes. He made clear his business to the door guard, a man of dark brown skin with a friendly smile whose size and stature were likely enough to deter trouble.

The guard opened a slot in the door and had a brief hushed exchange through it, then nodded to Samuel and let him know he would not have to wait long.

As Samuel waited, Maryana approached, emboldened by further drink.

"I know you were moved, love. You stayed. Has your cold heart been thawed?"

"The diva will receive you, sir," interrupted the huge guard.

She stopped. "So *that's* how it is."

Samuel peered at her with waning patience. "Do you ever stop?"

She nodded slowly as she glared. "Then I have proof, after all. You're a liar. You went on about only liking men, but you're here for her."

He clenched his fist; at first, he felt too angry to speak. That was a low accusation for her to make. Then he quickly found the words.

"That's definitely *not* how it is. I told you this was business."

She narrowed her eyes but smiled, satisfied to have gotten such a reaction.

"Sure it is. Even if it was, you know I have a deeper purse than some town musician. And that's not all there is to me, either. You've looked at me often enough to know that. What is your problem?"

"Do you know this woman?" Interrupted the guard.

Maryana pointed at the guard's face. "You'll stay out of this if you want to keep your job. My father's a shareholder in this venue."

Samuel interjected: "Don't threaten him. He's just confused. I'm the one telling you to go away!"

She was taken aback by a tone he had not dared to use with her before.

He felt like his whole body was shaking inside, both from an anger that forced its voice and a suppressed but internally screaming fear of the repercussions. He loudly continued: "How drunk must you be to insult me like this, calling me a liar about a fact so personal, and actually expect to win me over even if I was to be won? All you've made me do is regret ever having met you!"

Her mouth was agape and her left eye twitched as she absorbed the disrespectful tone and attitude from someone whom she viewed as below her, a prospective pet. How dare he not be grateful for her attention?

"Well, I know who to talk to about you, *Sam*. You can forget ever playing the Market Square again—or anywhere!" She crossed her arms and stormed away.

The guard looked at Samuel with concern.

"Friend, I'll let you escort me off the premises after the meeting. It should save your job. But let's not keep the diva waiting. I promise this should not take too long," Samuel explained. He might already have taken all the heat off the guard when he drew away her ire, but it was impossible to tell.

The guard glanced about with an exasperated sigh and let him past.

Now there was no going back. The castle might be the only venue in the capital that couldn't be poisoned against him by an heiress spurned.

* * *

"So," Adina said, "what did you think of the show?"

"Well, you have something excellent going on. You sure you can fit me in with your act?" He smiled.

Judit was quietly packing their instrument into its case, all the while paying close attention to the conversation.

Adina laughed. "You're a funny one. Really, what did you think of the show?"

"I've never heard anything quite like what you do, so I don't think we'll know how it all flows until we try."

"Well, it's your big job, not ours. Are you sure you want to take a risk?" Adina smiled. "I suppose if it falls apart on stage, you can ask after that admirer I heard you with. She would probably take you back and take good care of you at that. But then it's not about the money with you, is it?"

From her expression, he suspected this was a test. He could imagine how a similar conversation would have gone for her in the past. People who said it was not about the money didn't rule out the other simple possibility: sex. The discomfort he felt at the hands of Maryana might just be a taste of what many others tried with Adina.

His smile vanished quickly. He knew what he was about, but they had only recently met.

"We have a history, me and her. A past she'll keep trying to make present," he began.

She stared and waited. Did she expect a hilarious anecdote?

"I was younger at the time, and I hadn't quite settled into the realization that I like to be intimate with men, exclusively at that. And it's really the caring and connection I want most, not patronage. I already make decent enough money. Maryana refuses to accept that; she takes it all quite personally."

Judit nodded, believing every word of it from experience.

Adina blinked at the revelation. "You've trusted me with a lot, already. You can trust me with that. And I suppose that helps you a bit in my estimation, not having to fend you off. Or having to worry about Judit."

"Frankly, even if I didn't just like men, I understand what boundaries and consent are. I would still be a good enough person for you not to worry about, wouldn't you agree?" He asked.

"Of course—I've had a great impression of you all along."

"And am I right in supposing that you don't have similar motivations to my former friend out there, and you've been honest about your ambitions?"

Adina shifted uncomfortably. "You would be right, yes."

They paused for a moment, no one entirely sure where to go next.

Samuel broke the tension: "I'm sorry if I sounded upset. I feel like that was important to get out of the way, am I wrong?"

"I understand. I'm glad each of us knows where the other is at. This all sounds good, but I need to confer with Judit. And I believe you promised the door guard a quick meeting?"

"You heard correctly. Yes, I had better get going. Thank you for your time."

After curt and respectful nods, one to Judit and one to Adina, Samuel departed quickly.

Once he was gone, Adina breathed a sigh of relief, then remembered to look to Judit for final approval.

"Well, he's quite all right. A bit abrupt, but we're practically strangers, each made cautious by experience," Adina reasoned.

"I'm not worried about him," Judit replied softly.

6

ARRIVAL IN WANCYRIK

When Zinnia first entered Sir Wolter's carriage, her eyes watered from the floral perfumes dabbed everywhere.

Her primary assurance with riding in there was that her father accompanied them. This was just as well; there was only one carriage anyway. It was meant to be cozy, plush, warm, a different world than the outside one with muck and winds and horse droppings on the roads. To Zinnia, it was as if nobles with the wealth of Sir Wolter could afford to make everywhere a nursery, insulated from all else.

Luttwig was wedged in the seat next to her, since according to their papers, both were traveling as servants.

"That's one way to get family to travel with you on the cheap," Sir Wolter said with a sniff. "Very shrewd. Of course, my lovely bride Loren would never stand for being documented as a servant."

Willem den Holt exchanged subtle knowing smiles with

his daughter. It was both strange and telling that Wolter had taken so long to mention his ostensibly beloved wife, but Zinnia might breathe a little easier. If only the overpowering fragrances would let her.

Zinnia peered at Luttwig; this poor youth, having to follow Sir Wolter around and do his bidding. She wasn't sure she would accept any amount of money to do the same.

The freckled boy smiled at her nervously. He blushed and looked away. He was trying not to look like he enjoyed this as much as he did.

He failed, but she appreciated his attempts. He was young; he would learn. At least she wasn't wedged next to his boss.

Wolter continued further, his life's greatest skill being the gift of prattle.

"Not that I could really justify it, if questioned. Loren doesn't appear the type for service, nor does she have any particular skills. But your daughter, as I understand, can speak at least two languages, and looks fit to change a carriage wheel. And, given her look, she *certainly* fits the servant type—though a high class one, understand. What else have you taught her to do?"

Willem knew he should let Zinnia answer this herself. It should be her fun to have, if only there could be no negative repercussions. Willem was far too nice to say what should be said, and that's why all he cast her was a knowing glance.

Zinnia could construct arrows and a bow sturdy enough to hunt. She could sling a hawk out of the air and had once done it on the first try. She could wrestle most opponents face down to the ground within a count of ten. She wanted to relate this all with an air of warning, but she knew that wasn't the type of answer Wolter sought. Especially when her people were not supposed to learn how to hunt or fight. So she said nothing.

At her silence, Willem stepped in. "That credit should go to her mother; I only taught her reading and calligraphy, and hers has become better than mine. My daughter knows a breadth of manor upkeep activities and, I suspect, several traditional activities considered sacred by her mother's people."

Wolter frowned. "But that should all be below her station. Loren would never have approved such activities for any daughter of ours; what if she got sunburnt or scarred? I suppose you do it all differently out here, on the bleeding edge of the empire."

Willem pre-empted whatever barbed retort he could detect forming on Zinnia's tongue. "I preferred her education to include a healthy appreciation for all the hard work she would not have to do, so that she might be kind and considerate to our helpers. I was raised by such values in Bayrock, after all; there's nothing bleeding edge about it."

"Kindness?" Wolter adjusted his tricorn. "That makes for soft servants. They need austerity, and to feel the heaviest hand the moment they get out of line. It keeps them well-conditioned and vital."

Zinnia gave Wolter another quick glance, hoping she didn't look too doubtful to his eyes. "Is that how you became a knight, Sir Wolter? Service in austerity?"

Luttwig stifled a chuckle.

Wolter glared at her. "I hope that's not sarcasm I detect."

Willem intervened with his gentle voice. "I believe her

question is to be taken at face value. We have never had a knight visit, nor have we discussed the tradition often."

"Oh." Wolter said with a huff, not entirely convinced. "Well, it was difficult work, daughter-den-Holt. Strenuous and difficult work, which I shall not explain to *you* because I doubt you would understand or appreciate it."

Zinnia smiled sweetly and nodded in response. She doubted that he would last a single day following his own guidelines of service. Her father had, in fact, explained the ephemeral nature of Wolter's title.

Perhaps the King's friendship was a difficult and strenuous thing to live through.

Luttwig, who seemed fine stealing glances at her when she was not looking back, beamed with admiration. She could not read quite what his background or social class were, but he was not entirely foolish for his years. It must not have been admiration which landed him this role serving Wolter.

She didn't look Luttwig in the eye, but she smiled more sincerely for him. She expected her present face to live in his imagination for a long time.

"That's one thing I can respect about Wancyeks, Wolter mused, clearly eager to get away from the topic of his qualifications. "They can be downright rustic, but they're never far from hard work. They've stayed vital. It's the one noteworthy virtue they have."

Zinnia wondered if this worldview came with self-loathing or whether he considered himself exempt from his own expectations.

Wolter continued: "Can you imagine if they were our vassals, Willem? We could have them at the front of our army, striking the enemy hard before heavily armoured ranks move in to clean up; no one would stand in our way. Better than having to fight them..."

Zinnia sighed and looked out the small carriage window as they continued along the mountain road. The early part of the journey had been a consistent and gradual climb, but after that it was mostly level, sometimes hugging the mountainside where they had to go around a peak. This road was so vital to traders that it was kept two carriages wide and decently level by local workers who were paid by the nearest government or a prosperous merchant's guild. The window might show Zinnia distant valley landscapes, but she could always see the edge of the road which was never too close.

Their road soon intersected with another that went further up the mountain. Zinnia believed the massive walled city of Etrouk lay in that direction, but all she could see was the road winding up the mountain side until it was out of view. She knew very little of Etrouk, which was not much less than most others knew. Aside from their merchants, they were an isolated people, most of them content to live behind the outer wall of their capital and make the luxurious cloth that would line the very carriage in which she sat or make a cape for Sir Wolter. Etroukans were supposed to be related to Zinnia's people in some distant and unclear way; she thought the Etroukans must not care much about this connection, for they never once visited her father. Even their merchants would sooner head north to Wancyrik or set sail for Bayrock than travel through her homeland.

Unfortunately, this carriage ride still had a long way to go. Once they were past the mountains, they still needed to cross south Wancyrik to reach the capital. She hoped they would pick up the pace once they were heading downhill.

* * *

"YOUR PERSONAL LIBRARY, GOOD DUKE," the servant announced upon opening the door.

Lenn glanced quickly around the familiar space; a small shelf, but one with different tomes stocked on each visit; a long-cushioned seat that only saw use when he visited. He noted where the dust had managed to collect. It was nowhere obvious to the average pair of eyes, but diligent Piotr had trained Lenn up to higher expectations.

"All looks well," Lenn said with an approving nod before he heard hoofs and many men echoing from outside. With a look of concern, he went to the window to see what the matter was. Then he turned back to the servant.

"Was Duke Jarek summoned to this banquet?" Lenn asked.

The servant nodded quickly. "As a matter of courtesy, the great King Julian did not want to exclude him from receiving the Kensrikan visitors."

Lenn ran his fingers through his hair. Of course, for something as important as this visit, even diplomatically useless Jarek had to be invited.

"And is there a reason Jarek must travel with so many of his cohorts?" Lenn expected this question to be treated rhetorically.

The servant saw Lenn's agitation and shrank back a little.

"Well, uh, I think they won some sort of victory recently..."

"I doubt they come here to get drunk every time they burn

a few huts when they can easily do so back home. And having Kensrikans witness Jarek's bunch is an *excellent* way to make us seem friendly."

"I have no say in the planning, sir—"

"I don't expect you to. Don't mind my frustration; this is a private matter between nobles."

Then Duke Lenn snapped his fingers.

"I know a way you can help. Send a messenger bird to my home province and see to it that my riders get here with great haste. They have less than a day before the banquet. Mention Tibor specifically, and he'll surely find the others."

If Jarek was allowed to invite guests, Lenn ought to have the same privilege.

Someone had to make those rowdies stand down if they got out of hand.

IN THE THRONE ROOM, King Julian wore his most regal attire, all of it recently adjusted to fit him even more perfectly. He wore a blue silk gown long enough to cover most of his white wool trousers. On top of that was a heavy crimson cape with gold embroidery and fur trim. His long white hair was crowned with a heavy gold circlet; he owned a heavier and more jewel-encrusted crown, but that was meant for his coronation ceremony and public speeches. He only gave audience to family this evening.

Queen Monika sat on her throne, next to his, and her hand rested in his, which sat on a cushioned pedestal between them. She would still be with him, even through what she believed was folly. Her black-corseted dress featured gold embroidery and ended at a wide and ruffled white skirt that spilled out of a throne too small to contain it. She seemed to sit comfortably enough.

Off to one side of the throne room was a slender woman in green robes with her hair tied back in a bun. In front of her was a large instrument on a stand which had tightened strings like a lute or a harp, but it was laid horizontally. She sang various notes while hitting the strings of this instrument with a stick with a rounded head. It was light and beautiful and calming. She was the resident musician of the throne room, but never appeared for a banquet.

Lenn entered, bowed, observed everything, and found that Jarek had beaten him to the throne room and was sitting on the far-right, opposite the musician. Jarek was alone, probably to prevent his raucous riders from getting into trouble with King Julian.

Julian stood. "Ah, my nephew. I was wondering where you were. I take it one of the new books was to your liking, and it carried you away?"

Jarek nodded at his cousin with restrained amusement. Though not currently riding or on a battlefield, Jarek wore ornately engraved leather bracers on his forearms. Jarek and his riders were warriors wherever they went; they wanted onlookers to know that from sight.

"There's not a book you own that I have yet to read, but you certainly set out great ones for me to read a fourth time. Thank you, uncle," Lenn bowed lightly at the waist, then nodded at Jarek. "I'm told there's some cause for celebration, cousin?"

Jarek smiled slightly from his casual slouch. "An anniversary, you could say. You know well enough that it falls on a different day, but why not make use of the banquet that is already planned? I'm glad you can join us for it."

You know well enough... on that different day of which Jarek flippantly spoke, many years ago, the frontier wall was secured, and builders finished laying the last of the stone and mortar. This anniversary was considered a day of rest and optional feasting to remember the ones who died to make it so.

Jarek was already callous for bringing up the death of Lenn's father with a celebratory tone rather than gravitas. Now Victor's death anniversary had become an excuse for Jarek to bring his entourage when only the dukes themselves were called for.

If Julian had approved of that, then Lenn saw no point voicing an objection. He already knew what play he would make.

"You can expect some of my companions to join us as well," Lenn said. "I invited Tibor for the occasion, and he's sure to bring some of the others. The more, the merrier, right?"

"That's quite unusual." King Julian observed. "Do you have a victory of your own to celebrate?"

"I just hope to represent my dukedom in the manner that Jarek gets to represent his, so that we can show our diplomatic guests everything this kingdom is about in equal measure."

Jarek snorted. "Really cousin, I should think our armed

forces are already well represented. They are what Kensrikans need to see and to consider."

"If there was nothing more to this kingdom than warriors, what would they fight for?" Queen Monika interceded.

Jarek looked at his Queen with some agitation. "Then we should have invited my cousin to supply all the food, and some wonderful flower baskets for decorating. Do we really need his gang of ceremonial riders?"

"I wonder if that's what the Etroukans thought of his dukedom when they last tried to use it as a back door toward this very capital." Queen Monika said.

Jarek grunted. "Back door, certainly. No other practical reason to go there."

"And yet, your territory always has settlers in a hurry to leave and soldiers happy to go with them," Lenn said. "Perhaps, given what's on the safe side of the wall, they would rather take their chances with the mud fields."

King Julian stepped in. "Lenn. Jarek. This had better not be the sort of discussion our guests witness at the banquet. You two are also guests, and being invited to my castle is a privilege that I would not be pleased to revoke for either of you."

Lenn and Jarek stared at each other for a while. Jarek's expression said *you're not going to do anything; you never do anything; keep staring daggers...*

Lenn bowed again to his uncle. "I don't intend to make this your problem, great King."

Monika looked to each Duke, and to her husband. The bickering cousins still deferred to him, but for how long?

"I should step out. You know where to find me," Lenn turned, asking for no formal dismissal, and departed.

Jarek didn't even ask permission before following Lenn's example. He swiftly departed through a different door.

With the two most concerning witnesses out of the room, and eventually out of earshot, Julian let out an exasperated growl, balled his free hand into a fist and thumped it uselessly against the arm of his throne.

* * *

"THREE DAYS." He paused to exhale some of his agitation. "*Three days,* Monika; after so many years of those two getting along well enough, this is the time they pick to trade barbs. What in thunderclouds will the Kenderleys be here to witness?"

"Well, your goal is to make sure they don't see us as threatening, right?" Monika asked.

"Do I want for us to look completely inept? I think not!" Julian spat.

Monika let go of his hand. "You are the King. And this is your banquet. Be firm, command respect, and keep those Dukes in line. They answer to you. Allow me to manage the servants if you're so concerned. Is it that you want to resemble a stable ally?"

"We've been through this," Julian whined. "Unless you're implying that they need a friend to help swarm Etrouk, which would cost us far more lives than any plunder would justify, they have no purpose for allies here. The last thing they need is Jarek begging them for assistance in the way he already sucks from the golden teat of my wealth-stores. The goal is to look kept together, but not hostile. As if they should feel no dire need to attack us, nor do we give them an excuse."

She paused for a moment. It was the same old answer, as if he didn't notice she had asked a different question. Dissatisfied, she asked again. "But if there was a purpose for them to offer an alliance, what would you do?"

"You test me." He said, letting go of her hand and letting out another exasperated groan.

He held his head in his hands.

"You test me like *they* test me."

Monika shook her head. "No. I need to know your secrets if you desire the best advice. But if you are not in the mood, I suppose I should make sure preparations are going well for the banquet."

"Yes," he agreed, "please do that. Let me be alone for a while. I don't have the time..."

She stood and gestured to the court musician, who nodded. They departed together via the Queen's Entrance, leaving Julian in silence.

He leaned back in his throne and breathed deep. Some of the candles and torches of the throne room were burning out, and he felt that they were kindred spirits.

It was difficult, having two people in the room who deserved to rule more than he did. They should all kneel to Queen Monika had Wancyrik ever been matriarchal, like some of the Northern peoples were, and Julian would have aged gracefully, would stand taller without the constant weight on his shoulders. If only…

He hoped the new musicians he commissioned lived up to

the popular talk. Everyone in his court needed uplifting, none more so than King Julian.

DESPITE GOING DOWNHILL from the mountains, the journey to the capital of Wancyrik seemed to drag on. Lord den Holt had managed to fall asleep, and Luttwig was no doubt having pleasant dreams that caused him to mumble nonsense in his sleep, but Sir Wolter and Zinnia remained awake. She could not tell if the knight's gaze was off into the abstract, but it was in her general direction.

She didn't feel comfortable falling asleep while he watched. Nothing was going to happen in that carriage, and so close to their destination, but it gave her a bad feeling.

Perhaps he had learned to sleep with his eyes open, somehow?

The stress he caused could not immediately be solved, but she knew of one way to alleviate the tension headache. She slowly and quietly removed every pin she had placed in her hair, untied the tight bun she once built, then gathered most of the braids and coils into a loose and quick ponytail. Wolter never deserved to witness her in such glory, and the Wancyeks would just have to miss out.

Lacking any further way to help the situation; she passed the time wondering how her separate sleeping quarters might be furnished.

DUKE LENN LEANED on the library windowsill. He felt the Winds; he looked at the moon, waxing gibbous at the time; he thought he spied an owl on a couple of occasions, those nocturnal companions of the Winds. After some meditating, hoping to reconnect with powers beyond himself, he prepared to draw a curtain across the open window so that bats, those other nocturnal companions of the Winds, wouldn't fly into the library while he slept.

He could picture his father standing by the bookshelf. Victor would have been barely distinguishable from a western village man in his prime, but it wasn't like anyone else in the world could see or hear him anymore. Lenn could vividly recall the man's voice.

You know he's not the one who took me from you, the old man would say.

"No, but he represents an attitude that did. He's emblematic of the problem," Lenn muttered.

He does represent it. I just hope you understand your anger represents no solution.

"It's a reaction, not an answer. Tell me what solves this."

Keep your head. Survive. When the throne is yours, he will answer to you.

Lenn sighed deeply. Anything which sounded like doing what he was already doing, changing nothing about it, and simply waiting for the outcome, felt like it would maintain the same situation. He wished for a new course of action.

"I can't think of anything else, though. Not like this."

Then you should sleep. Perhaps it will come to you.

Before Lenn drew the curtain and doused the powerful reading lamp, he heard the approaching hoof beats and a full set of wheels. Sure, nighttime in the capital province had its revellers, but they were most often pedestrians, especially past that wall of privilege which had once served as a fortification.

He knew that Tibor could not have arrived by now, and with so few others at that; this was but two horses and one carriage audible against the stone of the road. By process of elimination, he expected this to be the Kensrikan contingent arriving at a strange time.

Lenn gazed thoughtfully upon the horses and the carriage they drew for a moment, then closed the curtain.

7

REHEARSAL AND ARRIVAL

The first rehearsal was about determining where Samuel could fit in the music. Even though he had the highest profile, there were two others and one of him, and what sealed it was the fact that he would not sing. Adina had the better voice and needed to be front and centre, with some possibility of baritone backup vocals from Samuel where needed.

When he could sing was a secondary concern, though. He first needed to know when his instrument could be of use. He needed to find a way inside the rhythms of Judit, which were not audible but implied in the timing of how they and Adina did things.

The more familiar duo would begin to improvise together, and Samuel attempted to form a fitting rhythm in his head and count himself in. Then he would gradually become more present until they had to stop.

"Is it necessary for you to play over us?" Asked Adina.

"No, and that's not my intention. Listen, let's start again. I'm going to begin as I did before, with single strings, flourishes, and instead of stopping me when it gets too much, stop me when it's just right. Or we'll just have to keep repeating the process until we work out the point of just-right." He explained.

Adina sighed. "I fear we may not see that point soon enough. But, if it's the only way, it's not like we have anything else to do, am I right?"

"This is the challenging part," Samuel reassured. "Once we're in the same town of sound, on the same sound street, that's when it will get interesting."

"Well, let's get ourselves in the same sound kingdom first, because I'm not sure it's just the timing or presence that we need to go for," Adina replied.

Samuel nodded. After a moment, he signaled Judit and waited. They would try again.

This iteration was nearly identical, and they stopped him at roughly the same point as last time, if not further.

But this time, Judit got Samuel's attention first.

"Adina, give him a low."

Adina paused, momentarily wondering how Judit could be out of tune in so little time, but she quickly picked up on the different pronoun and understood what else Judit must have noticed.

She looked to him. "Samuel, what do you tune off of?"

He opened his mouth, then closed it. Of course, as a solo artist his point of reference was his own voice; there was no standard tuning to learn, really. He alone had a feeling of where each string's sound had to be in relation to the others, and how to form chords.

"Sure, Adina," he nodded. "Give me a low."

He adjusted his lowest string to complement her low in a way that felt right, and incrementally adjusted the other strings by a similar shift.

Judit gave an uncharacteristic smile, pleased that he got their hint without much difficulty. Now they were all in the same sound village, if not on the same sound street.

"Well, I'll have to see if the notes change much for strumming," he said regarding chords.

"I think it shouldn't take me long. So, I'm going to be at the low end, yeah?"

"Let's try again, Samuel. Without that slight dissonance for a distraction, I think we can focus more on settling the other disparities." Adina said.

He grinned with satisfaction at their progress. "Don't be afraid to call me Sam. It's a friends and family privilege, you understand."

Adina returned the smile at that invitation.

They continued. Not every problem would be solved in one night, but they were encouraged by how they made such significant progress in so little time. They were well-introduced, socially familiar and getting comfortable, but their different sounds needed more coaxing.

AT THEIR NEXT MEETING, Samuel repeatedly butted his head against their sound; he was in the right neighbourhood, but the notes and chord shapes to stress were still unclear. He decided for some time to stop doing anything and listen to Judit's instrument, since Adina seemed to base her singing on the instrument's non-vocal cues.

It all made him feel rather auxiliary, a sewn patch on top of an otherwise functioning group; yet if that was the case and he wanted to make significant contributions, he needed to start from inside their sound and work his way out. If that failed, he was unsure what to try next.

"Judit, would you mind giving me eight different sounds, from low to high? Like eight that go well together, or a string of notes from a song you would usually play. You pick where to start; I'll try and figure it out." He asked gently.

Judit hesitated to consider which piece of music would work best. Then they counted themselves in and played for Samuel eight notes of their preferred scale in ascending order and looked to him for approval.

Samuel frowned and went over all eight notes on his fret-board, then considered a couple of two-string combinations, then three-string combinations.

"You know, I'd say that's half-Etroukan. I mean, it's genius, it fits an Etroukan sound snugly in with what I usually hear around here."

"Well, I am from Etrouk." Judit replied quietly.

He smiled. "That makes sense. I'm told they have excellent music there. All I usually get to hear are fragments which get stolen and replayed here by town musicians who are out of favour within a couple of weeks, once people remember that it's always the same fragments the last town musician stole. But I think we're travelling up the same sound street, now. And your preferred rhythms also sound like home, right?"

Judit nodded rapidly and grinned. Samuel thought the respect he was showing must not occur often, or not nearly as often as theft. He wished that wasn't the case.

Samuel gave his left wrist a few gentle turns as he said: "Thank you for sharing that. I'll work with it as best I can, but for this, you're the master and I'm your humble student."

"Well, that must be unfamiliar to you." Adina observed. "How does that feel?"

"Refreshing, actually," Samuel replied. "It gets dull doing the same old thing; I just hope my aging self can handle a new challenge. But I'm still in this if you two are, so what's say we grind it out a while longer tonight?"

By their third session, Samuel had cracked every aspect of his new role. He had down rhythm parts, a scale of sorts for soloing over various of Judit's more repetitive rhythm-like parts, and places where his voice could harmonize with Adina's without distracting from what she was doing. On such short notice, most of the trio's repertoire was songs he needed to fit himself into.

It was then that he humbly suggested the first song that gave him a turn as lead instrumentalist. This would become the first original song of the greatest musical act ever to come from Wancyrik.

They were three friends, the quiet inventor, the brainy strummer, and the unforgettable voice, ready to face their rulers in the castle of the land.

They had only the vaguest inkling of what they were getting themselves into.

It was dawn on the day of the banquet when they lugged their bags and cases up the street, knowing that most anybody who might otherwise get in their way was too hungover to be awake at the time, or able to walk at that. The few sober working people of the capital were out to set up shop, or bargain for early deals. This seeming lack of crowds left the musicians free to walk as quickly as they could with their instruments to carry.

And then, perhaps within the length of one laboured breath, there appeared a crowd. They came from a crossing of alleyways, and they formed a circle around the musicians. They were youths, mostly young men in shabby attire, wearing hoods common for street cloaks such that they were not easily distinguishable from the servant class.

From what Samuel knew, they were anything but servant class. Yet, in broad daylight…? He thought of one way to test this hypothesis, and he knew he had better hurry. He quickly handed his instrument to Adina, who accepted it with a look of grave concern.

"Well, what have we here? Three sellouts looking for their payday from the feeble King Julian, and one of 'em's even not from around here, looks like..." Said a tall boy who must have thought his voice was deeper and more intimidating than it was.

Samuel interjected, eager to head off trouble.

"Ignacy! Or does everyone still call you Iggy?" He called out the one whom he guessed was their leader; his volume also got some people out of bed to peek through the shutters of their windows, though the witnesses might not be deterrent enough.

The tough-talking masked youths took a step back and cast quick glances amongst themselves. They sounded shocked and dismayed, as if Samuel had just said something forbidden.

A figure of average height for the crowd, but broader at the shoulders, elbowed his way through the circle of troublemakers.

"No one alive calls me that. Except for you. Perhaps we need to fix that, boys?" Ignacy looked to the others with a crooked grin, as if his question was more than rhetorical.

Samuel remembered some years back when Ignacy got laughed out of a tavern and arrested for attempted rabble rousing. Whatever promise he made to the city guards in return for being set free was evidently false.

It would be youths whom Ignacy could rope in; restless youths tempted by clever older rebels. Who else would take the man seriously? Youths whose well-to-do parents didn't ask enough questions about where they had been. Perhaps a few slightly older losers saw the sway Ignacy had and wished they could be him.

"You want all these young men to take care of an older gent for you, Ignacy? Can't handle me yourself?" Samuel mocked.

Years ago in the tavern, Ignacy had sounded like someone who promised to help losers lash out with increasingly coordinated aggressive mischief against a society that had the audacity to bore them.

But the king of losers was the biggest loser of all, and Samuel correctly guessed that his direct opponent couldn't stand being called out in front of the losers-in-training.

Ignacy must fear losing the only measure of power he could trick anyone into giving him.

"So, a command performance, trying to show me up." Ignacy said. "I was never one for drama, here we do the real deal. Ball up those tricky fingers of yours and take your best shot."

Samuel did ball his fists, but he waited, suspecting that if he landed the first hit the young men would defend their leader, not run away. There didn't seem to be an easy way out of this.

Behind everything, Adina was silently trying to caution Judit to stay back. But Adina was neither their mother nor their boss.

"What, you not riled up enough to put something behind your words? All right then," Ignacy punched Samuel in the sternum with full force, winding the older man.

The string musician wobbled on his feet. His mind knew from experience he would breathe again shortly, but his body needed to catch up with that fact. He refused to fall.

While a chorus of jeers from the young men provided a good distraction, Judit broke away from Adina and swung their instrument case to the backs of Ignacy's knees. The instrument inside the case provided a fair deal of heft, such that Judit had to spin a little to swing it, torquing their hips, and Ignacy's weight was more forward than on his heels because he had just leaned into a blow. The attack threw him off balance.

Samuel got behind Ignacy even as he turned to look for his attacker. Samuel wrapped his right arm around his foe's neck from behind, a dangerous grip he had seen backstage security employ on occasion.

"You all keep back, or it gets a lot worse for him," Samuel grunted as he tried to keep a hold on his struggling foe without taking too hard of an elbow to the gut.

He didn't think the others would keep back for long. They might already suspect Samuel was too battered to employ this grip to its deadliest degree. Judit stayed behind Adina, who guarded Samuel's flank; Adina held the string instrument by the neck, prepared to bash it over someone's head.

The circle was edging in.

Then came the sound of many hoofbeats on the stone of the street. It sent the young men, who were thin of spirit, running to the alleyways and hiding places. The distraction also allowed Ignacy to break out from the rear choke and stumble away while blood resumed a normal course through his head.

Samuel wheezed, feeling the aftermath of several elbow pokes to his chest and gut after the earlier blow to the sternum. Adina sheepishly handed him back his instrument.

As Adina opened her mouth, Ignacy had already scrambled into an alley with his followers. Nobody chased them, preferring to stay and protect the accosted musicians.

"I'm sorry, I could have smashed it," she said, her voice shaky from what had transpired.

Samuel smiled painfully. "But you didn't... and if you did," he shrugged, "what else... could you do? I would've forgiven you."

The riders slowed to a stop in front of the musicians. Judit clutched their instrument case looking extremely concerned.

Samuel stood on one side of Judit while Adina stood on the other, so they knew they had friends at their side. Adina put one arm over Judit's shoulders; Samuel refrained, not yet feeling they were close enough in friendship.

"Thanks, Judit." Samuel wheezed softly.

The lead rider wore a golden-brown gambeson under light battle leathers. His brown hair was tied back in a short tight ponytail. "Good morning to you. Mind telling me what my arrival just broke up?"

"We were on our way to a big job when that group accosted us. The man who ran away, I think he was their boss?" She explained.

Witnesses at their windowsills began to call down confirmations of this. The lead rider nodded and put a hand up for this to cease, lest the cacophony prevent him from hearing the musicians' story.

"Iggy… and his troublemakers," wheezed Samuel. "No point giving chase… they vanish into alleys…"

The man nodded. "In broad daylight, and they didn't care that everyone was watching? How brazen! Well, I'm glad to have chased them away for you. My name is Tibor. I wouldn't mind escorting you to this big job. Hopefully we're travelling in the same direction?"

"Well..." Adina began.

"Don't worry, Adina," Samuel interrupted after drawing a good breath. "I know the style of their saddlebags and leathers, it's western. You're a rider with the good Duke, aren't you Tibor?"

Tibor grinned reassuringly. "He's not among us, but he summoned us. So, before we delay much further, where are you going, and can we help you get there safely?"

"We may be headed for the same place. Banquet, right? I would assume..."

"Our evening's entertainment, no less! I'm even more glad to have helped, and equally curious to have somebody explain this to me. That can happen along the way; I'm sure some of my men would volunteer to let you on, maybe carry your cases for you?" Tibor offered.

"Judit will carry their case, it's fragile and they know how best to handle it, and I should ride with them," Adina gestured toward the shortest of the three musicians.

"Well, Judit looks like the lightest of you, so that horse I'm gesturing toward shouldn't be overburdened with two riders plus that case. I can accommodate that; the current rider will have to join one of his fellows. Let's go to the castle, and you, sir, sound like you can tell me a bit more about this bizarre situation. So, you ride with me."

"So, you're Samuel, the fleet fingered," Tibor sounded amused.

"Do people remember me over in the west? It's been so long."

"We certainly get word of standout musicians, mostly from those of us who have gone here seeking glory and sent back letters full of superlatives."

Samuel considered that. "Well, it's nice to know my name gets around."

"So, I take it you hear lots of things in the capital, in your line of work. Might you know who attacked you, and why? A jealous rival, perhaps?" Tibor asked.

Samuel would have laughed if he didn't expect that to hurt. "None of them are that organized or brazen. I barely recognized the man I fought... but this isn't going to be one of those talks that will likely incriminate me, is it? Because if I'm going to tell you things, I don't want the extra effort of having to tell consistent lies," Samuel said.

Tibor chuckled. "And ruin the banquet? Listen, I just want to know about concerning groups of troublemakers in the streets, like the one that attacked you. I've been here before many times and never seen anything like it. If your venues are dodging the entertainment tax or something, I don't think that's the biggest problem by comparison."

"You would have to ask a venue owner, anyway. I only play in them." Samuel quipped.

The musician figured that Tibor would have spent any visit on the other side of the wall, the gate of which they had just ridden through. A visitor with the good Duke probably knew nothing about any trouble in the capital, firsthand or otherwise. Tibor also didn't look like anyone's easy target; troublemakers would think twice. Someone with that perspective would have no inkling of what went on in the city. Yet Samuel himself was shocked by the day's events on a couple of counts.

Samuel continued: "Being attacked during the day surprised me, too. And by that many people, with complete disregard for witnesses. But at night, sure, things have gotten worse over the years. I hear about more robberies and attacks than I used to, and perhaps the group you saw are the culprits.

I wonder if many parents have given up on their children. Most of those hooded folks didn't look like adults, except for the last one you saw running away, and a few who admire him."

Tibor frowned, believing what he saw but finding it difficult to grasp the meaning. "And what do you think makes bored youths and a couple of their elders want to swarm three musicians?"

"Eh. It's probably not us, Tibor. It's who we're seen to be working for, perhaps, who we represent. Word got out somehow of where we were going; I mean, if I hear so many rumours, guess what an inconspicuous person might hear?"

Tibor nodded. "Drink loosens tongues. You can't always remember what you've said to whom."

"It's not even that." Samuel continued. "Things said behind the stage, all it takes is someone hiding to overhear. I don't pretend to be able to keep a secret, but I must make the effort on my end and only tell those who need to know. If I'm overheard, well, I can't afford perfect secrecy."

"But, again, why are such people going after what you represent? Jealousy? Why would they have a problem with such kind rulership on the throne?" Tibor returned to the previous subject.

"If you want my guess, perhaps many youths are starting to lose their sense of purpose. Their clothes looked rather good for them to be living in poverty, so perhaps their families are well-to-do but not paying attention to them or offering them something meaningful or exciting to do." A part of him was so glad someone was finally interested in such musings, not that Samuel wished any of it was true.

Tibor frowned deeply at that. "But what about the Gods and the seasonal traditions, that which connects us with our ancestors? I may not come here often, but I never recalled such sacred things being supplanted by wealth. A means cannot become the end."

"I agree, but the way people look at traditions, the reasons people appeal to the Gods, can definitely shift in ways even our regents might not consider. Tibor, the larger this city grows, the less I get that feeling of community you have in the west; this capital's divided into households, many of which are rivals rather than neighbours. Does anybody try to explain to their children why one lives, why things are worth doing, why we should care? Because if all you're given is what money can buy, then life's all just living out your fun, doing what you want, sometimes deeply resenting what others get to have that you don't actually need. And if I remember anything about being a young man, there's a lot of frustration in you. You can see all the people who are somebody, who have respect, and you're so enraged about being nobody, and you despair of change even though it's constantly happening to you. And Iggy's older followers, maybe they feel left behind in life, but this secret group makes them feel like they're dangerous, like people should fear them; like they matter."

Tibor paused to make sure Samuel's musings were finished, then asked: "You get a lot of time to think about this, don't you?"

Samuel shrugged. "Well, you asked. I'm no scholar, but between jobs, I get time to ponder. Tough for me to ask the troublemakers when the first thing they want to do is kick my face in. Ask Iggy if you get the chance. He'll probably be flattered someone cares what he thinks, other than a bunch of overgrown children."

Tibor laughed. "If his name is Iggy, that might be why only children tend to take him seriously. But you called him something more formal at first, when I found you...?"

"His proper name is Ignacy. I vaguely recognized him after no one spoke his name in so long; a would-be rabble rouser we mocked years ago, forgettable to most. I called him Iggy to rile him up, and I will always call him that for what little respect he deserves. He must want the youths to grow up like him, to just be overripe frustration and rage and to break everything. But now I'm rambling..." Samuel admitted.

"It's fine, this is quite helpful. I hope this banter doesn't strain your singing voice."

"Oh, don't worry about that. I've got Adina singing for us, thank the Winds. And Iggy's elbows did far worse to my chest than this conversation."

Tibor didn't feel reassured by that. "Even so, I won't tire you any longer. I'll be sure to tell the castle guards and get you all looked after. Most of the day's still yet to elapse, plenty of time to rest."

"Just make sure none of them try to carry Judit's case. Don't ask. But I'll tell you, I didn't get Iggy on his knees by myself; see if they need any tools you have on hand, in case their instrument got knocked out of tune..."

They rode into the long shadow of the castle.

TIBOR WOULD NEED plenty of time to consider all these facts. Beyond what was discussed, why had nobody else escorted these musicians on such an important day, with such conditions stirring among the populace? That was not something to ask the musician. If a worldly man like Samuel was shocked, did the Capital Guard have any understanding? Did no one inform King Julian that extra precautions should be taken?

And yet, there was so much hypothesizing in Samuel's banter. The only thing Tibor witnessed was that the musicians were attacked by strangers who disappeared into alleys. He hoped Lenn would permit him to investigate further.

8
THE OFFICE OF THE QUEEN

Adina sat patiently in the office where the servant had led her. The cushioned wooden chair should have been the most comfortable place for anyone to sit and wait; certainly, Judit appeared to have no problem in theirs. There the two waited in front of an ornately carved wooden desk. On that desk sat a ready stack of the highest quality writing paper, an inkwell, and a fine quill pen. Nothing about the room was threatening unless one was concerned about accidentally toppling richly decorated pottery or an intricate sculpture.

But Samuel had not been invited to this meeting. The problem was not that she could guess exactly why. She wondered what to say. Much would depend on what questions she would be asked.

The servant who had brought them here opened the door and announced, "Her Royal Highness, Queen Monika Wancyek."

Adina and Judit stood to greet the Queen. She casually entered the room and politely asked the servant to wait outside for further instructions.

Once they were alone, Monika addressed her guests. "Please be seated."

They obeyed. Monika smoothed her gown and sighed happily as she sat in her own impeccably embroidered armchair, on her side of the desk.

The Queen looked to Adina. "I have been informed that your name is Adina, and that your partner has given you permission to speak for you both," she then looked to Judit with a sweet smile, "not that you are uninvited or disqualified from participating in this conversation, if you wish."

Judit smiled back without comment and gave one slow nod.

"Yes, your Highness, you have been informed correctly," Adina replied, silently concerned about her tone of voice, posture, and any number of other things she might have wrong in the presence of such a person; what should her hands be doing?

Monika seemed cognizant of the discomfort and continued to smile. "You may relax and call me Monika within this office. These are noble halls, but welcoming ones. I quite like the neck-line of that dress; is that what they wear in the city these days?"

Adina's self-consciousness soared for a moment; yes, the Queen seemed gentle and told her to relax, but the office of an employer was also a place of scrutiny.

"Yes, your... Monika, it's a matter of personal style. If it is ill-suited for noble halls, I would have no trouble wearing something different."

"No, no, keep it. To clarify, this meeting has nothing to do with your dress. Julian will neither be offended nor care about it either way. But you must know that. We do maintain a reputation for what we find suitable entertainment here." Monika lightly cleared her throat before carefully peeling a sheet of paper off its stack and preparing her quill pen. "And some talk of you has gone around, all of it favourable."

"Thank you." Adina nodded politely.

Now Judit paid close attention to the Queen, the manner of her motions, the way the feather of her quill pen caught the light entering from the nearest window; most importantly, they listened for any word on the purpose of this meeting.

"Tell me what you think of Samuel," Monika said.

Adina was correct about the meeting's purpose. How correct remained to be seen.

"He conducts himself in a most professional manner, yet gently; he insists we are not his 'backing band', and he would not stop until he found a way to fit his skills in with the type of music we already made prior to having met him."

"That's a polite and generous description. He's not in the room, however, and my purpose is to ensure that everyone working in this castle feels safe. We did request him, and he did bring you to this job, but we agreed to everything *before* someone complained to us about him."

Adina was entirely correct.

"Thank you most kindly. I meant everything I said. I suspect I can provide useful information on the one who filed the complaint, in fact."

Monika raised her eyebrows. "Oh? Do you know her name?"

Adina fidgeted, remembering again that she was working with hunches. "You're right, Monika, perhaps this is an altogether different situation."

The Queen put down her pen. "If there is more than one situation, I should like to hear about them all. Please tell me what you know."

Adina interlaced her fingers and tried to recall every detail perfectly.

"The agreement was, Samuel would attend our show and meet with us afterward to discuss his thoughts. As he was outside the door to the preparation area, this private space for musicians, he was confronted by this woman who apparently knew him from prior shows."

"Apparently?"

"From what I overheard, it sounded quite like they were familiar with each other from some prior time. He confirmed this when we spoke. He called her Maryana."

Monika nodded, dipped her pen in the inkwell, and began to record this story.

"I apologize for interrupting, but please stick with what you know from witnessing the altercation, not what Samuel told you, unless I invite otherwise."

Adina noted that the Queen was polite enough to apologize when she was entitled never to do so, which helped the nervousness a little. Now Adina was less concerned about how this powerful woman viewed her, and more focused on representing her recently met friend properly.

"She sounded livid, accusing him of spurning her in favour

of me, then something about the depth of her purse. I'm sorry that I didn't hear it all perfectly, or perhaps my memory is failing me from nervousness."

Monika paused. "You have nothing to worry about, dear, and I quite understand. This is all very interesting. A lover's quarrel, or perhaps he owed her money. Neither of which quite aligns with the story of her complaint. But he has never posed a problem for you or Judit, correct? And you'll not be afraid to inform me immediately if this changes?"

Adina blinked and replied softly. "Yes, of course, Monika."

"There is more to the conversation that I remember quite well," Judit spoke up.

The other two glanced over to see Judit leaning forward, posterior resting on the edge of her seat.

"Absolutely, friend," Monika assented, refreshing the ink of her pen.

"Samuel made it known he loves men. The conversation he had with the woman suggested that he had told her this before. She claimed his interest in Adina proved him a liar."

Adina sighed with frustration at herself. That was a huge detail to omit, but after all, she learned it from Samuel after the argument; Monika wanted Adina to stick with the altercation. Fortunately, Judit must have heard things better.

Monika heard that sigh and spoke while writing. "Be gentle with yourself, Adina. It's not every day you meet the Queen. Now, Judit, did you witness anything to uphold this woman's accusation?"

"He was only interested in making music when we met him and that remains unchanged. As for their argument, she approached him with a suggestive tone and words. She threatened to ruin his career when he asked her to leave. Then she threatened the door guard's job when he inquired about the situation. Her father is part-owner of the Market Square, she said."

Monika paused her writing and looked up from the page with a scowl. "A door guard, for the musicians' preparation area, correct?"

Judit nodded.

"I don't know how they normally do things on the other side of the wall, but the law is the same on both sides of it. If true, this sounds like a heinous abuse of power—on *two* counts. And she tried to mislead and manipulate me, the audacity. And that door guard sounds like another witness to a situation which seems inconsistent with anything she mentioned in her complaint. I might like to hear him confirm this."

"May I make a suggestion?" Adina asked.

"My pen is at the ready," Monika replied.

"While I agree that the door guard can be a witness, if it became known that he gave incriminating testimony about an heiress, her family would hold that against him. So would their friends. That sort of thing has happened before on the other side of the wall. I'm not sure what can be done instead..."

Monika swirled the tip of the quill in the inkwell, thinking deeply. "To hear tell of such corruption is disheartening, Adina, but I concur. An overt legal action should be kept for a last resort. However, such information and testimony could be leverage. You say her father is a shareholder of that performance venue? It's *his* authority she's leveraging?"

Adina thought about it. "Definitely, and I believe her father's other holdings and connections were implied in the threat as well."

"I wonder how aware her father is of the situation and its implications." Monika smiled knowingly. "I can draft a letter calmly making him aware of the truths I have uncovered and inviting him to discuss how we might resolve these accusations. Hopefully this will happen swiftly enough that the door guard is not affected; did the guard appear to take sides in this dispute?"

"Absolutely not. He asked an innocent question." Judit confirmed.

Monika nodded. "I shall make that clear in my message. However, I am not sure whether we can repair the damage made to Samuel's reputation. We can offer him safety within these walls. We can do our best to make sure the truth prevails over time. Much depends on her father's temperament, though I would not reveal that to him. Neither shall you mention this to anyone."

"Thank you, Monika. I think Samuel was counting on the safety of this place." Adina said.

Monika paused, then continued: "The idea of her repeatedly pursuing this man who has no interest in women, as if he had no right to refuse... a devious degree of entitlement. We enslave no one in Wancyrik; your regents govern with respect, and we demand that our subjects recognize each other's rights and own their responsibilities. I should like to invite her into this office personally for a lesson to correct her ignorance, her actions being so at odds with respectful conduct. Her father may be inattentive or doting, as I know many to be, or he may have enabled her attitude by neglecting to teach her properly. She might need to hear this from a higher authority who feels no obligation to keep her happy. I would handle this most delicately, of course, from an experienced woman to a younger one."

Adina considered this. "You are most wise, Queen Monika. I trust your judgement on this matter. All I know is that Samuel has given me the least reason for concern out of anyone approaching us for collaborations."

"No concern at all. He listens better, too," Judit added.

"Splendid. And you already said you shall tell me if this changes. Well, I shall not demand you sit here watching me write; I am sure you have rehearsing to do, or some preparation for the banquet."

9
OUTSIDE AND BEHIND THE STAGE

While servants readied the banquet hall, King Julian took it upon himself to escort Lord den Holt, Zinnia, and Sir Wolter on a tour of the castle grounds; Luttwig did accompany them, but he was tasked with remaining silent and veritably invisible.

The knight found it fascinating that he would get a tour from the King himself.

"It's quite unexpected, great King, for you to expend your energy and grace us with your time on a tour—please don't feel like you're obligated. But it truly is an honour, I mean..." Sir Wolter babbled.

"Oh, nonsense, Sir Wolter," King Julian replied. "I like to go for walks at times, go about my daily tasks myself. And the better part of it is that I have some company," he nodded to Lord den Holt and Zinnia, "who can experience my castle with fresh senses."

Sir Wolter nodded. He had been to this kingdom before,

but only to spend time in the capital with a diplomat of lower tier nobility. He didn't think he stood out too much from the revellers, though he was happy to now be received by the monarchs. It felt like progress.

"Out here, we have flowers planted, gifts from the west. And beyond them, down the hill, the stables, and the wall," King Julian gestured at the grounds ahead of the castle's front.

"Have you considered taking the wall down? Or putting more doors in it?" Zinnia asked, as some riders were seen filing their way through the wall's one opening.

"It just seems strange, this one way through, when you've already allowed some of the city to expand on to the lower castle grounds," she observed.

Wolter realized Zinnia had not been formally introduced, and Julian might see her as a servant speaking out of turn. Yet the Wancyek regent only smiled; perhaps the king assumed Zinnia enjoyed elevated status if she escorted her lord, which may include such privileges as speaking freely. Willem did not behave as if she had done anything wrong.

"A valid question; we have indeed discussed it before. Yet even if we never warred again, that wall has served us too well to be demolished. Think of it like the memory of victories past, which could be of use again someday." Julian explained.

"I rather like what the wall does for you now," Sir Wolter offered. "Lets you keep the riff raff on the other side, keeps the noble folk safe. Wish the forefathers of Bayrock had such foresight."

Julian looked away from Wolter to hide his distaste for the knight as they made their way inside.

* * *

"WELL, can you wake him up? What could possibly take him away from his one task on this most important of banquet days?"

Monika was livid. They had a Kensrikan delegation, one group of Jarek's men, and now a group of Lenn's riders, all requiring service in one massive banquet. That was challenging enough before one of the kitchen assistants failed to show up. With so much food to serve at once, and not enough pairs of eyes to watch everything, there was a great risk of burning the food or having it sit for too long before being served. Monika might not like the questionable purpose of this diplomatic banquet, but that didn't mean guests deserved bad food.

"He has headaches from the beating. We can't make him work through that. We aren't monsters, my Queen, he needs to rest," a kitchen servant frantically defended her brethren's absence.

"Beating?" Monika focused on the key word of that exchange; first the complaint about Samuel, now this? "From whom?"

"He would not say, he so feared for his life. It was bad enough what they already did."

Monika's tone softened in an attempt to soothe the distressed bearer of ill tidings.

"I can guess; we've invited belligerent persons into this castle, and the guilty party should never return. I will investigate. Is there another servant in the roster who knows their way around food preparation?"

The servant's panic was not made worse, at least. "I wouldn't trust the cleaners... but whoever replaces him, we would be short of their role instead."

"Never mind, just do your best to keep to the plan here. I shall go and find someone; let me worry about that. I'm your Queen, I'm in control." She said that last part as much to rally herself as anything. Someone had to keep their head.

Monika took a moment to feel glad that Julian managed to get himself away from such concerns when he was already troubled. She would search the halls for a suitable replacement.

What she failed to realize was that she had motivated the servant to conduct the exact same search, against Monika's direct yet quickly forgotten instructions.

"WELL, it's rather aromatic in here. I've noticed it since our arrival..." Sir Wolter said with uncharacteristic politeness.

King Julian smiled and took the comment at face value.

"I'm glad you noticed. Here we burn frankincense for special occasions, and I know that Kensrikans can be particular about the aesthetics, the scents as well as the sights."

Zinnia appreciated the change; the frankincense of the halls was refreshing compared to the overpowering floral scent of the carriage.

"Quite." Sir Wolter let the subject fall through, having nothing nicer to say, as they entered the corridor that went past the kitchen.

Just then, a servant lady left the kitchen, hesitated, but having already interrupted the tour, bowed apologetically.

"A member of our servants' roster, no doubt proceeding to her next task," King Julian introduced the woman with a bewilderment that he could not hide.

"I'm terribly sorry to interrupt what you're doing, great King, but our kitchen is a man short, and it seems to us rather like an emergency..." She didn't want to create a panic, while at the same time being in one, and couldn't help but let her feelings seep through her words.

"*Short?*" King Julian was at a loss for words, such a topic to bring up in front of the guests.

Zinnia read Julian's tone and expression perfectly. He looked fit to roar, and the poor frightened servant was merely a messenger.

"Ah, a tragedy." Sir Wolter replied smugly. "It just so happens we have a servant with us of whom Lord den Holt isn't in terrible need at this time, do I recall correctly? I'd offer Luttwig but he couldn't cook suitable rations for prisoners."

Lord den Holt looked at Zinnia.

"Well, I—"

"I can help if you need me," Zinnia said with an icy tone, trying to turn another Sir Wolter embarrassment into a more fruitful enterprise.

Lord den Holt looked to his daughter as if to say, *Are you quite sure?* But he understood that, technically, her papers, the very justification for her presence on this journey, marked her as a servant; she was not introduced as any proper lady, even though she should have been.

"Well, you have my deepest thanks." King Julian said, his tone taking on an edge that was not intended for Zinnia.

Wolter grinned sardonically, as if he had greatly inconvenienced a hated enemy.

Julian continued: "Let's resume our tour and put this bizarre moment behind us. There are rooms upstairs..."

Julian soldiered on, but he carried a thinly veiled abruptness for the rest of the tour.

How could it be that the kitchen was short staffed during this most important of days? And how could that possibly look to representatives of House Kenderley, who likely considered all Wancyrik rustic and martial to begin with?

And to have this happen during all his other troubles, the dysfunction between Dukes, the restless times, the arguments with Monika; now he couldn't even throw a banquet together.

Someone was going to pay. He wasn't sure who, but after this bumpy ride of diplomacy he would do what it took to find out.

LENN AND TIBOR sat at opposite ends of the long couch, whiling away the time left before the banquet. Both had spent the better part of the day resting; Lenn wanted energy for the broader social experience that he found draining, while Tibor had spent most of the day riding.

"So, we have Kensrikans here? Kenderleys or just Kensrikans, do you think?" Tibor asked.

Tibor knew the divide between the Kensrikan common folk and House Kenderley who ruled them; the richest and largest empire in the world was really its richest family, which could afford to own the largest tracts of land and an army of daunting size. It was not an army for the people, but it protected them insofar as protecting them protected the ruling family.

Wancyrik was not so different on the surface, but its people were closer to its armed forces; they lived together, the connection was more direct. The Kenderley Army practically had its own villages and barracks, and no lives outside their careers; they lived and died for House Kenderley.

"I've yet to meet them," conceded Lenn, "but I believe we have one lord or governor of some sort representing West Kensrik, one knight from Bayrock, and a couple of servants they brought."

"Well? Are they trying to head off a war or something?" Tibor asked.

Lenn shook his head. "I've not been made a party to whatever they plan, but if it was war, I would expect to have heard about it, and we wouldn't be inviting the enemy here. Nor would they send us easy prisoners for ransom. No, I've yet to understand what my uncle is doing, but it's suspicious."

"And what of Jarek? I take it he's the reason you invited me and the others? Is he more aggressive, somehow?"

"He's bad enough to begin with." Lenn paused to gather his words. "I suspect that something awful is going to happen, and we had best make sure it doesn't happen here."

"Or to you." Tibor observed in a hushed tone. "If your uncle appears too close to House Kenderley, and whispers get out, I don't see Jarek being suitable for the throne, do you?"

"We shall not talk about that."

Tibor smiled; the implication itself had not been refuted, just the act of speaking it. "Why not? Would you prefer to make things up on the go, when this *something* of yours finally happens? I can tell you this: there are other problems occurring in this capital, ones which would not serve any successor."

"Here, where everyone's happily drunk? And the gaze of power is so close?" Lenn asked.

"Drunkards are not particularly watchful, and no power of this world can see everything, particularly not through the capital's constant distractions. If I have your permission, Duke, I should like to investigate on my own. I have no taste for this banquet, and I can make sure the others are properly instructed for your protection."

"Granted." Lenn said. "What do you know so far? It sounds like you learned quite a lot, having only arrived today."

Tibor explained: "The musicians for tonight's feast were accosted, in broad daylight no less. They stood up well for themselves given the circumstances, but I caught a glimpse of considerable numbers surrounding them who then fled at the sound of our riders' approach. This does not just seem like a small band of pickpockets. We cannot afford to ignore this, Lenn."

"Shocking as that is, I believe you." Lenn assured. "But if the musicians were the target, and they're safely within these walls...?"

"That string instrument player seems to be well informed. He gave me the name of the suspicious persons' leader, and said this person was once arrested for rabble rousing. He also gave me some ideas about what they are up to and why, but only with constant reminders that it was all speculation. We must find out what's going on, and the scope of it, to make sure it's not the kind of rot that can spread to your province."

Lenn cast him a careful glance. "And, ideally, prevent the existing order of things from falling."

Tibor nodded quickly. "Of course, if this can support the best of all cases, peace and safety for all, that's ideal."

Lenn thought for a moment before giving further instructions. "I invited you and the other riders because I'm concerned about Jarek. I'm already taking a risk allowing your absence, but the good of the kingdom takes precedent over a questionable banquet, and over the way Kensrikans look at us. I respect your intuition that much. We have neither the numbers nor the jurisdiction to solve problems meant for the Capital Guard. I can let their captain know to expect you. However big or small this troublemaking group is, you will report anything you find directly to him." Lenn instructed.

"I have questions for him, anyway; for instance, why was nobody sent to escort the musicians, with such danger lurking? Samuel's testimony made it sound like corruption and theft are becoming rampant; a simple escort must have occurred to someone." Tibor said.

"Ask the captain with respect, Tibor. He should know the city enough to understand what's warranted, and no matter his thoughts, he must run things as my uncle instructs. In the meantime, keep safe. I should like to hear what you find and what the captain tells you."

Tibor went to the door but turned for a parting word.

"The longer corruption is allowed to stand, the worse it is for common folk when everything falls."

Lenn sighed. "I don't need to be reminded. If you're going somewhere, just go."

* * *

THE THREE MUSICIANS were each set to their own tasks in a backstage area that few ever got to see. Samuel thought that must be why it was so clean, without scorch marks or anybody having carved their name into a table or chair or ceiling beam.

Samuel was the quietest of the three, and he would remain so. He needed all the wind going in and out of his sore chest just to keep moving and to focus on the instrumental aspect of his performance.

Judit was hard at work, because their instrument had taken a bad rattling when they had used the case to take out Ignacy at the knees. They worked with little picks and needles, a small hammer to tap out any dents, and an expression on their face that suggested a keen absorption in the task at hand; nobody had said a word to them since their arrival for fear of interrupting the sacred repairs.

Adina was the least quiet of them, and Samuel was thankful for that. Her voice was a paradise for the ears, even during something so simple as vocal warmups and scales.

Then a slender and angular woman of perfect posture shuffled into the room. From far away, her head looked elongated, tapering first at the back of the head and then at her chin, and her shoulders appeared broad, but as she approached and went from silhouette to well-lit person, it became clear that her hair was pulled back into a bun and her cloak created a broad-shouldered effect.

"Is it time yet?" Samuel immediately asked her.

Time for the world to end or to begin. The walls of his performance anxiety were closing in, and these two others who together with him made up band, they were appreciated pillars; at least he no longer had to worry about holding everything up by himself. The sight of their confidence emboldened him.

"Good day to you all," the lady politely bowed her head. "I am Iris, the resident court musician of House Wancyek. I understand this is your first time playing in the castle; if you have any questions, I would be happy to answer them."

Something about her aspect was so quiet and calming that Samuel found himself relaxing somewhat. Not too much, since he found that a baseline cautious feeling kept him energetic and kept his efforts honest, but enough to let him breathe a little easier.

Adina examined this courtly resident. "Well, it's a pleasure to meet you. I can't help but look at your attire, and mine, and I did try to dress up a level from the tavern standard, but..."

The court musician smiled. "Fear not. I heard you from the corridor; though echoes distort sounds, I nevertheless think that nothing but misfortune could stop you now."

Adina blushed a bit. "Well, I don't know if this is all right with you, but..." she kept looking at the court musician's attire from every angle. "Do you think it would be awful if we switched clothes for the evening? Because the King and Queen must like what you're wearing."

"Ah, but if they wanted me to sing for the banquet, they would have asked me to." Iris replied. "They want to see you. If you dress like me, it's like they're seeing me again. Besides, it's not as if we have the same figure."

Adina blushed. "True, we do not."

Iris continued gently: "Here's a thought: I was gifted a scarf in colours that clash with what I tend to wear, thus they have yet to see me wear it. I think it would better suit your outfit's colours."

Adina's eyes widened. "Could you arrange, that, please? It would be great. There's just something so stately about you."

Iris smiled. "Oh, thank you, you're beautiful..."

Samuel stopped paying attention to the exchange at that point while shining up the part of his instrument which was all too often left with a grease mark from his right palm, right near where his wrist would rest as his fingers plucked strings.

The court musician shuffled back out to fetch that scarf.

"Oh, I hope she returns before the performance." Adina said, wide-eyed with worry. "Though she moves with such stately grace, there's nothing brisk about that walk."

"Adina." Samuel comforted. "You've done awesomely before without any scarf. Just be who I saw when I knew I needed you and Judit up here with me. If anybody can't see what I saw, they're foolish, whether or not they wear a gold circlet."

She quickly went up to him and hugged him around the shoulders, careful to avoid his bruises from the encounter with Ignacy.

"Sam. You're just adorable. Thank you."

He smiled and relaxed a little more.

"Maybe we could both learn something from Judit," Samuel spoke quietly. "I bet they could take the stage wearing sack cloth, yet they would bring the same excellence as they would if laced into the finest attire. Solid and unshakable."

Adina disengaged the hug, and her smile faded a little. "Well, as long as you understand why they might seem that way to you. We all have feelings here, deep ones at that. Judit's no different. But we support each other through them."

Sam quickly nodded, remembering Judit's pained expression when they didn't know how badly their instrument might be damaged after the fight. "I hope I didn't offend. I meant that as a compliment. I admire how Judit handles the pressure and I appreciate that support. Just let me know how I can help..."

10

THE BANQUET

The guests were escorted to the master table of the hall, where they could sit nearest to King Julian and Queen Monika. Dukes Lenn and Jarek were seated far from each other, kept apart by the important guests in the middle. They had been through the loudly announced entrances of the monarchs and the introduction of the distinguished guests. The soldiers, dignified by having been proven under steel and the rain of arrows, were given no introduction but occupied the same level floor as the others. No chair or section of floor was elevated from any other except for the performing area which needed to be visible from the back.

Wolter turned and said to Lenn, "I'm glad we get to have a dinner to ourselves, us nobles, and these hard-working fellows grateful for the privilege of our friendship. I was worried for a moment that you would let the servants sit with us, too; this banquet arrangement is so odd to me. At least servants know where they belong in life's great hierarchy."

"Ah. Would you like me to relay that message, so that they can decide how to prepare what you're about to eat and drink?" Lenn replied in question.

Wolter laughed. "Oh, I suspect it's already cooked, not that I'm inviting you to say anything to them. Well, you're a polite man to all types, quite dignified in his words, something I must respect and admit to lacking; the world has made a bit of a ruffian of me."

Lenn analyzed the man's expensive looking attire. Perhaps the knight understood that the most concerning roughness was rarely worn on the outside; that true nobleness lay in the virtues by which one lived and the dignity with which one treated others, and Wolter knew he should work on this. Or perhaps Wolter only pretended to recognize his own flaws as a conversational misdirect.

"So, you are the knight." Lenn observed, thinking this was the kind of man who would regale Lenn about his accomplishments once his title was recognized.

"Sir Wolter of House Kenderley, as introduced." He said abruptly.

After a patient pause, Lenn understood that either Wolter had no story or didn't wish to discuss it.

The knight then asked: "And you brought the fellows whose well embroidered outfits seem closest in style to your own, understandably sitting on your side. Not the veritable army that's still marching in and filling those other seats," he nodded in the general direction of Jarek's men.

"I'm Duke Lenn; I govern to the west. I did invite my riders. The north seems to have greater need of soldiers in recent years."

"The west, a province of craftsmen, bread, flowers, and baskets to carry the bread and flowers; I have read about it, though no occasion to visit. I like it on principle: civilized, hard-working, but endearingly humble, though I hope you take no offense at that."

Lenn shook his head for more than one reason. "Humility is a virtue; it has its place."

Besides, "endearingly humble" might have been the least offensive way Wolter had described anyone. If this was House Kenderley's number one diplomatic choice, Lenn understood why Kensrik would likely go to war at any moment. Then again, it would be just like them to treat Wancyrik as an afterthought and make precisely the diplomatic effort that they felt was deserved.

Wolter moved along at the assurance. "I've rather enjoyed your capital, like a prototypical Bayrock; I suppose in a smaller kingdom such as this, the carousing, the warring, and the more pleasant things each need their place. Your dukedom also stands to gain a lot from better trade with Kensrik; I imagine your surplus crafts would trade well."

"Just as long as trade is all that's on the table." Lenn said flatly; he didn't appreciate his homeland being perceived as small, cute, and destined to become a different place that it never needed to be.

Wolter laughed and gave a cursory glance to his surroundings. Almost all Jarek's men had finished filing into the room and ending their arguments about who got to occupy which seat of equal status at a front table scarcely closer to the stage than the table behind it. Some of them would begrudgingly occupy the rearmost table.

"Come now, Duke. We have our disagreements, but Wancyrik is a proper Southern Kingdom, albeit at the bleeding edge of civilization. It would be different if you were, say, Etroukan."

"And how would you see me different if I were a steadfastly religious man living in a walled city of untold wealth? Given your typically Kenderley love for gold, I should think you would respect them more than us." Lenn replied with a smirk.

"Bah." Wolter sighed. "You're going to keep me honest, eh? Not going to let me have my fun. I suppose it's less than sporting to speak ill of those who aren't present to defend themselves, and you're more noble for speaking on their behalf."

Lenn was not distracted by the compliment. The degree to which this conversation was sporting had not been a consideration when Wolter insulted the kitchen servants, and it could only be rhetorical misdirection now.

"But after all the times you had to push them back up the mountain to their city, at such a high price to your people, you *respect* Etroukans? Did they not cost your King one of his fingers?" Wolter quipped.

"As adversaries, they are too fierce to belittle; I'm glad they choose peace for now. It suits me fine giving them no cause to reconsider. If you don't believe me, ask King Julian, and he would say the same. Ask the Etroukans, if they ever let you past the wall, and I expect they feel similarly about us. Our ways are different, but our peace emerged from mutual respect. This friendship you seek with my uncle; I'm not sure what it emerges from, but I shall respect his decree."

Lenn smirked again as he observed Wolter's discomfort. Was that guilt or shame? Did Wolter consider Lenn too harsh? If King Jonnecht ever sent such a prejudiced man to Etrouk, his only purpose would be to bait them into war. Instead, Wolter seemed to have gotten a plum job visiting a king who already hoped they could be friends. Lenn could picture Wolter pestering Jonnecht for a high-profile task and Jonnecht finally sending the knight where he would do the least harm, just to shut him up.

"I hope they bring the mead out, soon. And I'm curious about this music," Wolter admitted.

Lenn relaxed a bit in his chair. "We can agree on that, at least."

He wouldn't get used to the feeling.

Lenn traded glances with Monika, who looked amused and must have been eavesdropping. He often wished she was the regent, given that her mind was as sharp as a dagger, and she was utterly blameless in all matters compared to her husband. Unfortunately, Lenn's own west being a simpler place rooted in traditions, and tradition placing a king in the supreme role, Lenn would find himself alone in recognizing the reign. Scholars in the capital would ask for legal precedent, which circled back to tradition. The inept-but-good-natured, led by the devious-yet-well-read, would unite behind whichever man first dared usurp her throne.

And knowing her wisdom, Lenn expected she understood these bitter likelihoods in a more direct way than he could ever know. She likely knew them before Lenn was born. If she devised a better solution, he would happily consider it.

He then looked further down the table to the Lord

Governor of West Kensrik, who appeared to be having a polite discussion with King Julian. Willem den Holt outranked Wolter by the customs of his land, yet felt no need to flaunt it. His governor's medallion on a thick gold chain was his only conspicuous accessory.

When it came to trade, that discussion made sense. West Kensrik merely needed to send wagons north, through mountain roads already well travelled; the route from Bayrock and the wealthier side of Kensrik traversed most of the empire before reaching the same mountains. Etrouk owned the stretch of beach at trade waters, and they knew well what tariffs were. If traders on behalf of the Kenderleys were like Sir Wolter, they were not going to pay an honest tax if they could find a convenient way around it. The knight probably haggled vigorously for the gaudy clothes on his back.

The King then rose from his chair, a throne for the banquet hall; this was built from dark mahogany, lightly dusted with gold, and thinly coated with lacquer.

Julian spoke: "I thank you all for arriving from far and wide, old friends from the north and west who make sacrifices and toil endlessly for our happiness; and a special welcome to our prospective new friends, who just a few years ago might have sworn never to set foot here, lest we sever said foot for stepping where it was unwanted."

Wolter fidgeted; where was that mead, already?

Julian continued: "In my advanced years, and during these uncertain times, I value life's simpler pleasures. The presence of friends, great food in abundance, and sounds pleasing to the ear. I'm informed that, for all our benefit, the best musicians in this capital, and most likely in this land, have graciously agreed to provide such music that no one here has ever heard. It would be terrible to go into such a new experience on an empty stomach, so let the eating and drinking commence."

As helpful as Zinnia wished to be, no one expected her to master the complexities of a different culture's cuisine in so little time. The kitchen servants had no such expectations and assigned her to the simpler but no less eventful task of serving platters. While any of the usual servers might know the cuisine better from experience than Zinnia, everyone expected a Kensrikan servant to bear platters as well as anybody.

Kensrikan cooking was complex like a carefully woven tapestry; Wancyek cooking appeared deceptively simpler, like cracking a hard shell with a rock to reveal a delicious nut. Zinnia saw meat covered in slices of fruit; she could tell they were using honey or reduction of mead to glaze the meat, too. She saw that they grilled and seasoned vegetables. That was the limit of her immediate knowledge, and even if she was a fast learner, no one saw room for a single mistake on this most important evening.

When it was finally time to begin serving finished platters out to tables, she knew enough to kindly request that she be allowed to serve the head table. They did not deny her the privilege. Most of the cooking was done, and after all, they feared glares from the King or Queen that could not fairly be directed at a generously helping guest.

* * *

TIBOR BEGAN his investigation under cover of darkness.

Knowing how conspicuous a horse would be, and how outsiders were expected to ride them, Tibor proceeded on foot. He hoped to blend in with other merry makers until he saw something to investigate. Given that he was not on assignment from the King or Queen, he also kept aware of city patrols. To their knowledge, Tibor might be a suspicious person.

The streets echoed with fragments of noise from different taverns and venues, but the actual number of people outdoors was limited. The time had come and gone to be on one's way somewhere, and the time for returning home would be much later. There were few eyes upon him as he took his walk, looking like he might be late to a party but not quite panicking about it.

He remembered what Samuel told him. He kept his eyes open for youths who were out so late.

He tried to relax the tension he felt from his unfamiliar surrounds. For a man from the western province, this was an unusual number of people to witness living in close quarters, milling about, and all of them strangers. outside of any formal barracks at wartime.

It was also an unusual cluttering of buildings, awnings, alleys, places to avoid the moonlight or blend in with the other flickering shadows and figures produced by the few street torches in mid-burn, places to hide and from which to watch passersby. There was so much to steal his attention.

And yet, he heard Bayrock sprawled much farther than

this, with taller buildings and many more people. Tibor was glad he only had to cope with so much.

He was never going to fit in with the group he was tailing, being hardly the type to take this Ignacy fellow seriously, but he thought they might return to the last place he saw them. He could follow them at a distance. And he suspected he could lay a sound thrashing on them, if need be, provided he was not vastly outnumbered. He only worried that they fought with no class, given that he saw them swarming three people; he would stay wary of low blows. Soldiers rarely thought much of that because their plan was to incapacitate a person with as few strikes as possible; the motto "one blow, one life" was meant to remind that one never struck anybody that one would not risk killing, for a direct and heavy hit on just the wrong part of the skull...

There, snapping Tibor out of his train of thought, were a couple of hooded figures with shoulders rather narrow compared to many adults. He could only make out that they spoke to each other, but not what their hushed voices said. They looked similar to those who attacked the musicians. They walked quickly, as if they urgently needed to be somewhere.

He hoped he was not just following them home to their concerned parents.

The sounds bleeding out of taverns covered his footfalls. He was careful to let his eyes adjust to the dimmer lighting as he followed them around an ally corner, careful to stay far enough behind them to avoid notice.

The next thing he heard was the grinding of metal on stone, and then they were gone. A moment's deduction suggested to him that the only cause could be a heavy metal object at ground level; it was being dragged closed, so it was not hinged. He wondered what sort of door would do that, and he carefully felt around the bricks of walls with no luck.

Then he felt an uneven spot underfoot and realized whatever he stepped on did not quite behave like cobblestone. He stood in place, shifting his weight, feeling it tip slightly in whichever direction he shifted; he heard a metallic rattle as it did so. Then he stepped off it and looked down to investigate this strange metal disc.

He found handholds and carefully lifted the disc, pausing momentarily to look around for others, and to listen for sounds echoing up from the opening below. There were none.

This opening led underground. Was it a cellar door to access the city's foundation?

The metal disc looked the same on either side, at least in the dark, so he would not have a problem replacing the cover from underneath. Nothing about its look would give away the fact that it had been disturbed. The mysterious figures no doubt found this convenient to their purposes as well. He carefully slid the cover back over the entrance as he descended.

Bricks that jutted out were footholds and handholds as he climbed to the tunnel below. He moved carefully because he could make out nothing once he replaced that cover. The climbing bricks jutted unevenly and haphazardly out of the wall. It would be too easy to bump a knee or a shin.

What was this passage? Not a sewer, though judging from the subtle smell, some waste had seeped into it. The aroma was more damp than filth; this was likely a drain for storm waters.

It was the only answer that made sense to him. A passage to the castle itself, with so many possible entrances, overrun by rough characters... someone would have bricked off the concerning sections long ago or built a new tunnel.

Heavy rain would carve up the streets in time, and it could instantly flood a cellar. Anything that placed the temporary creek's worth of water underneath would prevent flooding, and the good condition of those streets and buildings at this point was a testament to such expert planning.

Granted, some rain flow down the street would help to clean it, but above a certain threshold...

He reached the bottom and found this stretch of tunnel better lit thanks to wall-mounted tapers. The taper holders had likely been placed long ago by workers so they could see what they were building. However, the tapers were meant to die out soon after the use of those who originally lit them, so Tibor had to quickly to follow his targets or get stuck underground in the dark.

There was a thin pool of standing water in the middle of the tunnel, upon which he would be careful not to tread; left over from the last big rainfall, no doubt. He stepped around it to follow the line of increasingly bright tapers that marked the youths' path.

"THERE." Iris patted Adina on the shoulders, having perfectly adjusted the scarf that she let the younger performer borrow.

Adina shivered; she lifted one end of it with her hand and admired its embroidered details. "This is just... it's the King and Queen who'll watch me now. I perform in the tavern to get hooted at by the night owls; why am I here? Sam, why did you bring me here?"

Iris beamed at Adina with a look of admiration and approval.

"Just listen to me, Adina. I've observed people come through these halls for the decade I've been in residence. And I haven't offered all of them my help. But you're beautiful—inside and out. Go with Samuel and Judit; claim the glory that's yours. Be strong, now, or you'll have to reapply your makeup."

Adina nodded and blinked a lot. She tried so very hard to remain strong.

"This is a scarf of sorcery." Continued her recently found ally. "When you feel it gently hugging your neck, you feel that I'm there with you, to protect you wherever you go. You can keep it if you like..."

A servant stepped through the doorway to the backstage area.

"I hope you're prepared," he said. "It's your time, ready or not."

Iris smiled, bowed her head, and shuffled away.

Adina looked to Samuel, whose eyes betrayed an anxiety barely below the surfaces. Then she looked to Judit.

"Well, we shall do this, shan't we?" Judit asked, their head tilted a bit to one side with curiosity.

* * *

ZINNIA LOOKED to the other assistants and made sure they were ready.

Some music of an intriguing character had begun streaming into the kitchen at a trickle from the hall outside, mostly overcome by frantic kitchen noises. The other servants had been bringing lesser platters out and serving mead to all. The head table was served last as these regents traditionally refused to be served before their guests.

Everything was in its place and set to its proper moment. Zinnia led the head table servants out of the kitchen and headlong into the peculiar waves of music.

NO ONE SPOKE any longer at the head table as they all tried to make sense of what they were hearing. It was familiar enough to be music, but it did things that no music they previously heard had ever done. Some of Jarek's men were rocking and swaying in their seats a bit without realizing it.

All the banquet's attendees were uplifted to a transcendental state, life's problems no longer of priority.

The first to break from this enchantment was Duke Lenn, who considered it a minor miracle that anything could keep his attention for such a long time. He was of a melancholy disposition, and often found himself disinterested in the day-to-day. That detachment from his social surrounds gave him the power to observe the effect of the performance on everyone else in the room. During this grand temporary phenomenon, Lenn observed Jarek's men with a sharp memory of how brutish they could be; they looked so peaceful and delighted in their trance. Maybe they remembered some part of them that had been dying for a long time. That which made one forget for any length of time could not just leave a vacuum; it had to stir up something as a new focus.

And then Lenn glimpsed back toward the kitchen because the music could not make him forget his appetite any longer. When he did, he saw that the main platters were emerging, and he received a vision that fit this music and completed his experience.

There was this woman, and the way she walked fit with something in the rhythm of the music, though everyone in the room was likely following this rhythm whether they were aware of it or not; it was just as well the kitchen servants should do the same.

Her dress was distinctly Kensrikan in form and quality. Had den Holt brought her? Even then, it must have been some mistake; no servant was done up and dressed that well just to work in a kitchen, nor took such care with her hair. And she so casually carried such power in her form...

Lenn immediately wanted to ask someone who she was, but in an instant she was at the table, laying the platter down, and it seemed strange to ask someone else to talk about her when she was right there. He stared intently at the singer, because the servant might think him strange if he broke the spell that entranced everyone else. He tried to catch glimpses when no one was looking, but rarely, for he expected to be caught.

The woman on the stage helped him by locking gazes. Well, she looked inviting, but in a different way. He had no words to describe his feeling, so he was thankful nobody demanded any explanation. Everyone in the room save him was bewitched by the performance. All sense was gone. And then the stage siren had him, and he felt comfortable letting her have his attention because he knew she wanted it. She seemed happy up there, with her very capital province attire, and that courtly scarf...

* * *

"Who was he?" Asked Zinnia.

"Who was who?" The nearest kitchen servant asked in reply.

"A Wancyek at the head table, next to the gaudy Kensrikan. I'm sure this man was not one of the soldiers." Zinnia tried to narrow it down.

"That leaves the two Dukes as possibilities." He explained. "Might I ask why you want to know of either? Just a visitor's curiosity, or...?"

"He was clumsily trying to make it look like the musicians had his undivided attention, but just because I'm not looking directly at a person doesn't mean I cannot see them stealing glances from the corner of my eye."

The servant nodded curtly. That framed the discussion differently than he expected. Many people took a tragic interest in the perennially available Dukes. It was most often Lenn. If it was Jarek, that interest was more puzzling than it was tragic; he was neither as handsome nor as gentle as his cousin, hence why nobody called Jarek the 'good Duke'.

But to have a Duke take interest in you was a rare and beautiful thing. Now this kitchen servant was intrigued.

"Well, Duke Jarek... I would guess that it's not him. And between you and me, though everyone would concur, that's for the best, because it takes unusual taste to prefer him over—"

"Then let's not speak of him further. So, Duke Lenn?" Zinnia interrupted.

The servant smiled. "Not a problem, let's discuss the good Duke, then—what he's often called. He is melancholy, often lost in his own mind, reading his books. I suppose there was some sorcery in the air with that strange music from the stage, that even he could behave uncharacteristically."

"What do you mean?" Zinnia asked.

"I mean what I said. What would you really like to ask?"

Zinnia sighed. "Very well. Do I need to worry about Duke Lenn? How am I expected to feel about this?"

"Oh." The servant considered, reminded once again that Zinnia was from elsewhere. "I understand this is all new to you, so: Duke Lenn is known to be only the most polite, fair and gentle in his dealings with others. If he makes you curious, get to know him; approach him, talk to him, in a friendly way. If he is bothering you, tell him, and he'll apologize and go back to his books."

Zinnia smiled, possibilities stirring in her mind. "Thank you. That was most helpful."

"Are you two actually going to clean these platters, or are you going to stand there?" Interjected the kitchen overseer.

"Our guest had an honest question," the kitchen servant replied. "I gave an honest answer; I'm done."

"It's all very charitable, but this guest is the servant of our other guests, and servants work," cautioned the overseer.

Zinnia crossed her arms. "I am the," she caught herself before saying 'daughter', "personal assistant to Lord den Holt of West Kensrik. I am not to be considered any ordinary kitchen servant."

"Ah." The overseer replied, looking Zinnia up and down. "Then would you kindly go assist him? You're standing where people could be working. If you're not going to do anything else, I can't have you distracting the others while they should be doing their fair part of the cleanup."

"Gladly." Zinnia smiled coldly before walking out.

ZINNIA SAW no point in joining her father at the table when no place had been set for her, nor was it enjoyable to be the most sober person among drunks. Further, she had spent enough time sitting near Sir Wolter on the ride here; she felt all right avoiding him for as long as possible. That left her traipsing the corridor toward the safety of her guest quarters, hoping to reach privacy before any of those unruly soldiers could be staggering the halls. Granted that, she suspected, no banquet-goers might yet be able to safely stand from their chairs...

As the stairwell came into view, she encountered one person who defied her assumption.

"Ah, it's you," she whispered in puzzlement.

"I'm sorry to have startled you. I'm Duke Lenn."

"Oh, it's... well. Why are you waiting for me at the stairs?" She asked hesitantly.

He stood, having previously been sitting on the third stair up from the level, but off to the side; the stairwell to the bedrooms was wide at the base, narrowing slightly as it ascended, and bisected neatly by a handrail. He was mindful enough not to block her way, but why was he there?

"Here in particular?" He pursed his full lips a moment in thought, perhaps realizing from her hesitant tone what his unexpected presence had done but continuing anyway. "A reasonable guess. Some of the guest quarters are up there, down the opposite turn from the library. You were understandably busy during the banquet, and I also wasn't sure if talking to you would get in the way of others' enjoyment of the entertainment..."

She read his pause and remembered what the servant had told her; her shoulders relaxed, and she proceeded with greater confidence. "I noticed your glances. I'm somewhat more surprised to see you speak Kensrik's language so fluently, and to be able to stand for that matter. You were at the head table. I expected everyone sitting there to sleep in their chairs for the night."

Lenn smiled. "I felt no need to drown my sorrows tonight. The music did a wonderful job of that; I thought so much mead would hinder rather than help the experience."

He spoke only part of the truth. In fact, he wanted to be in better condition than Jarek or any of Jarek's men if they started a brawl. Fortunately, even they were too cautious to cause a problem in front of foreign visitors, just as Lenn felt too cautious to tell this stranger every reason for his choices.

She just nodded and paused. This remained a strange situation: she did intend to speak with him, but it was also late at night, and she didn't necessarily want to speak with him right that moment. Then again, she would depart for home tomorrow at some scheduled time never made clear to her, so when would that right moment be? Here they were, each with as much freedom and lack of scrutiny as she imagined they could expect. Opportunity didn't wait for a person to be ready.

"I've done something really awkward waiting for you like this, haven't I?" Lenn asked.

Certainly, she thought. "I was on my way to my room."

He glanced at the stairs and moved further aside as if worried he had inadvertently blocked them. No person in the world would have been large enough to block them by standing in place.

"I'm terribly sorry. I won't follow you; I won't ascertain where you go. I just don't know when we would have a chance to talk before you leave. I can take a stroll and return when you're past..."

"I did want to speak with you, actually. I may reconsider."

He nodded apologetically. "I'll take a quick stroll. If you still want to talk, I'll be in the reading-room; it ought to be the only other room in the hall with a lamp burning, at this stage of night. Do whatever you like, feel no obligation to me."

"Very well, if I need you, I'll find you."

Zinnia walked by and mounted the stairs.

She still had grease on her hands and dress and wanted some time to clean up. She thought it was important to make him feel uncomfortable in return for how his sudden presence had made her feel, but he seemed like a good man to accept her choice without argument or question. Let him be even more grateful when she found him again.

The moment Lenn saw her foot ascend the first step, he began his stroll.

While they both felt they had privacy, there had in fact been a pair of eyes to watch, but only briefly, and their bearer did not choose to listen for particularly long.

NEITHER MEAD NOR a long banquet night could dull King Julian's obsession with the absent kitchen servant. He waited impatiently and was satisfied when the Kensrikans finally retired for the evening, so he and Monika could depart right after them and finally discuss the matter. They left behind a mess of soldiers too subdued from song and drink to brawl.

"That ended beautifully, Monika. It saved everything. But we came dangerously close to failure."

"Failure at what? Having dinner? I don't think anyone can adequately describe what we just saw and heard; it was incredible. Let the Kenderleys have their complicated big bands. I would defy them to come up with something like that!"

"We just had someone else's servant help us out. Do you know how impoverished we look?"

She frowned. "Oh, that. You're really still on that, aren't you?"

She had almost forgotten, almost neglected to pass along her suspicions about the culprit. Well, at least he was already too obsessed about it, and she was not in danger of ruining his evening with the news.

"It's not my job to overlook a problem just because of some distraction." He said.

"I refrained from sharing what I know at the banquet because it would have soured the evening further. You understand, right?"

He nodded. "I applaud your deft social management. Now is the time, then; tell me all about it."

She explained: "I took the kitchen servants to task, demanding an explanation for the absence. I know for sure, by their account, that the missing servant is recovering from a beating. I should think it's a severe one, for who would fail to serve their duty on such an important day? No one holds spite for you, Julian; I caution that I have yet to see the recovering servant with my own eyes..."

"None of them would lie to me about such matters." Julian grumbled, though his ire was not at Monika but at her ill tidings.

He then asked: "Is the servant's jaw broken, or do we have any kind of word who did this?"

"Perhaps not his jaw, but his spirit. He's too afraid to say who did it." She conceded. "But we can narrow the possibilities down sufficiently, can we not?"

"No one who serves and dwells in this castle would ever do such a thing. Even if I misjudged the character of any guard, why would none have committed this crime before, yet suddenly do so now?"

"Agreed." Monika wondered if he would come at this in the most roundabout way possible.

Then again, he was supposed to be a just regent. Monika thought they both knew who they would prefer to blame, but it was important for Julian to reason through things, as if anyone else in Wancyrik had the authority to challenge his verdict.

"So, we have nephew Lenn's needlessly invited riders. As if they ever seemed the type, they rode all night to get here and slept most of the day; I don't believe any of them would have the energy or the aggression to do such a thing. And Lenn himself having his nose in a book and his mind in a daydream, no, we can rule out the lot," Julian reasoned.

"Also agreed. If you had said otherwise, I would have questioned your mind."

"The visitors on behalf of the Kenderleys are not particularly suspect. Granted, I hear nothing good about Sir Wolter, but his misdeeds are of malediction. I don't see him as the type of knight who earned it through any physical trials, no, he's the ceremonial sort that only a decadent kingdom feels the need for. And Lord den Holt wouldn't want to be inconvenienced, nor do I see his personal servant wanting to be trapped in our kitchens when she could be enjoying the banquet."

Monika nodded, waiting for it.

"That leaves Jarek and his men, such a large group that I almost wish it was anybody more specific. Is there a way we can narrow it further?"

"I think we can give Jarek himself more credit than that," Monika said. "Not so much for his moral character, but his sense of duty and basic intelligence. I can't believe he would jeopardize your constant support. Yet he must always corral his men. Remember the last time?"

Julian grunted. "Years ago; I hoped they would have learned from that. He doesn't have to tell them to be loyal to each other, though. Who can we get to tell on his fellows? And we don't exactly have the numbers to easily punish them all, should none confess. I think they would be equally aware of that. What do we do?"

"We must count on Jarek to be more loyal to you than to the soldiers from his dukedom."

Julian nodded slowly. "On the surface of it, that should be possible. The Kensrikans will leave first, while Jarek and company already planned to stay one more day to recover from their excess. We can settle this without further diplomatic embarrassment. Let the culprit relax and think he got away with it, or stew in his guilt if he has a conscience..."

Monika thought this might be more difficult than Julian was making it sound, but she was not willing to introduce doubt at this juncture. It sounded like he was forming a viable plan.

She worried that the tensions between provinces, between Dukes, might come to a head because of this. She found herself glad that Lenn's riders were likely to stay an additional day, as well. If they would not side with the castle guard in case of any dissent from Jarek's men, then there must not be anybody else in the entire world upon whom the monarchs could depend.

11

THE UNDERGROUND

Air greeted Tibor's foot where he expected stone should be. He felt an instant of panic; he pushed off the ledge into a forward jump using the trailing foot and made it to the other side with a two-footed stagger. He paused briefly to listen for any indication that he had been discovered, but there was nothing. Then he glanced behind him; in the dim light, he could see a pit. There was no telling whether it was a maintenance issue or a trap, and that was not important for now.

Tibor moved ahead as quietly as he could while keeping a pace that allowed him to make use of the tapers before they died. For a while now, he could see far ahead of him but not what was immediately in front, such as the narrowly avoided pit. He doubted that was the only one.

After a couple more turns, the near tapers were dead, but a mysterious light shone at the end of the forked tunnel that was bone dry in this last section. That light seemed adequate for this last leg of the journey. He kept making his slow way along until his eyes adjusted to the level of illumination, letting him know that a floor stone here and there stuck up from the others, and there was no effort put to making it look like any mortar lay in the cracks around such stones.

He navigated around the raised stones and felt the walls, and he learned more with his hands than with his eyes. He found openings where rope was wound to high tension; nearby were dusty clubs, like the helmet-crackers every rider carried, not quite flush with the wall. The mechanism was simple enough: an intruder stepped on one of the raised stones, and then some catch that held the rope tense would be released, and then a club would hit them. If they stumbled around in pain, they would probably step on the other stones and get swatted by all of them. A crippling, perhaps fatal set of blows.

Ignacy's group lacked the resources to build their own tunnels, but they had no problem modifying derelict things to their purposes. It fit the group's nature: a collection of derelict youths warped to dubious purposes...

Then he heard quick boot-falls against stone, distant yet approaching from the darkness he had left behind. It had to be people who knew the tunnel well enough to have memorized the largely uneventful first section, to skip over the pitfall, and not to need any tapers. Perhaps Tibor had followed new recruits. It might explain why they were so easy to track.

Tibor hoped this would work, having no better idea in a pinch. He carefully weaved back around the trick stones and began to nick the trap ropes with his dagger. He sliced them just deep enough that they would begin to fray, but not immediately spring.

He was close to the end of the gauntlet when different and distant voices echoed from the well-lit end of the tunnel. He fumbled his dagger with surprise, and nearly falling on his face in a vain effort to catch his weapon, instead managed an impromptu forward dive roll that carried him past the final trick stone. His shoulder screamed with discomfort against the hard surface as he rolled, and he scrambled back to his feet.

"Hey you! Hey!" One of the pursuers called as the nearest group rushed from the darkness.

Knowing which group would reach him first, Tibor faced the darker end of the tunnel and squared up to fight. He could tell that these runners were deft enough to step around the trick stones even in haste, but he hoped that the first part of his quick plan would bear fruit.

As the group navigated through the trap, one of them stumbled on the handle of the dagger that he left behind, stepping on a trick stone as he tried to regain balance. Stopped in his tracks by a sprung helmet-cracker, he couldn't get out of his friends' way, nor could they stop in time. They bumped into him and each other and stumbled about setting off every trap.

For a moment, Tibor was rather glad he dropped his dagger. It did more for him than nicking ropes.

He cast a quick glance over his shoulder toward the sound of the others charging from the well-lit end of the tunnel; they might soon be upon him.

A distant throng of reinforcements on one side; the other

way, two youths who managed to remain standing after the traps struck them. Tibor made a simple choice. His stealth was ruined; escape was the best option. At least his eyes had adjusted to the darkness.

Tibor slammed a left hook into the head of the nearest young man, a knockout blow; before the young man could fall, Tibor shoved him into the trailing attacker. After a further hefty push, the second man tripped over the prone bodies behind him. Though he wasn't knocked out, his unconscious friend had fallen with and on top of him.

Hoping that was enough to clear the way, Tibor quickly staggered over the bodies of those who had been hit by their own wall mounted traps, brazenly albeit correctly assuming that every trap had been set off. One assailant, down but still conscious, grabbed his ankle; Tibor stepped on this man's wrist with his free heel, breaking his grip.

Tibor hustled forward, not counting on the others to be hindered for long by their downed friends. His route of escape had become total darkness, but he could no longer afford to go slow and careful. He braced his forearms in front of him to avoid hitting the wall head-first where the tunnel made its corner turn. While he knew there were no more helmet-cracker traps this way, the pitfall remained. He knew it was on the other side of this corner and closer to it than to the traps he left behind, and the sound of running water grew near, but that was all he had to go on. Making his best estimate, he prepared to take a running jump.

His last step came on what turned out to be the edge of the pitfall. He flopped over to the other side, bracing himself with his forearms and preventing his face from hitting the stone.

He scrambled to his feet, noticing distant tapers the moment he did. He kept running, his boots causing familiar shallow splashes.

Now past the traps and the pit, Tibor had a different problem. Even if he could find the entrance he used, he remembered jumping down after a point and landing in the middle of a tunnel, so it would be more difficult than finding where the passage ended. The new tapers he saw could reveal another exit. It could also represent another throng of attackers.

The attackers he knew about were chasing him. He could only keep running and hope for the best.

Tibor sped down the tunnel, assured in the better lighting that nobody set traps or pitfalls in this direction that went so far away from the hideout he had failed to reach. But those who lit these fresh tapers soon came into view. Tibor saw the terror in their young eyes as he rushed toward them from the darkness. They turned and fled.

He hoped they would. Then he could find their different entrance, which, given that they fled back to it, must also be an exit.

He caught up beside the slowest of them and ran him hard against a wall; he left his quarry to crumple to the floor, hoping his pursuers would stumble over their friend.

The second quarry was a few footholds up the climbing wall to the exit before Tibor unceremoniously yanked him to a crash landing and started climbing as rapidly as he could.

By the time Tibor felt the hard metal disc above him, there was a clamour immediately below him; for a long moment he felt trapped like a bug in a bottle. Given no time to think, he struggled to keep his balance, push the heavy metal up, and occasionally kick downward at whoever was trying to grasp his boots. Tibor just nudged the metal disc at the top and let it roll away as soon as he had lifted it out of place, since he had long abandoned any pretense at stealth.

Now he wouldn't mind the city guard observing him. He expected them to see his pursuers and to get the right idea.

He was half-way out to street level when someone got a firmer grasp of one of his boots. He kicked it off, then accidentally used someone's face for one last foothold as he scrambled above ground. Then he hurried to standing and loped along, one foot booted and the other not, following the sounds of carousing drunks towards the main street.

"The rain-tunnels! They're down there!" He shouted as he stumbled into the street.

People stared at this odd panting figure, one boot off, dripping with water all the way up the front of his outfit, beard peppered with chunks of unidentified debris, palms of his hands lightly scraped from the fall he took in the tunnel. What was that about the storm drains...?

Tibor stopped, checked behind him, and realized that nobody followed him; there was no visual explanation for his frantic shouts. As far as they knew, he was a drunk who had fallen into a tunnel. It was clever: Ignacy's people would just let him stagger out there so that the general populace could frown upon his condition and not listen to him.

He immediately regretted that he had gained anyone's attention, but at least he escaped. The street looked slightly familiar at this juncture. The direction he needed to go was predictable, given that the castle was at the top of the incline.

All he had to do, now, was limp uphill some indeterminate distance to safety.

He removed his other boot and resolved to carry it. He felt better with an even step. Walking in wet socked feet was hardly going to feel much worse than the rest of his body already did.

By the time Tibor identified himself to the night guards and made his way to the castle, he no longer had the energy to recount his tale. He hoped he had set them back for a time, given them doubts to stew on while they nursed their injured.

For now, he had his own injuries to tend to.

12

NIGHT AND MORNING CONVERSATIONS

Lenn stopped reading, distracted by that which he had initially hoped to distract himself from. He shifted his odd sitting posture on a far corner of the reading couch and closed the old book. He cast a quick glance at the still-bright flame of the reading lamp in its glass as if it might reveal some answer. The lamp sat there on its sturdy short table and did nothing more than its job.

He ran his fingers through his short straight hair, anxiety overcoming his usual melancholy, tempered by the euphoria and magic bestowed upon his senses by the evening's festivities. It averaged out to a slight sense of wonder, a slight contentment, and a hope that he had not entirely ruined things with this strange woman whose name he did not yet know. He accepted that given his dissatisfying social approach, he was owed nothing by her and was left to her mercy.

It all would have left him too awake to go to his sleeping chambers even if he had not promised to be in the reading room. His recently abandoned book was a time-tested favourite, the cartography and memoirs of G. den Hoogezand. It was a masterwork by a man whose frustration could only be darkly hilarious to anybody that didn't have to put up with the same. From a newly established island port, he attempted numerous excursions to the 'legendary North'; vast uncharted territory far past the eastern frontier wall of Jarek's dukedom, far north across the sea from Kensrik. Den Hoogezand's obstacles included miscommunicating with peoples of cultures unfamiliar to his Kensrikan eyes, political borders that shifted more rapidly than he could map them, and Kenderley suspicions that he had fabricated his travels and pocketed their generous patronage. After a final ill-conceived embarkation in storm season that wrecked multiple ships, he quit under heavy duress.

Lenn found it darkly fascinating. Den Hoogezand could be the luckiest man to have survived so much, only to be loathed and neglected during his autumn years by the people for whom he had done everything...

Then out of the corner of his eye he saw unexpected motion at the door, doubly startling from how preoccupied he had become. He jumped a little in his seat and bounced on the plush couch's cushions. He then remembered that this was the visitor for whom he waited. He must have lost all track of time.

The door opened slowly on its well-oiled hinges, making little sound once it was unlatched. This being a small library and not a bedroom, there was no lock, just a catch that could be accessed from either side to keep the door from swinging open due to a breeze.

"Good evening." Zinnia said with a smile, and added: "Apologies; have I startled you?"

Lenn smiled nervously, understanding he deserved the momentary discomfort for what awkwardness he had earlier caused. "Welcome. Enter if you like, please latch the door back closed either way."

She entered, pulling the door shut behind her.

"Have a seat if you like. Or you could stand, or you could sit, and I could stand, whichever."

"Given the seat," Zinnia observed the long couch with its slightly faded crimson cushions. "I think it might be proper if I sit on the far end."

"Certainly. So, this is a personal library. I know it's small, but the main library is really just a storeroom with no good place to sit and barely enough light to read by."

Zinnia looked around. "Ah. This is, rather, the place to bring your books and read them. A big couch just for yourself, or do you often have company?"

"Everyone living and working here is literate, but only some enjoy reading. I come here as a guest and don't usually have responsibilities while I visit, other than showing up where I am invited. Before such events, and after them, I have time to spend. I don't think this was ever intended as my library, but I guess it's become that."

"I think most of my people can read, these days," Zinnia said. "There isn't much around the city to read, but Lord den

Holt thought it was very important that we all learn how, even if we have to take turns sharing what few books House Kenderley deigns to give him."

"You're West Kensrikan, of the local populace? I wondered about that."

"Do I look like a Kensrikan?" She asked.

He paused, then replied: "I've never been to Kensrik. I know the place has many different types of people."

Zinnia understood. "Sir Wolter is the only Bayrocker of us three, so if you saw anything past his garb you might understand the type. Lord den Holt came from part of the empire close to the mountains in the southeast; you can tell them apart by their names, and their features if you know what to look for."

"We might have a few types in Wancyrik, but they've been living amongst each other for so long that most people don't pay attention to the difference."

"Ah, and you are from the north?" She asked, suspecting she guessed wrong but more interested in making light conversation to calm him; she could feel his tension.

He shook his head. "That's where Jarek's from. An easy way to remember is, the north's where we always seem to make war. The west, where I'm from, is the place that feeds everybody. And I suppose to complete the picture, this capital province you're in right now is an entirely different world that I'm not even sure King Julian recognizes at times."

She shifted a bit closer to him and examined his face. His eyes were a brownish amber she was not used to seeing. They seemed to open a bit wider after she had moved up the couch, where before they seemed so relaxed; his full lips pursed a moment, as they had done during the conversation by the stairs when he was nervous. She stopped where she was. He seemed oddly unready for this conversation, given that he was the one who first courted it. She hoped talking more would help relax him.

"Is King Julian your father? But you're not a prince... but I see some vague resemblance, more so than Jarek perhaps."

"Our family is complicated. King Julian is mine and Jarek's uncle; Jarek is not my brother. My father was Julian's brother and died when I was young."

"I'm sorry to hear that."

Lenn sighed. "Don't be, it's not like you're responsible."

"Did King Julian raise you?"

"Oh, no, I wasn't orphaned. My mother lived for a very long time. It wasn't easy, but we adjusted to the loss after a while." His shoulders had gradually eased as he spoke, and he appeared more relaxed.

She shifted right next to him for a better look at his eyes, his strong nose, the squareness of his chin, the angles of his cheekbones. He was a severe kind of handsome. He looked like he might have held back how nervous he still was, as if he wanted her to be so close yet had no idea what came next.

"It's been a pleasure to meet you, Duke Lenn. You're a good man, I can tell. I hope you understand, how do I say, that I would like to learn much more about you."

He blushed. "How much more?"

She slightly raised her eyebrows a moment and paused to consider her phrasing. "As much as you feel comfortable with, of course."

"I don't really know what else to tell you."

She leaned forward and gave him a short, cautious kiss, noted his lack of resistance, then leaned back with a glorious smile.

"Tell me you also want this."

He let out a heavy breath, at first relieved by nothing but a taste, yet this only served to whet his appetite. Then, feeling no confidence in what words he might choose, he simply nodded in agreement.

She patted the side of his face. "Relax, lie down. I should undress and leave my attire clean for the eyes of others tomorrow. You should do the same, no?"

He blinked, confused for an instant by the effort to process his unfamiliar emotions and her words and his environment all at once. Then understanding soothed his nerves like a balm and he removed his shirt with trembling hands.

THE CRIMSON COUCH had been built to serve different purposes; one could sit upright while reading or lay on it stretched out fully for a nap. It was never built for how they had just used it, but the impeccable craftsmanship held up well.

He let her in the way he had never trusted anybody else to do, and he regretted nothing. He felt a oneness, a completion, that he only ever read about before; something he thought he was too broken to feel. As they sat upright on the couch once again, he wanted her to know that she didn't have to remain anyone's servant.

"But I don't need you to title me, Lenn. I'm already a lady, according to House Kenderley."

His eyes widened again, but she began to answer his question before he had time to ask.

"I feel I would be a lady without their social order, anyway, but it's a formal title like your own. I was adopted and raised by Willem den Holt. As for how I ended up serving platters at your banquet, I saw people in need, and I read how upset your uncle was; I did my best to help the situation." She grinned mischievously and looked him up and down. "And look what an adventure that became. Well worth the trouble, no?"

"But the rest that you told me before... all of it is true? You work for your people's independence not just from within his manor, but as his daughter?" He examined her again as if only now did he truly know her.

Her smile faded; he knew then that he was correct, and hers was a risk she understood and took seriously. It was not any kind of game.

She locked gazes with him. "Yes. All of it. Do you judge me for that?

He needed no time to consider his answer. "I judge you to be the boldest person I know. If I didn't observe you to be so caring, as well, I would be greatly concerned about who I just let love me."

In fact, it soothed him to understand that they were closer in status than he once thought. He had only gone through with this because despite how he vastly outranked her, he placed her comfort in the highest regard, and he saw her pursue this enthusiastically. Even then, a part of him wondered if he had done something wrong until she told him the truth.

"I want to help you, Zinnia. Tell me what I should do. Absolutely anything." Lenn said.

She leaned in and kissed him again. Then she retreated until her face was a hand span apart from his and she said: "You'll stay out of my way and have nothing to do with my people unless we invite it. And hopefully your uncle does the same. If this is the case, there is nothing else you need to do for me." She retreated further and awaited his reply.

Lenn stared back. "From what I've overheard, all House Kenderley wants is reassurance that we'll not strike them while they address an enemy alliance to their east. I believe they would only need such assurance for a war that requires most, or all, of their army. I can hope that peace with us is all they ask, given how accommodating Julian appears."

He observed her smile lightly at that. Perhaps he just confirmed something important to her.

"What happens when they object to your freedom? I know your father was kind to your people, but the regent he serves is entirely different. Does your plan account for that?" He asked with deep concern.

She casually stood and prepared to clothe herself again. "You don't need to tell me the nature of House Kenderley. Even if I had forgotten for a moment, Sir Wolter's presence on this visit would remind me." While she dressed for the walk to her room, she continued: "Perhaps I need something else, Lenn. I need you to trust me and to ask no further questions."

He ran his fingers through his short hair. That would be severely difficult.

But he said he would do absolutely anything.

Before she left, she approached him once again, unclasped her necklace, and placed it around his neck. She did up the clasp and patted the pendant that now sat against his upper chest.

"Keep this to remember me, and what you have promised."

* * *

HE TOLD her everything she needed to hear. Now she knew what was asked of House Wancyek. It helped for him to reinforce the rumours about the imminent war on the opposite side of Kensrik, one which should prove costly.

The council did not completely agree about whether they believed House Kenderley would accept the loss of a deeply expensive and unprofitable region. They intended to draw no blood and for Willem den Holt to return safely to his people, a show of good faith. They had traditional weapons, but they might have little time to organize any army, let alone one capable of deterring Kensrik. This was a risk they were willing to take for their freedom.

But Lenn didn't need to know that. If he did, he might interfere.

* * *

LENN DID NOT QUESTION AT FIRST how he ended up in bed; in his own half-awake mind, he still felt that he was lying in a grassy field bathed in the light of a generous sun while cloud castles revealed themselves to him. It was a blissful and innocent dream to have given what it followed.

As waking overtook sleep, the previous night's festivities quickly surpassed such innocent wistful memories. He wondered where Zinnia was. They had been in the reading-room, and then...

He opened the curtain and then the shutters and looked at the bright light of the dawn that shone through the window. Were the visitors already gone?

But something of the distant past remained. He could not help but be haunted by it.

Does the day feel new, son?

"Every dawn heralds a new day," Lenn grumbled.

A bad time; apologies. You can always talk to me when you need it.

Lenn shook his head. "I'm just glad I didn't think about you a few hours ago."

Fortunately, his clothes had travelled to this room with him. He had been thoroughly infatuated, not drunk, though that banquet music was intoxicating enough by itself.

Thinking ahead to whether he would meet with his guests again, he took off the necklace she had given him and put it in a safe pocket among his belongings. If any other guest noticed its absence from her neck, she could claim she had lost it, but not if they saw it hanging around his.

SAMUEL WAS unsure of whether he had slept for any relevant span of time that night. As far as he recalled, he had been lying awake in his hastily prepared guest room through to the dawn. His thoughts raced, and he felt euphoric from the novelty of which he had recently been a part; this was tempered by the crash of it being over. As far as his musician ears could tell, the band engaged sorcery little known even to themselves. Through them, the spirit of music itself brought a miracle the likes of which had never been heard in his lifetime.

Unfortunately, that alone made no guarantee of what would happen next. His judges were not expert musicians, nor expert critics, if such a thing existed. Just as life in the capital province typically went, one lived at the whims of fickle wealthy people who went by a felt sense more than musical knowledge.

But why wouldn't they feel what the whole room appeared to have been feeling? Why would it be any different from what he felt now? What made him nervous when all indications pointed to a successful show?

Then again, rejection had not been the only thing absent; any thanks or resounding acceptance was absent as well. When the band departed the stage, they left an audience that could no longer stand for any ovation; an audience the majority of whom had chosen to drink themselves comatose.

But was that because they loved or hated it?

Samuel had a mind forever searching for reasons to justify his inherent tendency toward nervousness. When there were no immediate reasons, his mind worked doubly hard to make some.

At some point, though, the night was officially over, dawn beckoned, and he felt it was time to wash up and see what answers the new day held.

THE CORRIDORS between various rooms in the castle joined at one main hall where there were chairs for those in waiting. More than a century ago this had been the throne room, until one of the more prosperous kings decided to finance an entirely new throne room with the riches won from a peace negotiation with the Etroukans. The old throne room was now the main hall or the waiting hall, depending on who was talking about it.

Duke Lenn descended the steps to the corridor, passed the closest entrance to the banquet hall, and made it to the main hall at a brisk pace. He was puzzled to find no one there but the string musician from the previous night.

The man straightened but did not stand. "My apologies. I don't recall if I'm supposed to stand, salute, or bow. If you'll excuse my memory lapse, I think it's been a long night for everyone."

Lenn found his candidness refreshing and eased a bit. He hoped he could help this man relax with some humour.

"Don't worry about it. So, are we both terrifically early, or terrifically late?" Lenn asked.

"I've been alone since I got here," the man answered, visibly easing at the shoulders himself, "I haven't seen nor heard from anybody. May as well sit and relax; I take it you're a lighter drinker than all the others to have recovered from the night so quickly, sir...?"

"Duke Lenn of the West." He took a seat on a plush cushion near the musician.

The musician raised his eyebrows. "By the Winds, the good Duke himself. I should know exactly what you look like, I used to live in your province. Now I'm embarrassed. I'm Samuel."

"Samuel the fleet fingered?" Lenn smiled in jest.

The musician laughed. "Not at this time of morning, I can tell you that much."

"Your show was magnificent. Did this band form recently? I know you're well established by yourself, and I just haven't heard of the other two."

"We put that show together in haste, with a lot of hard work. Good to know our efforts are appreciated by a respectable person such as yourself," Samuel beamed.

"I don't just trade flattery. Nothing easily keeps my attention, Samuel, but your act had me for a good length of time. It took me to another world..."

The other two musicians interrupted Lenn's compliments with their arrival. Lenn felt the need to stand again in a polite fashion. Samuel felt unusually relaxed from the conversation and had already abandoned all pretense of formal greetings; he stayed put.

Adina curtsied, while Judit just stood there and cracked a friendly smile.

"The good Duke; we're humbled and honoured. My name is Adina, my nearby friend is Judit; I suppose you've already met Sam."

"Sit on any of these giant cushions and see how difficult it is to get up," Samuel cracked.

They all found seats near each other.

"Well," Adina began, "I don't drink at shows, I don't believe my bandmates do... what brings you awake at this earliest part of the morning? I'm not sure any other banquet-goers could get up now for anything."

"I'm a light drinker, myself..." Lenn was reminded of his awkward conversation with Zinnia by the stairs.

He quickly shook off the memory and continued: "I can't say the same for the others. Jarek and his men were celebrating a solemn anniversary, while my uncle and aunt celebrated the presence of our Kensrikan visitors. I hoped to have a word with the visitors and was concerned they had already left for home."

Adina smiled; Lenn thought it was a knowing expression. Before he could ask why, they were interrupted by visitors for whom Samuel could feel the urgency to stand. Julian and Monika arrived only slightly less formal in attire than they had been for the banquet, which was nevertheless twice as prim as the average commoner: an ornate blue silk gown for Julian, a black corseted dress with a white skirt for Monika, and each wore a circlet.

"My nephew. It's good to see you up early. And these grand musicians, with whom I see you're getting acquainted," King Julian observed.

"King Julian. Queen Monika." Lenn bowed respectfully to each of the new arrivals, and the musicians followed suit.

"Please, all of you, return to your seats, don't let us disrupt whatever you were discussing." Julian instructed, before looking at his nephew: "We shall breakfast with our visitors in the private hall. You may arrive with them as they walk through here, if your present conversation is too engrossing to end. It should be great to have at least one of our Dukes present."

Monika smiled and nodded. She expected them to assume that Jarek was still recovering from the banquet, when in fact he was not invited. It was better for them to think so.

"And as for the famous capital trio, after the breakfast, you are all invited to the throne room on an important matter. At the appropriate time, I shall send a servant to collect you."

Samuel perked up at that, trying to determine whether Julian's description of them was polite or full of awe. That throne room meeting sounded like as good a time as any for his hopes and fears to be confirmed or denied.

Adina and Judit traded glances. The two wondered if a completely different matter had been settled, of which their bandmate had little idea.

THE MUSICIANS HAD some time to converse with Duke Lenn about his home province, of which two bandmates knew nothing, and the third only had memories from his farmhand days.

"I really just remember a profound flatness," said Samuel. "It was like if anybody wanted to sneak up on you, they had better be shorter than the wheat."

Lenn chuckled. "It barely changes. Sometimes you have fields of flowers, grown for festivals or orders from the capital province, fields of colour instead of grain. But not often, nor shall it ever be, unless people decide to eat blooms more frequently. People may change, but it feels very cyclical: the fields are planted, they grow tall, the harvest... the same old houses just need repairs, and the winters are increasingly less fun with age."

"I'm not sure I could last in a place like that." Adina said. "Where everything's visible for far around and is just... unchanging, unchanged, except for me getting older. I need a life that can change with me. Nothing really stays the same in the capital, except for the castle, and even then, it gets some wing added to it occasionally."

Judit liked the feel of this conversation but felt no urgent need to contribute. They would run their fingers over the thread decorations in the wraparound skirt of their outfit, or they were happy to examine the vastness of the hall with its high ceilings and buttresses.

Then Judit noticed other guests approaching.

LORD DEN HOLT WALKED SLOWLY, Sir Wolter practically shambled, and faring the best of the three was Zinnia. Luttwig was too young to have seen a drop of drink and remained his usual self.

It was the first time Lenn and Zinnia had seen each other since their night of passion. Lenn betrayed nothing with his expression, nothing beyond what anyone could have observed at the previous night's banquet. In the daytime, Lord den Holt and Sir Wolter were the honoured guests, and

Zinnia was supposed to be an afterthought, just like the goofy looking youth who expectantly followed Sir Wolter around. Lenn could pretend not to know Zinnia. It was not easy, but it was possible.

Lenn stood. "Good morning."

"Good for whom?" Wolter mumbled.

Lenn ignored him and briefly addressed the musicians.

"The breakfast calls. I hope we see each other again before I need to go home. Unfortunately, I have no banquet hall out west, or I would happily arrange a show. The next harvest festival, perhaps."

He then turned to Lord den Holt; it took considerable effort to focus on the official leader of the diplomatic group, who was neither its most interesting or beautiful person.

"Do you recall the way to the private dining hall, sir?"

"Feel free to show us the way," Lord den Holt replied tiredly.

Lenn nodded. "Right, it would be my pleasure."

As the dignitaries followed Lenn, the musicians turned to discuss things amongst themselves.

ADINA QUIRKED AN EYEBROW. She knew of an energy in that brief interaction that no one else could, but it was no one else's business. Only pure coincidence had made it hers.

Samuel observed none of his bandmate's mannerisms and spoke first. "So, they want us in the throne room after they eat. What do you suppose that's about? I may just be used to people handing me money by the door, but..."

Adina let out a sarcastic laugh. "What, do you think they'll knight you, or execute you?"

"Neither. I just don't understand the level of formality. Whatever this is, it could be big. Perhaps another show?"

"Would be great to play a wedding," Judit mumbled. "Big royal wedding. Don't really see much opportunity for that, unfortunately."

Samuel smiled reassuringly. "Maybe they'll keep us around long enough for that to come true."

Adina hesitated, wanting to reassure Samuel, yet hoping not to reveal their meeting with the Queen.

"Do you really need to know what it is? Couldn't you just be content with the likelihood of it being a pleasant thing? We will not have to wait for long."

"I want to." Samuel admitted. "I wish I could. I know better than to try, at this point. I hate to say it, but given where I grew up, I'm a product of the good Duke's realm: predictability, routines, cycles; this excitement may be more to your taste."

"Ah, Sam. You poor worrier. Look, we're both here for you. No matter what it is, you won't have to face it alone. And did you notice how the King himself referred to us, not too long ago?"

"Yeah. He also didn't remember our names. I would be surprised if he remembers terribly much from the banquet."

"The good Duke's a light drinker, so he says. He remembered. His verdict was the same," Judit offered.

"As he said, he doesn't have any place to hire us in residence." Samuel said.

Adina shook her head. "You're impossible, you know that? Quite something."

He sighed. "I'm in this to the end. This, however, is who I am; none of us can change our personality within the turn of a moment."

"Fair enough. As long as you understand that we care." Adina said.

13
TENSION AND CONFRONTATION

Breakfast became an awkward affair where Lenn and Zinnia tried not to gaze at each other.

Today, in front of her father, theirs was a dangerous secret. He would keep it with the utmost loyalty. With all his heart he trusted her to do the same.

Lenn caught Zinnia casting the quickest glance at his neck, and he knew why. He gave the lightest smile of reassurance that he hoped nobody else would detect. It seemed these hungover men weren't paying attention to her, anyway.

That must not be the only reason. No one should be in a hurry to inform Julian that the guests loaned him not only a kitchen assistant, but the lord governor's daughter. Even Wolter should know better than to mention it.

Well, one would hope.

"This has been a phenomenal look into the way another southern culture does things," Wolter said. "I mean, you're northern by the map, but in my eyes, a proper and civilized

Southern Kingdom. A frontier land, right at the edge of civilization, doing daily war with the forces of darkness. It's truly admirable."

Lenn patted his own lips clean with a cloth napkin. If ill-conceived warfare was going to be the basis of Wolter's positive impression, then Julian had invited the wrong Duke to the breakfast.

"And you, Duke Lenn, with your sturdy, hardworking bread-basket province of craftsmen; I see the trade opportunity. Well, maybe not for Bayrock, but for West Kensrik." He looked to the lord governor. "Wouldn't you agree, Willem?"

"It should make King Jonnecht happy if we do some trade. Not too much of it, mind; Kensrikan traders must consider it a measure of power to be our primary supplier of goods, and should we get too close to Wancyrik, some gold counters might start feeling insecure." Lord den Holt said.

"Oh, nonsense," Wolter said. "Just food, better clothes. I don't see these noble people riding in to occupy your homeland any time soon. Besides, Wancyrik seems quite busy already with its fair helping of conflict."

Lenn wondered what would happen when Zinnia and her cohorts finally hatched their plan. He wasn't told the specifics, but she just seemed smarter than the agent from Bayrock and, though they were closer in intellect, her own father. What sort of trade would there be, and who would recognize the new southern land?

He could recognize their independence if he were king, perhaps grant it cautionary protection. And invite the wrath of House Kenderley. That would be a splendid mess. Lenn couldn't see his uncle doing any such thing.

"Well, I'm certainly glad you've enjoyed yourselves. If there is any place on the grounds you would prefer to revisit, don't let me hurry you out past the wall." Julian said.

Wolter smiled. "As much as I would love to stay and try to understand that strange music you've invented, my life runs on a strict schedule. I'm needed in Bayrock, and there's a ship chartered to depart from the Etroukan trade port at a very particular time. It's fairly expensive, getting their permission to land there."

And more expensive, Wolter knew, to be caught sitting at anchor for too long when you didn't pay for any permission to land anywhere. Least expensive of all to arrive on time for the boat, and make sure it left from a more secluded section of the beach before anybody could catch up to it...

"We could give you a full rider escort out of the capital," Lenn offered.

Julian looked puzzled. "I don't think that will be necessary..."

"Agreed. Riding behind two horses is quite enough without making it a stampede." Wolter concurred with Julian.

"We will require you and your riders for a small matter of ceremony after our guests are seen safely away." Monika informed Lenn.

"*All* the riders?" Asked Lenn. "Tibor is still—"

"We'll discuss that afterward. I know of Tibor's condition." Julian cut off his nephew before there could be any talk of the nature that Tibor raved about to castle guards; nothing that needed to be said in front of the Kensrikans, for sure.

There was a brief silence where most were too tired to

carry the conversation themselves, and those who were most awake dared not share what they thought.

Julian clapped his hands as a signal to kitchen servants. "Right, I believe we're all finished our helpings. Servants will see to it that you leave nothing behind in your guest quarters..."

* * *

THE MOMENT TIBOR could drag his aching self out of bed and clothe himself, he requested to meet with the captain of the Capital Guard. He spent the next long while sitting on the modest bed in the cozy quarters allotted to a visiting soldier of elevated rank, sipping water but eating no more than a small bun for breakfast. What he had to say felt more important than hunger, and if guards returned to summon him, he would not be caught in the midst of a meal.

Then came a firm rapping on the door of his quarters.

"Captain Bruno has agreed to speak with you." The guard's voice resonated through the door.

Tibor replied with an affirmative and sprang up uncharacteristically quick given what parts of him still hurt. He donned his boots. Patting himself when it felt like something was missing, he realized he no longer had his dagger. The story he needed to tell Captain Bruno would explain why.

The guard led him along a path inside the wall of the privileged section of the city. The Captain's Office to which this path led was attached to the Armoury yet accessible with its own entrance, an ornately carved wooden door through which the guard announced Tibor's arrival. After

Tibor was granted permission to enter, the guard waited outside.

Tibor cast a circumspect glance at the office's interior. The painted portraits and nature landscapes on the walls and the warmly toned wood furnishings contrasted with the bare and functional looking exposed stone visible outside. Captain Bruno sat in a dark wooden armchair behind a desk which appeared sturdy but also weathered with age; the lacquer was lightly scratched in places.

Bruno did not stand to greet him but gestured to a chair on the opposite side of the desk. "Hello Tibor; I know you're one of the good Duke's riders and he let me know to expect you; you needed no introduction. I heard you ran into trouble in the city last night." Bruno glanced carefully at him. "Are you well? I heard no request for a doctor."

Tibor winced. "Well, I fared better than some of my attackers, at least."

Bruno nodded quickly; he had a pen at the ready and he looked at the paper on which he was about to write. "Tell me all about them."

"Young men, wearing hoods; I first saw them in broad daylight accosting the musicians who performed at the King's Banquet, whom I ended up escorting to the castle. At the time, they fled at our horses' approach. Then, later on—"

"Wait." Bruno knitted his brows and glanced up from his paper. "The musicians were accosted, and during the day? This is the first I've heard of it. Did you tell someone to pass this information along to me? Because I should have a talk with whoever forgot."

Tibor's eyes widened a little. Did Lenn only tell Bruno to

expect him, but not relate a single other reason why? Perhaps this was best characterized as a harmless oversight.

"I saw fit to escort them myself, during which time one of the musicians told me what he knew about who the attackers could be. After my arrival, and with most of the concern for the security of the banquet, I asked permission of Duke Lenn to quietly investigate the attackers myself. He instructed me to report immediately to you once I learned anything."

Bruno sighed and gave a curt nod. After this pause, he said: "I understand that you take orders directly from the good Duke, so I cannot fault you for your loyalty. But I hope you understand how irregular it was for him to instruct you as he did, instead of telling you to report such things to me immediately. What you just said is absolutely unheard of. This isn't Kensrik."

Tibor wanted to ask why the lack of escort, even if they were not in Kensrik. Was this man, who oversaw the city every day and heard every report, so absolutely sure of the musicians' safety? Even if he was, would Julian not have asked for that?

But Tibor remembered Lenn's instructions, and Bruno was already rankled.

"I will pass your complaint to the good Duke if you like."

Bruno put up his free hand for a moment and shook his head once. "I see little point in that now, but you might like to mention this to him if he asks for any further quiet investigations; I'm sure he knows whose jurisdiction this is. Let's move on to what you learned, and what happened to you last night." He readied his pen once again.

Tibor was grateful to return to the point of the meeting. "I quietly moved through the streets near where the musicians were attacked, and I noticed hooded youths resembling the attackers. Following them at a distance, they seemed to vanish around an alley corner. Then I discovered a... metal door in the road, a way into this underground system you have."

"The storm drains, is that where they went? Curious. Please continue." Bruno interrupted as he took his notes.

Tibor shifted uncomfortably in his seat; given the type of falls he had taken, sitting in a chair was not entirely comfortable. "Yes, they were lighting tapers to see the way and I followed them a good distance down the tunnel until I was discovered. I never found their destination; it was all I could do to fight them off and escape."

Bruno quickly nodded; his eyes trained on the paper. "A veteran soldier like you against some youths; I suppose some of them would land a lucky blow, but they stood no chance overall. Did you count how many of them you encountered? If not, just estimate it for me."

"With my own eyes?" Tibor hesitated. "Maybe a dozen I could make out. They had reinforcements chasing me, too, but by that point I was running and looking for an exit."

"Ah, a mob stampeding like that would be dangerous even to a fully grown soldier. Smart."

Tibor doubted he impressed upon the man how dangerous this truly felt, but gut instinct was hardly adequate proof. "Captain Bruno, I'm certain there must be more than I saw. I just can't tell you how many more. I mentioned I spoke with one of the musicians, Samuel, because I first thought he had been attacked by a jealous rival. What he told me was worrisome."

"Then let's hear it." Bruno replied calmly.

"Samuel said there might be a group of disillusioned young people, and perhaps a few of their elders, who are not just thieves or pickpockets but following a man named Ignacy. And he even testified that it was Ignacy who assaulted him that day."

"Ignacy, the runt we once arrested years ago for attempted rabble rousing?" Bruno paused for a moment, then put down his pen.

"You know him?" Tibor hoped he had gotten through to the captain.

Bruno grinned sardonically, and Tibor's hopes sank at the sight of this expression before he even heard why they should.

"Ignacy who got laughed out of a tavern, convincing no one, and who got on his knees and begged and cried and claimed it had been the liquor? Ignacy whom I let free because it can hardly be called rabble rousing when he couldn't even rouse rabble?" Bruno leaned back in his chair and steepled his fingers as he examined Tibor. "I even got him to praise me for making sure nobody in the tavern beat him for what he said, though nobody found him worth the effort. And someone thinks this man has followers?"

"But Samuel thinks he could. Would that not be a concerning threat if true?" Tibor protested.

"Did he prove that to you at all? How does he know Ignacy didn't just join a small band of thieves?"

Tibor paused, speechless. No, Samuel offered no proof, just anecdotes, but Tibor felt no different about the matter after reconsidering. Yet what was he supposed to offer Captain Bruno?

"Listen, Tibor. I realize the Capital Guard is here to protect the city from external threats; our patrols, our community problem-solving, it's something we do mostly to keep an eye on the drunkards at night. But at heart, we're no different from people in the west. Our gods are the same and we take pride in who we are, and we care about our community. Our young people learn the same values here as they would in the west, and I give them way more credit than to follow some loser. Maybe you think it's different here because this is a wealthy city, but wealth is neither good nor evil. It never corrupted anyone, not even Kensrikans. All it does is enable the virtues or vices of whoever possesses it."

"I never said wealth was causing a problem." Tibor said.

Bruno appeared to calm at that, as if he had accidentally voiced an insecurity and realized he had reached a premature conclusion. "Perfect. Then what do you think is really the problem? What would you ask me to do?"

Tibor sighed, adjusted his posture with a wince, and thought carefully about his next words. "If a dozen or so thieves are attacking people during the day, that can't continue. Now you know they're hiding in the storm drains; you have some idea where to look. You can flush them out. And if you know Ignacy is one of them, that's someone people could watch out for; you might catch him and get him to betray the others if he is soft as you say."

Bruno smiled with satisfaction and began to write on his paper.

"An organized group of thieves brazen enough to attack in

broad daylight is certainly a problem worth solving. That system is extensive, but I can spare guards to do a thorough search. If we find Ignacy, we'll not let him off so easy this time."

"Let them know to be careful of pitfalls and traps. I encountered a couple in the dark."

Bruno shrugged. "We can bring tapers. If there's nothing else, this meeting is concluded; just make sure you trust the Capital Guard to do its job, and report anything suspicious to us first. All right?"

"Yes, sir." Tibor agreed, supposing he was due for a proper meal anyway.

"Rest up some more. You've been through a lot."

THE SUN WAS WELL on its way toward noon when the enclosed carriage bearing Lord den Holt, Sir Wolter, Zinnia and Luttwig rolled away. Lenn watched it leave and wondered if he would get to see Zinnia again.

The wall's portcullis cut off his view of the carriage.

In the same courtyard of the grounds, Jarek's men were lined up for inspection.

"Soldiers," Julian said, "in light of our banquet to congratulate you on your victory, it seems a pity to have to punish any of you now."

The expression on Jarek's face turned completely sour before Julian had the chance to continue.

And continue he did: "However, inexcusable wrongdoing has occurred within my castle's walls."

Julian walked a slow path in front of the line of soldiers, his face stern and cold.

"I have little notion of how you carry on up north, nor do I pay it much mind. You do a noble task for Wancyrik, a constant attempt at expanding our borders in the only direction suitable. I trust Duke Jarek to govern you in his province. While he normally does a grand task of keeping you honest during visits to the capital, I understand only too late that he cannot be everywhere all the time."

Julian had been looking at the path in front of him, but now he turned and locked gazes with a series of soldiers before he continued.

"Nor can I, though why should we be? Soldiers are men of discipline, are you not? More to the point, soldiers are people, creatures of empathy who should wear killing with a heavy heart, as a grim necessity to protect our way of life. But perhaps one of you has become an animal, and animals need to be tamed."

Jarek tightened his right fist after hearing that. Julian returned to a spot about ten paces in front of the center of the line

"I, King Julian the Fifth, hereby declare that the man who beat one of my kitchen staff within a thumb's length of his life should step forward and accept his punishment. Should he fail to do so, or should a knowing soul fail to make his identity apparent, all of you must be punished."

A murmur began amongst Jarek's men. It was difficult to ascertain who said what, but the gist of the soldiers' anonymized utterances was clear: they wanted to see evidence of a person having been beaten, moreover, they were not about to take punishment as a group for the crimes of the one.

Julian's cold expression became a glare that swept up and down the ranks.

"Is that how it is? That not one of you will speak up for justice? That you can look into the eyes of your King, knowing the wrongness of assaulting one of the King's own servants, and stay silent? So I should suffer the indignity of explaining to you how much deeper this runs politically than one person's life, as if that life should be held up for measurement against anything? Very well, you force my words.

"We live in different worlds, House Wancyek and House Kenderley. They can keep theirs. But when they visit, when we have use for making a positive impression on them, that's the first day in history we end up having to borrow one of their servants. What kind of castle needs to borrow servants from their guests to run a banquet? In their eyes, this is now that kind of castle. We must look like we're incapable of managing our own affairs. Whoever you are, you have embarrassed us all."

"Great King," Jarek interceded, "this display, it's completely unnecessary. I will handle this matter in my province, and I give you my word that the culprit will be found and duly punished."

"You've said that before." Julian dismissed, not even awarding him a quick glance.

"So I have. Does my word mean nothing to you?"

"Not when the prior incident failed to be the last, as you promised it would."

Before Jarek could further protest, one of the soldiers called out.

"I did it, it was my crime; lay nothing upon my fellows."

The speaker emerged from the line, to stand separately from the others. He could otherwise easily have been mistaken for any of them; another northern soldier of average height, dark hair that framed his face and went down to his neck, and a stocky build.

Julian approached him, brandishing a helmet-cracker. "On your knees!"

And Julian began to lay a beating on the man, swatting him on the forearms and on his buttocks, and then to the sternum, knocking the wind out of him yet mercifully not hard enough to crack ribs.

Jarek stormed toward the king. "Lay not another blow upon him! Put down that club, I tell you!"

"You tell me?" Julian growled back. "You dare talk to me that way? Don't presume to decide when enough is enough in my home."

"I need him to be able to fight. There's been enough of a punishment today. Let me handle any further reprimands," Jarek argued, with a menacing undertone to his voice.

"Do you submit yourself to the remainder of his punishment, then?"

"Uncle, I—" Lenn interrupted.

"Not now Lenn, I don't need your advice on this matter," Julian spat before pointing his club at Jarek and adding: "I should beat you on your own account, for insubordination. Now shut your mouth."

Jarek scowled. "Old man, don't give me a reason to defend myself."

"Old man?! I'll take one of me over ten of you. You don't know how to war against a real enemy. You would never have survived against Etrouk. I ought to..."

Knowing the club had a short reach, Jarek backstepped from the first swing, which was meant as a surprise but was too predictable in its execution. Jarek kept his weight forward to immediately rush Julian and crowd the weapon wielding arm.

"Stop, Jarek—both of you!" Monika called out, only to be ignored.

Jarek struck the back of the wrist of Julian's good hand, causing him to drop the helmet-cracker.

Julian clutched his good hand with his bad. He stared at Jarek in shock.

Then Jarek slapped Julian hard enough to send him to the ground.

There was silence amidst the soldiers. Monika rushed to Julian's side in tears, calling out for guards. Lenn himself was frozen in shock. He thought Jarek took pride in everything they did in the name of the regent. Had his cousin lost his mind? Or had Jarek finally come to understand what the King secretly thought of him? That didn't make it acceptable.

As if not yet satisfied, Jarek retrieved the club and waved it at the fallen King, then at his soldiers.

"Whose men are these? Do they belong to the gold that backs them from a safe distance? Or do they feel true fraternity with one who rides among them, commands them from the front lines, and braves the stones and arrows and spears of barbarian lords and bandit kings? I should punish you further for mistreating my men when you had no right. If you don't get out of the way, Monika, I'll deal with you too."

Julian whimpered from the fault line of pain he felt in one of his hips. Not under his own power could he right himself.

"I can't believe... you would dare..." Julian gasped.

Lenn's shock finally gave way to fury. "Toss that club, Jarek, or I'll have to make you."

He moved toward the conflict, his companions following a dozen paces behind.

"Lenn, stay out of this," Jarek said. "You are a respectable weakling, at least. Don't make me remind you of your place."

"And what about you? Do your men know of what's supposed to bind people together, whenever there isn't a war? They can never learn if the war never ends. And it's a war in such a loose sense of the term."

Jarek tossed the club to the ground. "There. I did that to shut you up before you could bore me to death with your usual nonsense. Are you satisfied? Besides, what could you possibly teach me about war? How to weave a shield from twine?"

Then Jarek turned his back on his cousin and moved to stand with his men.

Lenn held up a palm, gesturing for his companions to stay back. Jarek's ire was turned away from Julian, and toward Lenn, which was his first goal. The second goal was in progress.

This needed to remain between them.

"So, you retreat behind your men. Interesting." Lenn remarked.

Jarek stopped in his tracks but did not turn.

"You'll not hide behind a wall from an army of bandits, but you'll hide from a 'basket-weaver'. Is that how you were taught to fight?" Lenn asked with facetious simplicity.

"Keep talking like that and I'll sure teach you something." Jarek said; he supposed if Lenn tempted him further, he could ignore the familiar sensation of moderate hangover for a quick fight.

While the cousins traded barbs, neither side of this conflict was alarmed by a few servants quietly crossing into neutral ground and carrying Julian to safety. Lenn pretended that Jarek had his undivided attention, but was glad to notice this rescue. Jarek was willing to consider the old man already dealt with, now that Lenn was being such a pest.

"Turn around when you speak to me," Lenn said, arms now crossed; his plan had worked thus far, but the most challenging part was nigh. "You slap an elder to the ground and threaten his wife and you really think anyone in this courtyard doesn't take you for a coward."

Jarek scanned the expressions of his men once again. As disciplined as they were, he spied a few raised eyebrows among them. That would never do.

"You're going to regret those words, cousin," Jarek said as he turned. "I don't care how formal this is, I'll beat you in any manner."

Lenn scowled and doffed his gloves. "Bare your knuckles, then, and we'll waste no more time. We fight until one of us can't. I promise I'll treat you just as well as you treated our King."

Jarek grinned mischievously as he doffed his gloves yet

kept his ceremonial bracers on. The fight must be bare-knuckled by tradition, but no one had said anything about forearms. Lenn observed this but said nothing, hasty and eager to redress the years of grievances that built up to this moment.

Every capital guard within earshot began to arrive, reinforcing Lenn's companions, but no side would interfere. Between Lenn and Jarek, there was no question of insubordination, territory rules, who commanded whom; two nobles similar in age and of equal rank agreed to settle this unassisted. It would end when one of them surrendered, in the best case.

Lenn immediately drove toward Jarek throwing punches, who absorbed these strikes with his thick, leather-bracer-clad forearms. Lenn felt only the vicious intent that he put behind each blow. Jarek stood his ground through the assault hoping to creep inside Lenn's guard, waiting for an opening; for the price of enormous bruises, his head was thus far spared. As Lenn stopped advancing, Jarek moved forward, trying to close the gap between them.

Seeing his cousin's advance, Lenn reflexively stuffed Jarek's gut with a lead leg front kick. Jarek was too well-conditioned to be felled so easily, grunting as he took the kick, then launching some quick punches of his own. Lenn snarled with frustration as he slapped each punch off-target in the same exaggerated fashion with which he had launched his prior furious blows, but Jarek eventually caught him on the cheek with a light and whiplike punch. It lacked the force to knock Lenn out, but it would leave a bruise. It only made Lenn angrier.

These glorified feints did what Jarek needed them to do. He had brought himself close enough to grab Lenn's arms, stopping the unequal exchange of punches, and close enough to jam any kick. Then they struggled in this deadlock, each trying to move his grip up behind the back of the opponent's neck while trying to stop his opponent from doing so, trading moves to the inside grip, resisting, feinting, pulling. Each loudly grunted as he struggled; Lenn would fight to his last breath if he must. Neither man could push or pull the other off-balance. Lenn's stocky figure held great skill, but perhaps Jarek could outlast the anger visibly fuelling his cousin.

Lenn managed to clasp both hands together behind Jarek's neck. Jarek tucked his chin down to resist being choked by those forearms that squeezed together. Then Jarek quickly braced his forearms down, predicting the hard knees Lenn was about to throw. One cleanly landed knee from a man of such size could have ended the fight, but Jarek bought himself time by letting his already bruised forearms take further punishment.

After trying a few heavy knee strikes, Lenn paused from his exertions, wondering for an instant what pain he must inflict to adequately punish his hated foe; this gave Jarek enough time to bring his arms up and pry the faltering forearm squeeze open. Jarek popped his head free of the grip. Lenn brought a knee to Jarek's midsection before he could back out of range, but it lacked the same power without the target held close.

Lenn reached after Jarek with a kick. Jarek sidestepped this into a crouch, then drove forward to grab the kicking leg and attempt a tackle. Thinking quickly, Lenn set his kicking foot to the ground and shifted most of his weight on to that now-leading leg. While Jarek struggled in vain to topple him, Lenn boxed Jarek on the side of the head a few times, irritated that their closeness to each other prevented Lenn from putting decisive force behind this type of strike. Jarek still had to retreat for the sake of his head.

The two men stood straight, and each took a cautious step back out of the other's reach, aching and breathing heavily, thankful for the pause but unwilling to give up.

The throbbing in Jarek's head had been quiet enough to ignore at first. It screamed at him now. The previous night's indulgence meant more than he expected it would. Did he already regret this fight? Not enough to admit it.

"I'm going easy on you, Lenn. Always felt sorry for you. Like I owed you for your dead father. Will you really risk being broken? For him?" Jarek gestured toward where he noticed Julian had been moved.

"Remember our noble surname, Jarek? Same as his. Being noble, we live right. We respect elders. We respect the law. But first, we respect what's right. It's more important than ourselves—"

While Lenn had been drawn to talk, Jarek rushed him again, believing they were both too tired for deft footwork. Lenn saw the punch coming and slapped it down with his left hand before socking Jarek in the eye. Reeling from the sting, Jarek swung another sloppy punch that tired Lenn could barely dodge.

As Jarek recovered from the miss, both his hands momentarily out of position, Lenn cuffed his cousin with all the force that his stocky frame and a bit of hip torque could deliver.

This blow landed butt-of-the-wrist to corner-of-the-jaw and sent Jarek sprawling to the ground.

Lenn towered over Jarek and observed the tears his cousin now shed. For a moment, he remembered when Jarek first saw him cry. But Lenn was unmoved; he knew Jarek deserved those tears.

"How did that feel? Like something fairly done to an elder?"

"He's fallen! Just stop!" Monika called out. The capital guard and Lenn's riders, among whom she stood, looked ready to draw swords. Even with these forces united, they barely matched the numbers of Jarek's group.

Lenn's tone was calm, but no quieter or less menacing. "I'm a man of my word, Jarek. I've done no worse to you than what you rendered upon our King. Is this what you prefer? Or do you miss my usual 'boring nonsense'?"

Jarek panted and blinked away his tears. He had no come-back for that.

Lenn respectfully backed away. "You get to decide how the next part goes. You know what I mean."

"Name your terms, cousin." Jarek wheezed. "And whatever I felt I owed you, I consider us even; this is for your fair fight and mercy only."

Lenn stepped backward slowly yet confidently, letting Jarek's hesitant men help their battered leader stand. The traitor in front of him should be imprisoned for treason, perhaps executed, but he doubted Jarek's loyalists would let that happen.

"Those are your men after all, Jarek. They proved that when they stood idly by while you injured our King. Take them and go home to your province and your never-ending war; even that sore one who took his precious time admitting his guilt. None of you are welcome here any longer. You have until the next turn of the seasons to deliver your unconditional apology and surrender to the proper authority of the crown, or you'll be permanently expelled from the capital as well. See what it's like to supply yourselves."

Jarek smiled, finding false bravado the moment he was no longer alone. He spoke for all to hear.

"Oh, that's all? I'll gladly ride out of here, as will my men. You, Lenn, won a fair fight and proved your worth, and it's for you alone that we leave in peace. We shall never return, not if it means suffering the authority of that false king. We'll take care of our own home; see what it's like to defend yourselves, to shield this decadent land from greedy foreigners. Or maybe that fallen old man's Kensrikan friends will do it for a price."

"Then shut your mouth and get out." Lenn said before pursing his lips and gritting his teeth; if only his glare truly burned Jarek and the northern men as they hastily departed, they would be ash.

Lenn was quietly thankful it ended at that. He might have the will to force his tired body through another round, but for what? He protected his aunt and avoided a courtyard melee. He had Jarek's assertion that they would leave and never return, which everyone heard.

But what was the value of Jarek's word, which King Julian knew better than to trust?

14
A MEETING IN THE THRONE ROOM

King Julian insisted on continuing with his daily planned duties. Servants provided him with a dose of medicine to numb the pain while keeping him conscious. They built him a sturdy splint to protect his injury, which could be anywhere from that leg through the hip to which it was attached. There might be multiple fractures; it was unclear to anyone where best to wrap the limb.

Lenn's companions provided all the assistance asked of them, including lifting Julian to his throne. The nature of the King's injury made it unclear where exactly supports could be placed for comfortable sitting, but once on his throne, he was able to brace himself using the arm rests; the elevated leg lay across a footrest. A troubled Monika took her place on her throne, but he needed both his hands and dared not place one on their hand holding pedestal.

"Stay in audience, nephew. I'm sorry to have dragged you into the worst of the day's proceedings, though grateful in the end you were there to help me. You may as well be rewarded by witnessing a sweeter moment."

Julian nodded to the resident musician.

"Iris, summon the three from the capital. I can't be any readier for them, and none of us can know if a better day will come." Julian wheezed; he was lucid, but one could hear the power of the drugs given him.

Iris bowed as deeply as her posture allowed and shuffled away at her customary pace.

Monika sighed hard and blinked a lot, forcing herself not to cry after hearing her husband speak. Ceremony could wait for a better time; she walked over to Julian's throne and lightly placed one hand on his nearest shoulder.

When the King and Queen were alone with their nephew, Lenn looked to his uncle.

"What do we do now?" Lenn asked softly.

"We wait. We are not equipped to act against Jarek, and even if we were, you named your terms and we all heard him accept them. Jarek will not attack us, as that would mean returning to the capital. And he will continue to fight his northern war, not for us, but for himself." Julian said.

"And what of the Kensrikans? The Etroukans?"

Julian slowly reasoned this out for himself, then said: "The latter, they stay put. They would not hear word of this even if it reached their city wall, and it might only be a mild curiosity to them. Attacking us would expose them to the former, the same reason we haven't warred since I was a much younger man."

"And House Kenderley, I suppose we hold favour with them now." Lenn observed.

Monika gave him a disapproving look, a warning not to go there at a time like this.

"Kensrik plans to make war on their eastern border," Julian said. "If that went as well as they hope, it means they will march uphill crossing mountains and needing all their resources to ensure a victory. All they came here to do was to ensure that we would not stab their backs while they settled matters with other old foes. To say *I am not your enemy today,* is not to say, *I am your friend every day.*"

Lenn nodded slowly at the further confirmation of what he already believed; the Kensrikans had asked for nothing else, after all. "And what happens when they're finished with the east?"

"Hopefully, that will be a problem your grandchildren are well equipped to face. The east may look small on a map, but what it lacks in length and width, it gains on all counts in height. Flatten out those mountains, and it dwarfs our kingdom even further in its breadth."

"I cannot be comfortable with this consignment of our future. We need to repair this kingdom somehow, and when we do, we need to strengthen. We need better reasons to feel safe than our enemies viewing us as too feeble to be a threat."

"Lenn." Monika would have said more, but it was difficult to reprimand the one who had gotten justice-in-kind for her wounded husband.

Before Julian could form an answer to that, Iris returned with Adina, Judit, and Samuel. Iris stood with them as they took their bows and curtsies.

* * *

"PLEASE RISE, stand proud. You can't imagine what fun it is to be able to stand without pain; I would give you that much," Julian commanded and complained.

Samuel had different questions, now, unrelated to his own fate. Even Judit, often of placid expression, was visibly concerned for the King. They saw the bruise blooming on Lenn's cheek and observed his outfit looking rougher than it did when they spoke with him that morning, though it was nothing compared to Julian's condition.

Julian continued: "I wanted to make a much longer speech for you, but today has taken a lot out of many of us. So, I will keep it brief.

"Iris wishes to retire. I have given her my blessing, safe passage to the west, and parting funds to help establish her new life. And she has persuaded me that you three should replace her. As court musicians, you are entitled to live within these walls, and servants are preparing long term quarters for you. I'm informed that this past night's banquet was your very first show together. It excites me to imagine what you will do with more time and patronage."

Samuel nearly wept. Here was the greatest validation he could ever know.

Adina blinked, seeming to be lost in a trance, such that she only noticed Iris sneaking away just as the retiring court musician passed through a doorway.

"Iris, wait." Adina broke away from the royal audience and pursued her.

Judit ran after Adina.

Samuel looked after his friends, then to King Julian.

Julian sighed. "Yes, go after them. Make sure whatever's

the matter gets decided swiftly; I need my court musicians to be in good sorts."

"Is my presence still required?" Lenn asked after Samuel departed. "I think it's time I had a discussion with Tibor about what happened to him last night."

"Indeed, look after your man. Just make sure not to depart for your manor until Iris is prepared to join you; she has already told me she wants an escort to the west." Julian said.

Lenn offered a slight bow on his way out.

The King coughed, then winced.

"Everyone is running off today. I'm definitely no shepherd of the people."

Monika leaned and put one arm around his shoulders and held his closest hand.

"Your people are definitely not sheep. And you're being too hard on yourself."

* * *

"IRIS!" Adina caught up to the former court musician. "Iris, are you really going? After we've only just played one show here? Can't you stay for another seven days, or five at least?"

"Adina. Thank you so much for setting me free, but it's my time to go." Iris replied tenderly.

"Go where? And leave us here with one night's experience?"

Iris smiled sweetly, but a certain relief showed through, as if she might be glad to depart. "You don't need me to hold your hand, Adina. You played a show with such tension in the air that I could never dream of handling it. What more do I need to teach you? Always remember to breathe, and keep good posture as a singer... You know it already."

Adina hugged her. "I shan't let you leave. I'm not going to let go, I'm going to keep you here."

Judit then tugged at Adina's dress sleeve.

"Adina," said Judit, "let her go. She's weary of this. And this is what we want, remember?"

Adina reluctantly let go, unable to argue against the wisdom of her friend.

"There, see?" Iris said. "But remember the scarf I gave you and its powers; I was with you on the stage, and through that garment, I shall be as present as you need."

Samuel had arrived, but most of the necessary conversation had already elapsed. He was unsure what to add but he settled on something. "I want to thank you, Iris, for everything you've done for us."

Iris just smiled in response, as this said all that she needed to say.

"What will you do?" Asked Adina.

"I will have to think of something. But yes, I go west with the good Duke. It's more peaceful there, the crowds are smaller if they are to be found. If I am not to stay in the castle, then I know my quieter fare is not for the rest of the capital province. Perhaps I will play for none but myself." Iris looked distant, as if she had other things in mind that she kept to herself.

"Well, if peace is what you seek, that's what the west has in abundance. The good Duke said he has no banquet hall, but there are festivals..." Samuel considered.

"We should let you go, then. Have safe travels." Adina said.

Iris turned before she left.

"These are uncertain times. If the troubles get worse, head south until you reach a great forest."

* * *

"OH, BY THUNDERCLOUDS." Tibor slouched. "Because the very last thing we needed was to have the better part of Wancyrik's army vanish from service. Just one detachment of Jarek's forces outnumbered the castle guards."

"The castle guards, plus me and the western riders... even in number, just about," Lenn concurred.

He then asked: "But is there some great reason for this to be any immediate problem? Apparently, House Kenderley favours going after their eastern foes, and they merely wanted to ensure we would not strike them while so committed. They probably sent the diplomatic party here just to make us think we were ever being evaluated, but I doubt my uncle would wish to belittle his fragile triumph of a banquet by considering that it might have been unnecessary. And the Etroukans keep wisely aloof of our troubles."

"Ah, well allow me to explain again how I wound up in this condition," Tibor began, "missing a boot and a fair deal of wind. There's a group of troublemakers, headquartered somewhere in these tunnels this city has for the purposes of conducting rainwater away. Having talked with the Captain of the Guard, I'm no longer sure what to think; how many there are, what they want, or who leads them. All I can tell you is that a few nurse injuries, and Bruno promised to flush them out and interrogate whoever his guards capture. Bruno firmly insists we let him handle it all from here, and he is rather put out that I didn't come to him first." Tibor quirked an eyebrow during that last sentence.

Lenn nodded; he was acquainted with Bruno, and he understood perfectly. "I'm sorry if you bore the brunt of a lecture, friend, when I was the one who deliberately left things vague so he would have no chance to interfere. The man takes great pride in his responsibilities. He also has a point; I guess we leave it in his hands."

Tibor looked uncomfortable with that. "If Samuel is right, these are not just thieves, but something far more sinister. I believe him, but I have no way to prove that. I feel like I was so close to finding out."

"Tibor, give the Capital Guard some credit. As remarkable as your intuition is, it may not matter who these trouble-makers are; you told Bruno where to look for them and he can settle it." Lenn reassured.

"I suppose. I even mentioned Ignacy, whom Samuel named as his attacker and claims could be the leader. Bruno knew of him."

Lenn nodded again. "There you go. If he doesn't remember what Ignacy looks like, he can ask Samuel. The guards should be able to break up a bunch of barely organized young adults. Is there anything else you recall that might help them, before we go?"

Tibor came around to this idea. "We may as well let them solve it, sure. But should we leave when Jarek might not keep his word? And I know you have no taste to hear it, but we also have an old king who is broken in a manner that causes men to die from bad blood, from internal rot."

"It's not suitable to talk about this before it has happened, Tibor."

He refused to let Lenn stop him from finishing his thought. "I give the great King until cold weather, the turn of the season. And I know Queen Monika will support you."

Lenn paused for a deep sigh, making sure his friend was absolutely finished. "I like that you're always a crafty tactician. Someone needs to think like that, sometimes. But if it's all to happen within due course, Tibor, then such talk is not only distasteful, it's useless. You know me as an agile tactician. Circumstances change and I give due consideration to that."

The conversation concluded. They would prepare their horses and saddles, their riding leathers, their escort formation for Iris.

Lenn knew something that Tibor did not. In fact, Zinnia was the only other person he had met who was aware. What she planned to do could change everything.

He would keep it safe. He felt a sacred loyalty to her. He would stay out of the way.

But she had also asked him to keep away if her plan went sour. That was one promise he doubted he could keep.

15
THE REVOLUTION AND THE JOURNEY

The remnants of the fire still burned in the Council Round after Zinnia gave her report and the others finished discussing what was confirmed. Roc departed with satisfaction; after years of slow and frustrating talks, the impulsive younger leader could finally prepare to act. Helynn, too, was satisfied: the older man felt reassured by Zinnia's report that the Wancyeks would not just swoop in and establish an outpost on this land.

Glyn did not depart with the others. She made sure Zinnia stayed a while to talk.

"That was a lot of knowledge. And well-detailed at that," Glyn began quietly.

Zinnia nodded to the matriarch. "Thank you."

"And for you to have absolute certainty in it, that you would swear by it..." Glyn smiled.

Zinnia blushed. Glyn's intuition seemed impeccable. Was

the matriarch really going to make her describe anything further? If so, at what level of detail?

"I can tell by your face, even only by firelight, that you know what I'm getting at. Was this always part of your plan? It would make quite the improvisation."

"It had crossed my mind; the opportunity had always existed..."

"I don't judge you. You were not the only one who had considered this outcome. How do you think we got unanimous consent for you to go? Even Roc understood."

"Oh, him." Zinnia pursed her lips; his was the last name she wanted involved in the present discussion.

Glyn couldn't tell if that dispelled the blush or transformed it into a flush of anger. She said no more. If Zinnia had a story to tell, she would keep nothing from the matriarch.

"He worshipped me, Glyn. At first, he didn't know who I was, believing me a servant, but he acted like my feelings were the only ones that mattered. Nothing changed when I told him my surname."

"You told him who you are? What else did you tell him? Should I ask what you didn't tell him?"

Zinnia breathed a hefty sigh, unable to look Glyn in the eyes. At least no one had questioned her about a missing necklace. This might have betrayed the depth of her affection.

Then Zinnia said: "He promised not to interfere. If he intended to spoil our plans, he could have given me away at the next morning's meal. We pretended not to know each other. He cannot have told father, or the repercussions would have kept me from here. And he would have nothing to do with the knight." He had almost as much distaste for Sir Wolter as she did.

Glyn paused. "I know it all worked out. It's why you're still here. It's also why I had the others leave before getting you to admit the risk you took."

Zinnia blinked rapidly. The stress of the conversation pushed her. "Thank you, Glyn."

"Don't worry, girl. But you should quietly come to me if you begin to feel sick, or any of the other signs."

Zinnia then looked at Glyn, observing the dance of firelight and shadows across the short and slight matriarch's features; her once-black hair turning silver; the crow's feet next to her eyes; her pursed wrinkled lips; all marks of experience, of wisdom.

"Thank you. I will immediately find you if this comes to pass."

Glyn smiled sweetly. "Of course, you only just returned. If things do happen like that, we can still act, but we must time everything strictly. You wouldn't want to be anywhere near labour when you speak for us all. Nor would you want to work through sickness of the early stages. Provided that's what happens, but we must not be caught unprepared. I shall come up with other reasons for the timing..."

Zinnia nodded slowly and looked into the firelight as she thought of something.

"If I end up being with child, should I not send word to Lenn?"

Glyn's smile faded. "I know he was sweet to you, but men can become protective of what they have decided is theirs. You made him promise not to interfere. This would tempt him otherwise, and in ways that could be most unhelpful."

Zinnia pursed her lips for a moment. "Yes, but if that temptation made him watch our backs against the Kensrikans, I would understand."

"This, from the person who was loudest to insist we should never let Wancyeks interfere. But he can't decree such a policy in his land even if he wished. His uncle is their King, as you mentioned, and his uncle is cozy with the Kensrikans, as you also mentioned. Lenn could, however, feel at liberty to raid our land to kidnap your hypothetical future child, even if you assume he never would. I see no point for now. One day, if Lenn takes the throne, we could have this conversation again..."

Zinnia looked down and nodded, but she would give much thought to sending word even if Glyn did not advise it.

They would wait months for better weather and for every plan to be perfectly rehearsed.

FOR WILLEM DEN HOLT, it started off as a quiet morning. He woke up alone, donned his robes, and went to the balcony to survey this paradise of progress. This city was his grand experiment, there to prove that with the proper tools, resources, and opportunity to education, anybody could be civilized.

And there it was, visible in the distance: the aqueduct, finished and fully functioning. Instead of continuing to irrigate a useless swamp, a stream from the mountains was artificially redirected to where the masses could use it for washing and drinking; some buildings had already gone up in the drained land where the nearest swamp used to be, and the direct road to the mountains no longer had to be built precariously of dredged mud and halved logs, the ruin of many a carriage wheel and suspension.

Some saw spoils and riches to gain from imperial expansion, but Lord den Holt saw a humanitarian opportunity. Kensrik surely had the best quality of life to be found, and all the best opportunities for education and wealth. Was it humane to let the people of the continent live in mud and huts, in filth, and worse, under threat of conquest from some other kingdom or culture that would only exploit people without improving their lot?

No, Willem believed, conquering the world was the regretful means to making it better. Now these people had sturdy homes and better hygiene, proper clothes on their backs, words to speak and to read, good food to eat every day... the list went on and on. And after receiving such gifts, did they rise to overthrow their conquerors? House Kenderley no longer had to spend a speck of gold dust on security for people who gladly guarded themselves, and purely out of ceremony. The Wancyeks would not dare test their old foes for a land they had resoundingly lost. And the Etroukans, as a Kensrikan saying went, slumbered.

It was a quiet morning but for songbirds, with some humidity in the air likely brought by last night's terrific thunderstorm. Soon, his people would be out and about, bartering in markets, hard at work building with wood and stone, bringing in grain and meat or greeting the merchants who occasionally bartered whatever they had failed to sell in Bayrock or any wealthier part of the empire.

There they were, now, beginning to stir in the streets. He was so proud of them!

He would record some of this uneventfulness in his diary. Perhaps, one day, this carefully documented model would be reproduced in various sections of the vast North, bringing a better life to people who were unfairly written off as intrinsically hostile and foolish.

He wondered if Zinnia was awake yet.

"WILL you be able to speak for us today?" Asked Glyn.

"I can and shall carry out all the tasks set for me." Zinnia recited.

"We know you intend to do so, but be honest with yourself. This will be a great and challenging moment. Will this make you ill?" The matriarch pressed.

Zinnia paused, in the hopes of appearing to be deeply considering what she had already decided.

In truth, she would not mind if the day's events caused the baby to be born ridiculously soon. If anything in the world could do that, the stress might, but not likely. There would be that new struggle, completely foreign to her, which many told her was extremely painful, during which it was entirely possible that she would die even with the best of care. She might prefer one deep trial of pain, knowing it could last one day, to the feeling of unease and unsettlement she had lived every day.

Not only did she have to be with child, but also to pretend the father was a mystery. Glyn was the only other local person who knew the identity. Zinnia was unashamed, but she had to keep her pride to herself. She even had to hide the pregnancy from her father, which would have been entirely impossible if the conspiracy for freedom did not run so deep within the manor. She might not have managed another day of that, but fortunately, the ruse was about to end.

And lying to her father was nothing compared to what she was about to enable. But he had raised a good and caring daughter, and she loved him as one loves a good father. No harm would come to him, the others promised, unless it was in self-defence.

"My commitment to our freedom is absolute. I can speak and I can stand; it's not like you're asking me to go to battle." Zinnia said.

"Very well," Glyn said. "I hope you remember later that we asked you again, in full consideration of your feelings, in case you later regret your choice."

The meeting concluded with reminders and double checks of various sorts. They all knew what was expected of them.

THAT MORNING, as he most often did, Willem den Holt started his day by standing on his balcony. He would most often observe with pride everyday folks commencing their daily tasks in this city he had helped them build. Today, however, they began to crowd right below him, looking back at him.

Did they want or expect a speech? Did he plan one for that day and forget, and if so, what was the occasion?

No, they began a resounding chant. The words that they chanted were not in Kensrikan.

They were words they had always known, in a language never to be forgotten. Willem knew barely enough of it to understand them.

"We're taking back our land!" The call grew louder as the crowd swelled. People from all parts of the city, all walks of life, gathered together.

He stared in disbelief. Was this a dream? A strange joke? The guards should have heard this, but he had yet to see any arriving to disperse the crowd.

Some of them might not be chanting upon arrival but had simply come to the commotion with a happier curiosity than that of the governing lord. The new arrivals adopted the chant. It was simple and it was for everyone.

"Our land! Our land! We're taking back our land!"

Now Willem might have tasted what the local populace once felt when faced with numerous invaders yelling demands in foreign tongues. Yet he could never fully know this as they did.

"What is the matter with you all?" He yelled at last.

He spread his arms wide as if to embrace them, and every building, every thing he had begged to have financed for them.

"Is this city not yours? Did you not build it? Did I ever take it from you?"

His voice was drowned out by the chanting.

This could not be allowed to persist. He needed to find the

guards; they practically lived at the manor; they should not have succumbed to this madness. Perhaps it was not too late to establish order.

And where was Zinnia? Now he wondered if she was safe.

While the congregation grew in the streets, an impassable mass of people, Willem retreated from his balcony, shut its door, and slid a panel of wood into the door handles to bar it shut. He then left that room and locked its door, as if he expected them to climb the balcony and storm the manor that way.

"Zinnia?!" He called out.

He went from this room to that on the bedroom level, shutting every door, locking every lock, and found no sign of Zinnia, or anyone else for that matter.

Where were the guards, the servants? Yes, they tended to remain on the lower level. Yet he heard no commotion from downstairs, no indication that they heard his calls and were also searching for Zinnia; no warning calls, no one barricading the doors, no one rushing to warn him.

How could he be alone?

The banister was the only thing steadying his panic-stricken hands as he descended the grand stairwell of his manor, calling out for Zinnia, for anybody whatsoever. Left to fend for himself, he locked the way to the kitchens, the front door, the door to the stables; he would stay inside, alone against the chanting horde outside, if he had to. He was determined not to give up on his sacred mission.

But he shouldn't have to stand alone. Where was his daughter? Had they kidnapped her? But he had heard no screams, no sounds of struggle.

He sat on the stairs and wept bitterly. He pinched his arms then slapped his tear moistened cheeks, hoping to awaken from this vivid nightmare, but even as he did so he knew these actions were farcical.

Then the main door lock turned, the terrific grinding sound of hinges badly in need of oiling as someone muscled the door open from the other side.

The guards entered the manor with Zinnia, and the chanting seemed to die down.

He stood suddenly. "Oh, by the Sun in the Sky! Thank the heavens, Zinnia! They brought you back to me!"

He rushed to her with unquestioning joy and embraced her for a moment, then spoke orders to the guards: "You have my undying thanks for bringing her back. Have you got a handle on that crazed group outside? I don't hear them anymore; have you got them to return to their homes?"

The lead guard shook his head slowly.

"It's your turn to go home. By the authority of the liberation, mister den Holt, you are under arrest. If you cooperate, you will be escorted to the border and allowed to return peacefully to Kensrik." The warning sounded so calm for someone carrying a deadly weapon, as if he already knew Willem would comply.

"But this is my home!" Retorted Lord den Holt. "I've lived here all my life, by what possible authority can you just throw me out? We lived together; why would you betray me?"

They waited stoically for him to comply. They might not wait forever. They would not have to.

He looked to Zinnia.

"Oh, they must have made you do this. Must have made

you surrender, just so they wouldn't hurt you. That's why they bring you to me now, right? You can come with me. None of this is your fault, I will assume full responsibility before the King..."

She drew close to him and kissed his tear-dampened cheeks.

"Thank you for everything, father. But this land doesn't need you."

"What do you mean by that?" He asked, but the answer slowly came to him.

It was in the way that when he first embraced her, she had just passively accepted it, not returned the embrace. It was in the way that just like the guards, she had been missing, and only now returned. Her betrayal was unbelievable at first, but undeniable.

Lord den Holt felt such a tightness in the middle of his chest that he thought his heart would quit at the truths that dawned on him. Sadly, his heart still beat.

There was a sudden hush outside. The crowd must have seen the door open and must be waiting expectantly for the outcome of this exchange.

"Zinnia, didn't I love you like you were my very own?" He asked softly, while wondering if they could see how much he trembled inside from fright.

"You have to go home now, father," she said, nearly choking on her faltering words.

He stepped past her and glared at each and every guard in turn, and asked in a desolate and crushed tone that was all he had left to muster: "Didn't I love you all? Didn't I fight for you and give you absolutely everything? Did we not build something beautiful together, and now you throw me out?"

"Yes. Now we have a capital in a land of our own. And now you'll return to yours," the lead guard said, his fingers shifting their grip on his springbow, a growing sternness in his voice warning that he would not ask nicely again.

Willem walked past Zinnia and nodded to his former guards.

"Take me away, then. There is nothing left for me here."

"Father," Zinnia called after him, "I'm sorry. Please believe me..."

He paused. He remembered a little girl he once knew whom he promised to protect from dragons and sea monsters. He couldn't bear to look at her now.

"She shouldn't call me that. She doesn't need me anymore." He muttered to the lead guard.

The lead guard raised his eyebrows, puzzled at the statement, but den Holt was agreeing to go quietly. He motioned for the other guards to lead the man out the door.

Zinnia said nothing else as she watched them lead him away, then heard the roar of the crowd outside at the sight of him.

Could a man who claimed he wanted what was best for the people fail to understand that they did not wish for his governance, and in fact would be better off without it? Could a man who adopted and raised her, such a kind and caring man, fail to understand or to appreciate the sacrifices that Zinnia had to make, and how this was difficult for her? And in his parting words, deny what he had been to her?

Zinnia took a seat on the same steps where her adoptive

father once sat, feeling such despair when so many of her people were happiest.

"The people will need you to speak for them, Zinnia. However, you may as well take your time to reach the balcony, as the people will be unable to hear you over their own cheers for a while. I'll go ahead and unlock all the doors," instructed a former guard.

Zinnia just nodded. She had many emotions to sort through before she could hope to stay composed, and to serve her last duty on this historic day.

* * *

THERE WERE NO LONGER any locked doors in the manor, and all were free to roam it in principle, but most were gathered outside below the balcony to hear the day's proclamations.

Zinnia appeared to a wave of excitement and waited a moment for the noise to die down. Once it did, she began her speech.

"Today, we all get to feel something unknown since before the occupation. We know how it feels to say aloud, and without reprimand: this is Our Land. We are not imperial subjects, not in the process of being reclaimed from nature, not Kensrikans-in-training; no, we are who we have always been, and we need no longer hide it."

She paused for a moment. None of them would feel this day the way that she had to suffer it, but she was glad no one else had to. She refused to let the crowd see it on her face.

"Let me be clear: we feel no ill will toward mister den Holt, but it was past time for him to return home, and he has agreed to do so in peace. He may have inadvertently helped us along the path to freedom, but he governed on behalf of occupiers who should never have been here. To make use of anything he did for us, we must redefine the meaning of his lessons. There is no evidence that he intended to teach us craftsmanship, literacy, or language, merely for our own good as we know it; he saw only potential in us, something which prepared us to be well-functioning servants of the far-away House Kenderley, speaking their language, dressing in ways deemed suitable to their eyes, becoming echoes of them, and to what end? We have always been more than that."

There was sporadic slow nodding, the occasional cheer or clap, but only that which would show their support for her without drowning her words.

"Our peoples' elders have kept and passed down many sacred oral traditions, but their predecessors had been driven into hiding across villages, each knowing an incomplete story. Our scholars have been bringing those stories together, recording their words so all can learn, so it will never be lost. We have a greater need to remember who we are than to know the history of our most recent occupiers.

"And why do I deserve to deliver this speech?"

She paused to push down her sorrow once again. Some in the crowd cheered her on; she had worked for this moment, had earned it, should never doubt that.

Then she finished: "The privilege I enjoyed under mister den Holt is undeniable. I speak to you therefore not as your new leader, nor even as one who will participate in the new governing structure that will respect our many different identities, which had previously been glossed over by the invaders and reduced to one. I speak to you as a living bridge between the old way that brought me up, and the new way that you will live and pass on to your children. Welcome to the new day! This was never the Valley of Garnecht! This is Our Land!"

She waved and blew kisses to them all and made it back through the balcony door and into the manor with a heaving chest. She had been strong for her people while they could see, while she needed to be. Her duty finished; she was free to weep.

The crowd did not disperse until dusk, but there were other doors out of the manor that had been unlocked. When Zinnia had calmed, she departed unnoticed by the multitudes.

She never returned to her childhood lodging, instead making a home with a small family that offered her a room and future help raising her expected child. She would not have lived alone, given her correct intuition that there were few weeks remaining before childbirth.

Whatever happened to them next, she no longer wanted any part of it.

FOR THE REVOLUTIONARY COUNCIL, the days after the departure of Lord den Holt were days of renewed negotiations. While the former lord himself was expected to deliver a bitter message to Kensrik, they needed to draft and agree on their statement of independence in short order; once agreed upon, this would be sent to Kensrik. In all cases, the message would travel by land.

There was some debate over whether they needed to raise any army, and how soon; a timetable was agreed upon, though priority was given to settling the political structure. Loose boundaries were drawn on maps, as peoples once forcibly united were now free to assert relevant difference; yet they knew that prior to occupation their ancestral territories overlapped in places. Sharing was a tradition.

When the meetings ended, each elder went home to their territory to deliver news of what had transpired in the city, and to solidify the new arrangements in territorial council structure.

THE GUARDS BROUGHT Lord den Holt to the end of their new territory, where the uneven land gave way to small Kensrikan farmhouses and barns, mill wheels, and greener grass. There they left him to make his own way, and this is where he thought their ignorance of the rest of the empire was absolutely glaring. Now, unless he wanted to lose days going around it, he would have to proceed through those expansive and dangerous woods where various clans of thieves went to hide.

After the guards left him alone and on foot, he tucked his chain and amulet under his shirt, then produced some gold coins he had hidden on his person in such a manner that they would not jingle or clink; each was surrounded by its miniature pocket of cloth, hidden for just such an emergency as this.

He bought a slow and sad looking horse from a farmer,

not because he couldn't have haggled for better, but because the horse reminded him of his own melancholy, and he imagined some mutual feeling of sympathy.

On the back of this horse, he rode through the woods, solemnly and slowly, until he stopped at a lone figure blocking his path.

"Excuse me, sir, but these are toll woods. If you would please render a small payment."

Willem looked tiredly at the figure in the shadows. "Are they? That must be new."

The man chuckled as he stepped closer, into a shaft of light that went through the canopy. He wore a wide brimmed hat and a mottled looking cloak of greys and greens that might blend in well with the surrounding forest.

Then the man brushed his cloak open and placed his hand on the hilt of a sheathed blade.

"Well, consider yourself freshly acquainted. Now get off that horse." He said before strutting toward Willem.

The former lord complied. "Please, mister. They already took everything from me. I just have this old horse; it would be nothing to you—"

"Interesting. Then what was that loud jingle I heard under your shirt when you dismounted? Did you think you could fool me?" The thief swept his dagger close to Willem's neck and felt the amulet under Willem's shirt with his free hand.

Willem gasped; he realized that even after such a crushing day, he could still fear. "All right, that governor's medallion is what I have left. My name is Willem den Holt, former lord of West Kensrik."

The thief cocked his head slightly to one side. "Former?"

"My head belongs to King Jonnecht Kenderley. I am delivering myself to him."

"Oh, so I can ransom you instead?"

Willem's eyes widened. "No, you don't understand. If he discovers I was lost or captured here, he will raze these woods. He would kill anyone who deprived him the satisfaction of slaying me."

The thief stared at him for some long and uncomfortable moments.

"Please, sir." Willem begged.

After sheathing his dagger, the man wagged a lecturing finger yet spoke softly. "I would hate for that kind of trouble, you know. And you look exactly like you cut the lies once I got the blade out. I'll tell you what: no one else ever tried that story on me, and you sold it so well. So if you're still lying, I'll let you through for being a master thespian and an original at that. And if you're telling the truth, well, Sky have mercy on you, Willem. I'll pass along word to the others in any case, I'll say you got nothing else. Wait here to the count of fifty."

Willem counted aloud as the thief swiftly vanished into the woods.

Jonnecht was more than likely to take Willem's life, but he would savour every living breath on this fateful journey to Bayrock.

After an uneventful journey past the woods and a ride on a river ferry for which he bartered his horse, Willem den Holt arrived in Bayrock. He approached some waiting coachmen;

these got their business from ferried folk who needed to make the next leg of their journey by land.

"I am Lord Willem den Holt; I require urgent passage to the Kenderley Palace. I seek audience with the King himself."

The men noted the unmistakable medallion he wore over his ragged clothes. They looked among themselves and found one who was most idle and had already done well for himself lately. A lord was at once presumed very wealthy yet too important to charge any fee.

Willem smiled as they prepared to take care of him. He savoured the good treatment. He thought this might be the last time he could expect it; little did they know what they escorted him to.

The streets of Bayrock reeked of fish, suggesting a superb haul from the bay and trade waters. The view was beautiful precisely because there was no single type or theme to what one saw: people hawked their trades all the way from Etrouk, from the islands, from the ports of the Eastern Kingdoms. House Kenderley might be at a diplomatic low with the East, but everyone had a good relationship with impartial merchants. The wealthiest politicians in the land had long learned to let wealth flow, a golden age for middlemen.

Guard numbers were lax around the Palace; security was ceremonial, and it made its presence known, but heavy stone masonry, iron fences and gates did most of the work.

Willem wondered if he should get used to the sight of iron bars.

The coachman was allowed to drop off his ride just outside the gates, for though the security was lax, King

Jonnecht had preferences about who was allowed to set foot on the grounds of his palace and for what purpose.

This next part of the journey was to be made on foot.

The walls were draped with tapestries from the new school of thread work, where historical figures engaged directly with the viewer. Willem felt judged, silently but coldly, by these long-dead onlookers. Here were the Kings of Old, whose victories created the expansive empire that existed today. The same empire that was about to learn it lost a large stretch of territory.

The oblivious guards led him to King Jonnecht's office all smiles. Willem took a breath before they opened the door to his fate.

16
FLOWERS

Duke Lenn only fell deeper into melancholy when he returned to the grounds of his manor and the thoughts and memories that came with it. After the euphoric sorcery he had experienced during and post banquet, he returned with unexpected chagrin to this place with its time-worn books and perfectly kept gardens. How could he feel like this life was enough when he knew a better experience?

Maybe he didn't want everything to be the same anymore. Maybe things needed to change.

But there were obligations to his province, duties as a duke, expectations in a land of routines; he might cause a ruckus if he changed things too quickly. They might think he had lost his mind, even if his usual way felt tired and he ached for different things.

So Duke Lenn pretended to like the old norm until he convinced even himself. As weeks went by until he stopped counting them, without any word about King Julian, he settled into familiar routine. He was not without the occasional pang of loss, but it was nothing that a drop of mead couldn't dull. He took care of Piotr, who took care of his grounds; he ordered new books whenever possible and reread old favourites; he solved the occasional dispute between common folk whose problems had escalated to such a point that they troubled him with them, rare as that was.

Occasionally, he sent for word of what Iris was up to. Their ride together to his dukedom had been quiet and pleasantly uneventful. Now Iris had gone from playing in the throne room to appearing in the occasional festival, celebrations of village or household gods, kitchen dances. The word returned was often enough just vague messages that all was well, nothing profound or substantial. Lenn trusted that nothing was amiss, for his people tended to be a good and orderly people who did not take kindly to lies or trickery. As one who governed a province with a hands-off approach, Lenn appreciated that it was better for her to do well than to ask him for things. He let it go.

And life fell into this groove, until the day he received two unexpected visitors.

DUKE LENN WAS GAZING with a furrowed brow upon one of the new works of fantasy, which was of that spectacularly dubious quality that commanded him to read how much more awful it would get, when the gradual crescendo of Piotr rose as the man approached, until this finally stole Lenn's attention.

"Rider approaching! Rider approaching!"

Piotr staggered through the door, panting and sweating but unhurt.

Lenn smiled knowingly at him.

"Well, there's a rider. Approaching the grounds. Just thought you should know." Piotr explained sheepishly.

Lenn nodded in polite acknowledgement. "Thank you, Piotr. I appreciate that."

"I'll be in my quarters for a rest," the groundskeeper pointed towards his destination.

"Absolutely. I'll only knock if it's really important."

When Lenn stepped out the front door to see a horse and a rider already in the front yard, he knew this must be a matter of great urgency. Piotr may have seen that horse from terribly far in such flat countryside, but it must have covered so much ground before Piotr could sprint into the manor.

"Hail, Duke Lenn!" The rider said before dismounting. He wore a light brown gambeson, but not battle leathers; he was evidently more worried about the bite of the wind than that of arrows.

"Hail to you, rider. What business brings you here today?"

"By the order of King Julian the Fifth, and in his defense, you and all the riders you can spare are summoned to the castle of the capital province," the rider recited solemnly.

Lenn considered this. "It must be a long siege the castle's under, if he has time to call upon me."

"There is no immediate threat to the great King himself, good Duke, but you are summoned in anticipation of a need not made clear to me personally."

The duke stared off into the distance at fields of grain

rippling in the wind. Julian was alive, or had been when the message was sent. Lenn felt certain that if this were not the case, word would have arrived sooner and emphasized an immediate need.

Just as he had acclimated to the old norm, something had come to end it once and for all. Of this, he was certain.

Lenn nodded. "If it's not immediate, then he can wait for me to round up some volunteers from the villages. Is this not so?"

The rider hesitated. "Take the time you need, but make haste thereafter. I'm told there's some unusual news."

Lenn nodded at that. He would consider this semi-urgent.

"Is there anything else, from Captain Bruno perhaps?"

The rider snapped his fingers as if he nearly forgot what else there was. Then he checked his saddlebags and brought out a bundle of cloth. He walked toward Lenn, carefully unwrapping a dagger but leaving it flat on the cloth so as not to appear threatening. Lenn still looked at him cautiously.

"Bruno would like you to know that some of us swept through those underground tunnels exhaustively, and we found no traps, just some holes in the walls and pitfalls where the masonry must have caved in over time from the elements, a maintenance issue. We did find this dagger with a western pattern carved on the hilt. Bruno thinks your man must have dropped it when he was down there."

Lenn nodded slowly. Tibor might not like the sound of that, but if so many guards found nothing, perhaps there was nothing to find. Or perhaps Tibor's presence had caused some thieves to abandon their hideout, leaving no trace. Lenn carefully accepted the dagger.

"I'll return it to him. Best not to trouble yourself with anything further, then," Lenn advised, though his mind was now consumed by guessing the news he could only learn upon arrival; here he had first assumed that Jarek had broken his vow, or that some informant had let his uncle know of such imminent treachery.

Now Duke Lenn was certain to move as quickly as he could, for other reasons entirely. Was it unusual news from the south? He had not forgotten what was there. Regarding what the matter could be, he had knowledge no one else in Wancyrik was privy to

The rider saluted and mounted his horse again.

"Are you sure you don't want my groundskeeper to whip you up some tea?" Lenn asked. "He picks the flowers and herbs himself, which he grew, and you only just arrived."

"I must politely decline. By the King's decree, he must know as soon as possible if you are on your way. I will relay the message."

Lenn shrugged. It was that man's horse to ride, and that man's posterior to ache from too much continuous riding. It was that man's choice to make whether duty came before health or comfort.

"Very well. Send him my tidings and let him know I'll get my affairs in order as hastily as possible, for I was not prepared to travel."

The rider nodded, hailed again, and rode away.

And before the rider had disappeared, which was a mighty long time in such a level land, Lenn cast a lucky glance in the direction of the nearest village only to see a different approaching horse, a different visitor.

* * *

THIS HORSE WAS SLOW, the rider gentle and careful. That gave Duke Lenn many long moments to contemplate what had brought Iris to the manor without so much as a letter sent ahead of her.

As she approached, her smile became apparent, and they locked gazes.

"Iris." Lenn nodded. "You're fortunate to seek me so soon. Within the day, apparently, I'm to head back to the capital."

She nodded respectfully. "Good Duke, I have always benefitted from timely fortune. I come to discuss a private matter. Provided you have time, and interest, of course."

"You are most definitely welcome, Iris. I'll have my groundskeeper prepare us some tea; he picks the flowers and herbs—"

"Thank you. I don't believe I require tea."

She stopped in the yard and beckoned for him to help her dismount. Her attire was none too different than what she had once worn in the royal court, terrible for riding and for movement in general. He offered assistance, of which she seemed to require rather little.

"I would appreciate if we could give this matter the utmost privacy," she said.

He refrained from quirking an eyebrow. "Well, now I possess the utmost curiosity. Follow me."

He opened the door for her and showed her into the manor, but as soon as he closed the door behind them and followed her in, he easily walked past her. She doubled back and had no trouble finding a quite common and easy-to-spot bolt mechanism, and she locked them inside.

"All right." He said as he observed this. "In that case, allow me to bolt the back door as well."

"Please." She said with a smile, before she roamed about shuttering each window.

He finished his task sooner than she, and he lit some lamps before returning to his desk and chair.

She found herself a chair to place on the opposite side of his desk.

Iris smoothed the front of her dress after finding a seat. "Excellent. I have a sensitive matter to discuss with you. I want no listeners, no lookers."

"I do have that impression, yes. Folk around here are too mild in manner to be spies, and I wouldn't worry about Piotr. But, if you feel safest in the dark, then speak of the matter."

"The sky is so open here, and the world so flat, that the sun hides behind nothing," she sighed, then continued: "I wish to retire in Kensrik. I know in some eras, to admit so was treasonous, and I dared not make this request of King Julian..."

The duke felt sudden relief. It was far from any era where that should matter. Even if it did to someone, Iris had approached the right authority figure.

"I suppose it was shocking, once," Lenn said. "But given my uncle's decision to invite Kensrikans into his very castle, we can hardly say he has an antagonistic attitude toward our neighbours. On the other hand, might he have become jealous, and forbid you from leaving? Who knows?"

"I shall take the road along the far coast for the view, around the City in the Valley entirely. It will take much longer, but that city doesn't interest me; my destination is further south."

Lenn nodded. He hypothesized a better reason not to chance going through the City in the Valley at that time, given what the earlier of the two riders had told him, but it was better not to mention that. He had no idea what the unusual news would be, nor whether they had to do with Zinnia's plans, but who knows what would happen there or when?

He leaned back in his chair. "Since we have complete privacy, I'm curious to know what would make you move to Kensrik."

She paused, but he was right: they were about as safe from eavesdropping as they could get. And if she was safer than she thought discussing a move to Kensrik, this next part was nothing.

"I have some contacts who want to establish a community for artists. We're hoping to quietly gain some musicians, actors, playwrights, any talent we might find. We want to build a place where we can attract regular patrons, look out for each other, and not subsist on the whims of a specific noble or wealthy person. I hope you take no offense at that, good Duke."

He thought of every lower noble who had ever crossed him, and even the likes of Sir Wolter. It was one thing to work for kind and gracious regents like his uncle and aunt, but it would be terrible to find oneself trapped, dependent on an awful person.

"That sounds like a boon to common folks, great talent in a convenient place, instead of it being hidden away in a castle.

And hopefully at a rate they can afford. I suppose you'll work that out with your partners. You have my blessing, Iris."

She smiled. During that moment's pause, he thought about his departure from the manor, and he thought about an important problem he had yet to solve.

"Do you still have heavy travel cases to bring with you, as you did on the journey here? I imagine it would be quite a lot for one person to move alone. You might appreciate a helper," Lenn began.

Her smile remained, but her brows furrowed.

"I was summoned to the capital, and I have compelling reason to suspect I'm meant to stay there for good. You might recall the condition King Julian was in, though I'm glad he has stayed with us this long and the messenger said he was still alive back when that message was sent. There are too many other aspects to share in a brief time, even if you were allowed to know them."

It took Iris a moment to piece this together.

"Your manor will be unattended until a duke is named. And you have a groundskeeper. I understand this much; please tell me more. You can't just give me his services. And I'm not yet sure I will have grounds to keep where I'm going."

"Correct, Piotr is an adult and free like any other, and he must agree to it. He has a wide variety of skills, and he can definitely learn new ones, but let me tell you about him..."

Lenn brought out a small, cushioned seat for Iris to sit and wait near her horse. He had no idea how long this conversation would take.

Piotr's warm-weather quarters were cozy and wooden and sat on one corner of the property; this small cabin was quite sturdy. The groundskeeper had modest needs, but Lenn would never have forced him to live in a tent or some ramshackle hermitage. During unusually frigid nights, Piotr often stayed in the fireplace room of the manor.

Lenn knocked on the door of the quarters. Piotr knew who it was. No one else tended to ask after him, and no one in the dukedom who disliked him would dare trespass on Lenn's property. Piotr answered the door.

"Hello Piotr. Can we walk together? I have a visitor who needs to meet you," Lenn offered gently.

"All right, sir."

They walked together, and Lenn began: "Everything is about to change, because I have been called away and I'll never return. Don't worry, I should end up living in the capital instead, it's not anything bad. Not necessarily."

"Ah. Never is definitely a long time." Piotr considered.

"I know in the past I have left you with what you need, but yes, never is a long time. I'm not going to abandon you without a plan; you're family. One of the most trustworthy and reliable family members I have. So, there are a couple of things that can happen, but you have a determining say in your future. One is if you come with me to the capital."

Piotr visibly tensed at those words. "I don't think I like that idea. Not if there are many more people who are just like the townsfolk here."

Lenn stopped walking. "I thought you might say that. The fact is, the capital could become an even more dangerous place, but you can follow me there if you insist and I will do what I can. There's a safety behind the castle walls, it's like a village within the city."

"Nothing you've said about the place makes me want to go there," Piotr replied.

Lenn nodded. "That's true. I don't particularly like it there, either, but I have duties, just like you've had duties here. The other possibility is, I have this visitor who wants to meet you. She needs help to bring and protect her trunks and valuables when she travels to Kensrik. I have told her all about you and she understands. She also talks very softly, more often than I do; she's very gentle. And she knows how to be direct while being gentle, to put things simply. I respect that about her."

Piotr stood there, wringing his hands a little as he thought. "But then if she doesn't like me, and that's who I have to work for all the time?"

"That would be terrible to think of, but it's not going to happen. It is true that people need time to get used to each other; remember when you first moved in here?"

"Oh yes. I don't want to, but I do."

"I'm sorry we had to go through that, but we understand each other, and we get along, no? She's definitely not the type to be awful to a person she needs; I have never witnessed her being awful to anyone, for that matter. And she will greatly appreciate your help, and if it doesn't work out, she can arrange something. She got a courtly pension from being their musician; I'm sending some gold with you, too, so you can have a fresh start. But a big gold purse is another reason why it might not be safe for her to travel alone, Piotr. And why it's good for you not to be alone, either. You two can look out for each other until you arrive, then you can agree on the next steps; stay together or part ways."

"I want you to understand something, sir. " The groundskeeper said, breaking lockstep and walking toward the garden. Lenn followed.

Piotr gestured at every perfect bloom.

"These, these are the best things. I know everything they need."

"I know that Piotr. There aren't any better flowers in the kingdom."

"Let me finish, sir."

Lenn paused, gesturing with sincere apology for having interrupted.

"I don't ask for a lot. I just... I always want there to be flowers. Do you understand?" Piotr hesitated, not sure how else to phrase that he was no happier about change than Duke Lenn had been all along.

Lenn waited until he understood that his long-time friend had spoken his peace.

"I understand. I always used to want them too, Piotr. I wanted nothing to ever change, because it meant everything to her, and then it would be like she was still here. And him, too."

"Mother, you mean. And your father. I never did meet him," Piotr considered.

Lenn nodded. "You helped me like no one else could. Nobody takes the care that you take because no one else thinks it's important, but you know better than anyone else and that's why I trusted you to stay here. You know every little detail matters. And you helped me care for her while she was still here. I'm sorry, maybe you had a better place to be in your life and I kept you here for my convenience."

Piotr shook his head once. "There's never been any other place for me. You know that."

Lenn paused. That was the crux of the problem. There were some truths he could say: soon enough no one would live here, and Lenn would not be able to protect his friend from ignorant townsfolk.

But Lenn knew better than to try and force agreement through fear. Lenn sought a better way.

"This woman, her name is Iris; she has no family. I never asked her about that because it's a sensitive question, the likes of which she never asked me. She could use someone who cares as much as you do, takes the time to do things right, and knows that every little detail and instruction matters. I would trust no one else to go with her. And I'm aware you can fight, and just the sight of a big person like you with her would deter anyone looking for easy robbery; you know how nobody ever tries to fight you one on one. I told her everything you can do for me, and the way you speak, and how best to speak to you; everything. I was wondering if you could try being her family."

Piotr hesitated as this was a lot of information to take in, however reassuringly toned and phrased.

"True. Maybe. You know, I think I heard her sing for a bit once, a couple weeks ago; one of those times you sent me to town for dinner with a stamp. She sings nice. I like her instrument. But what if she doesn't like me anyway? Just because you told her things..."

Lenn carefully patted his friend on the back. "Well, can I introduce you to her just to talk? I told her this would be your choice. She will not assume anything. You know, they love gardens in Kensrik. Some of them have manors like mine, or bigger, not growing a single fruit or vegetable on the land, just flowers. Iris might really love a garden one day, wherever she settles down..."

* * *

THE RIDERS AMASSED on the edge of the manor property.

Tibor squinted toward the waving figures in the general direction of the sunset.

"That's your groundskeeper, departing with the lady." Tibor observed. "Who's going to keep the place up while you're gone? I know you don't let the slightest dust settle on your books."

Lenn smiled. Unbeknownst to the others, one of his pockets held a marigold from the garden; one of Piotr's perfect blooms.

"It was time for him to move on, to do something different. The lady shall make a journey, and there's a lot to bring with her; he has strong arms for lifting and carrying, and more skills than he gives himself credit. And this will be someone else's manor soon."

"For the better of the possible reasons, I hope." Tibor said. "I figured, given Jarek's betrayal..."

"Let's not speak further of it before it's necessary." Lenn interrupted.

Lenn then continued: "I have a different task for you, Tibor, one which I once thought to embark upon myself. But it will take too long for an impatient monarch. You must ride to villages and declare us to be in a state of war. Round up volunteers, have them travel in wagons so we don't take all the horses with us. Bring them to the capital as stated reinforcements for the capital, then wait for my word."

"Are we at war?" Asked Tibor.

Lenn shook his head. "No, not yet anyway. But these folks might not understand what's happening, and that explanation works well enough. Just make sure you carry out this task and do no other; no running around in damp tunnels fighting with troublemakers. Got it?"

Tibor sighed. "Yes, my Duke. I get the suspicion we'll all be fighting Ignacy's people in the streets, instead. Am I wrong?"

"Doubtful; the Capital Guard found no trace of them, and you just might have spooked them into disbanding given your description of a bunch of youths. But if so, you will not be alone this time, and we shall be more than a match for street brawlers. Just focus on the task at hand. Do you need me to repeat what that task is?"

"Not at all. In simple terms, we're going to war, and we need volunteers."

"Right. Just keep with that, and we'll begin to understand the more nuanced truths of the matter after you arrive." Lenn signalled the other riders.

And they were off, most of them, toward the capital province, with the sunset behind them and the moon just preparing to light up the nightscape.

Tibor turned his horse in the opposite direction.

"We're going to war." He mumbled. "War with ourselves, probably."

He pondered this as he cantered toward the nearest village.

17

BEGINNING THE END

The horses moved slowly through the night by moonlight and torch, no rider hasty enough to risk an accident in the dark.

Lenn rode into a capital that felt almost unrecognizably different in its tension, an anxiety that crept into his shoulders. There was a new cautiousness to people in the streets. Homeowners shuttered their windows at the riders' approach. Once-outgoing pedestrians whispered among themselves at the sight of strangers. It was unusually relieving to reach the wall, to pass through that gate, even though it meant the possibility of being trapped inside. It was better to be trapped with friends and allies if it came to that.

After they left the horses in the castle stables, most of the riders went to their usual guest quarters, while Duke Lenn was immediately summoned to the throne room.

He wondered what to expect. He envisioned three musicians standing where Iris used to, easing the King's pain with their sounds; the two thrones, King Julian seated in one, his Queen still seated by his side, their hands clasped over that special cushioned pedestal if he was comfortable enough to do that yet. Jarek's usual seat would be empty, a vast improvement.

The sight that greeted him instead was a quiet throne room where Queen Monika sat alone. She looked ready for a public address or a banquet, from the flow of her long skirt to the crown over her pinned up brown hair. The fact that she wore the rarely seen formal crown instead of a circlet gave him a strong hint of why he was there. This would be a ceremony.

Monika stood to greet him. "Nephew. Welcome. We have much to discuss."

"My Queen. From the looks of it, more to discuss than I first anticipated."

"No doubt. There are certain things best kept secret, even from trusted messengers. In this capital, not everyone is as good natured as I hear they are in your dukedom."

"Have things gotten that bad?" Lenn asked.

"Come closer, that I might speak the truth in hushed tones," she commanded as she returned to sitting, and he obeyed.

She continued: "Your uncle is bedridden. Has been, mostly, since you were last here. The pain in his hip will not go away, though it is dulled with the strongest medicine; he is stricken with fevers that come and go unpredictably. He wills himself on, but his body grows weaker. We know it from his faintness of voice and manner. And word got out to the people about him, and about Jarek."

Lenn looked at the smooth tile of the floor, though the edge of her long skirt remained in his peripheral vision. His uncle did not have a fighter's reputation, yet Julian survived the battlefield in years long past. Julian chose to govern peacefully and with care because he knew the alternative intimately. Now he fought for his life.

Her voice was hushed, but not weak; it most often carried an underlying firmness, a strength that had become second nature to her expression. "I have been administrating and resolving disputes in his absence, but my authority comes from representing him and his remaining days are few. I therefore invited you to live here, and I'll select a steward for your province until a new Duke can be nominated. You are Julian's approved successor; it is already documented."

Lenn looked to her eyes. "Dire tidings indeed. Might I inquire what qualifies me to rule, beyond being the last remaining Duke in this land? I should think you would be up to the task."

"I'm happy you think so, and I concur." Monika said. "However, I doubt any reign of mine would be recognized; tradition and legal precedent being what they are. And the people are waiting for you, Lenn; they respect you. I'm willing to make myself available as your advisor for the rest of my days. I will select a suitable Queen for you and see to her training. All you need do is obey this royal decree, with which your uncle already agrees. For the sake of decorum, you will wait for his passing to claim his title."

"Let him keep the crown for as long as he can. I have never looked forward to wearing it; granted, I would less look forward to Jarek doing the same, and I cannot think of anyone else."

"You get no choice in the matter, so don't worry about it."

Lenn nodded curtly. "Then that settles it."

"Kneel." She said as she stood once again; he obeyed promptly.

She produced a sword that looked little different from one which every rider would carry: of middling length, the heftiest thing anybody could comfortably wield with one hand, but her blade showed no dents or scratches or signs of wear, and it had rubies embedded in its hilt.

"Do you swear your life to the service of leading Wancyrik?" She asked.

"I do so swear."

"Excellent," she said.

With the blade, she tapped his left shoulder, his head, and his right shoulder.

"On behalf of King Julian the Fifth, I append to your previously established title of Duke: heir apparent to the throne of Wancyrik. You may rise, Lenn." She said as she carefully put the sword away.

Once he stood, she put her hands on his shoulders and kissed each of his cheeks.

"I know how you govern, nephew. Worry not. Things will be as they have always been. Your one task will be to follow my instructions. When my time is done, if you've still not learned what's needed by then, you'll have a wise Queen of your own for advice. In the meantime, stay strong, stay here, and enjoy all that this castle has to offer."

* * *

TORCHLIGHT FLICKERED in a side tunnel of the capital's rain system. Weeks after frantically destroying their few traps and waiting for guards to abandon their search, Ignacy returned with his followers.

Within that tunnel was a movement of greater size than Tibor could ever imagine that had forgotten any hesitation it once felt from his intrusion. The survivors of this attack stood nearer to their leader, sporting their scars and lasting signs of injury and gaps in their teeth like badges of honour. An agent of the crown did this to them, and surviving his violence made them feel ennobled, justified. The injured became role models, people who made the movement real by taking pain and suffering for it. They reinforced the belief that accepting pain and suffering for their cause was worthwhile, a truer nobleness than any held by the castle's occupants.

Standing on a wooden box before them was Ignacy, pale as he had ever been from the time spent in hiding. He was their charismatic leader, whom they hailed when prompted. He alone tapped into this undercurrent of frustration at being considered small and ineffective, without power, without choice, bearing an inner streak of aggression that had not died since his adolescence. He never forgot what it was like to be them; he learned to use that knowledge instead, gaining their trust and adoration.

And the few among them who were his senior, whom he took in and gave purpose, stood rapt with attention. They had always been afraid to act their darkest wishes until they witnessed his boldness and aggression. He was their catalyst. They wished they could be him.

"Have you heard the thunder of hooves from above?" He asked rhetorically, to the sounds of sporadic cheers, then continued: "I know why they come. They know we're an army. You bring soldiers to fight a battle. And they bring all their bluster because intimidation is the only hope they have of defeating us. But they don't dare bring their horses down here, nor even their agents anymore, and we can get anywhere above through our system. They hide behind their walls, and it limits their reach. We are not afraid. We do not hide. And there is nothing outside our grasp."

They all cheered at this declaration. He crossed his arms and scowled impatiently as he waited for them to quiet down. Then he resumed this carefully written speech, his best work.

"We are on the threshold, here, this family we have chosen ourselves. This family where they never dismiss you as small or cute, where it matters to them where you have been, and where we always take you seriously. A proper family which saved you from corruption, spared you the temptation of drinking the Kenderley goblet in fellowship with evil as this royal family must have."

Someone yelled, "Kill the royals!" before being elbowed in the ribs and told to shush.

"There is nothing more serious than death, than fire, than destruction. Our enemies have all the weapons they can afford, but where have most of this kingdom's soldiers gone? Most spent their time with the brute Jarek, and it's no surprise those soldiers departed with him; the one who rode with them, the one who knew their pain and was most loyal to them. Not the ones who paid for them. Does the decrepit old man or his crone know anything of fellowship, or shared suffering, when they think loyalty can be bought? But after all, they follow the same example as our most bitter enemies, the decadent Kensrikans. And haven't they all along? Look at what the streets were before the decadent began to fear. They wanted to build a new Bayrock right here, a city of sin.

"And now the puppets are frightened. They should be. We are going to cleanse this city from the inside out, my family. And those who survive, those who are *healthy* and *vital,* will inherit the new world. The strong are unfazed by death; they overcome the weak. You, fortunately, have come to me before they could make you weak; you are made strong. Follow the example of our lieutenants, who lost teeth, who may never talk the same way; we are not children anymore, not to be thrown against the wall like water for washing, nor discarded like toys."

He shook his right fist in front of him as he spoke the conclusion of the speech.

"Our movement is about to come of age, my family. And when we have our say, we will not be ignored. A new day will dawn in this land and those who mistreated us will be purged."

IMMEDIATELY AFTER HIS throne room summons, Lenn returned to his personal library. He barred the door, shuttered the window, and unbuttoned the collar of his shirt.

No one would intrude, but he did not feel alone.

"She's not going to be happy if I must do what I think I will need to do," Lenn spoke softly.

No matter what you do, something will go poorly. I'm sorry, son.

He shed a tear as he imagined his father's voice.

Lenn could picture him standing by the bookshelf. Victor wore the striped pants and cotton shirt typical of farmers in his dukedom. He was only ever as old as he had been when he left to fight for the frontier wall. He never got to age further.

"How do you know?"

Time works differently where I am.

Lenn paced back and forth as he tried to think through how it would work. Then he stopped.

"Like a book already written, turn a page forward or back, read a line or a page, yet all the words in that book exist at once, unchanging; is this how you see it? Like fate? Do we fall no matter what I do?"

Not precisely. You are free, but we see where all possible choices would go.

Lenn paused and blinked, now curious. "We? You and mother—she would be with you, yes. Can either of you tell me what I should do?"

He liked the thought that they were together. He most often thought of speaking with the one taken from him all too soon. His mother lived decades longer, dying peacefully among people who loved her, and he felt her presence in the way his manor and grounds were kept.

In your place, we would have no idea. We never faced such a situation. Either you will choose in a way that befits your personality, or in a manner entirely unlike you. You have yet to surprise us.

"Is that bad? Father, do I disappoint you?"

Never. I doubt you could do that unless you intended it. And I would surely speak up.

Lenn slumped on the couch and wept. Everybody might be counting on him, everybody might believe in him, but for the same reasons that they did, they all might be doomed. An honest person would not let injustice stand. An honest person could still die in a battle if Jarek, with his majority share of soldiers, changed his mind and attacked them.

True, being good by itself cannot save your world. But the people know you will never sell their freedom. You are who they want. They live with the consequences as much as you.

He shook his head. "I know. You tell me what I already think because I would give anything to hear it from you. But I don't feel I'm solving a problem anymore, speaking to you like this. When we converse again, perhaps it will be face to face. "

I would be happy, but sorry, to see you again that way. Do not think you make me impatient, nor your mother. Time is not the same here.

"Tell her I love her."

She knows. You always have.

Lenn dried his eyes, opened the window, and unlocked the door; no longer might anyone enter to find him talking to himself.

No matter what happened next, he needed to plan.

DUKE LENN, heir apparent, found himself roaming the grounds often. The library in the castle was smaller than he would like, and the city beyond the wall was a different kind of stuffy, despite being outdoors. As he roamed, he pondered what gardens should be planted once he ruled.

When the hottest days subsided, he dressed in a nice light jacket for his walks, observing gardener servants trimming shrubs and trees and wondering how Piotr was doing.

One day, as he went outside, he found someone waiting for him. The dominant colours of her wraparound skirt, shades of green, reminded him of Iris. Adina must remember her predecessor fondly to have commissioned such a piece; enough not to care that her scarf's colour loudly clashed with the dress.

"Good Duke." She bowed her head slightly. "We meet again."

"Adina. Always a pleasure."

She adjusted her scarf, and hooked elbows with him.

"Walk with me, then. We should talk."

They shuffled a bit, neither one wanting to hurry or slow the other, until they found a common pace.

"I'm not sure this castle suits you, if you don't mind my saying so," she said.

He smirked at her observation. "I don't mind, I much agree. If I had my druthers, I would build a castle surrounded by farms that could be fitted defensively in a hurry. And leave the city separate. So that if any make war with us, they can keep war to the castle and to fields and let the city alone. Chances are, nobody in that city had any hand in the cause of the war, so why should they suffer?"

She nodded. She had another topic in mind but hoped to segue toward it.

"You could spend a lifetime moving this place, stone by

stone. But it's an interesting dream. You come out here for walks to dream, don't you?"

"It's in dreams that I find the most peace, yet I cannot always sleep."

She slowed. "Ah. You prefer a measure of solitude. I hope I have not stolen that from you."

Lenn smiled. "It's not a problem. Sometimes I wish for a distraction from the kinds of thoughts I have these days."

They each felt like it was time to stop, so they did.

Adina said, "I like the feeling of connectedness in the capital, but I must say I don't miss living outside the wall. I lived a comfortable youth, but my parents disapproved of my dream and kicked me out. They disowned me; wouldn't speak to me even after I became popular."

Lenn briefly furrowed his brow. "I'm sorry they wouldn't support what you do. Should I take this up with them?"

Adina quickly shrugged. "No thank you. I quickly learned to support myself, and one day I stopped looking back. But precariousness gets tiresome. I love knowing where I will perform and the guarantee of a friendly audience, and not worrying about where I will sleep. I would love it here even more if only the times were happier, which I hope they shall one day be," she adopted a lighthearted tone for this next part, "but I suppose we are ill-suited for each other in the end: you prefer the quiet, I love the crowd. Yet few noble marriages necessarily base themselves on love..." She cracked a smile.

Lenn did not even need to take a quick glance at Adina to remind himself what impression she had first given him, which went unchanged. She was delightful. He knew that her remark was about the traditions and procedures of the nobility, not the fondness her words explored.

"True, love is not always where the wealth tends to be, though my family has been fortunate enough to know both. But I would settle for nothing less than love, as wealth is not anything of which I have a desperate need."

And if he was unlucky enough to find love, he would have to accept Monika choosing someone for practical purposes. That was the deal he accepted when he became the heir apparent.

Seeing no one else around this corner, she stepped in front of him, held his hands, and looked him closely in the eyes. Did she think he didn't believe she was serious?

"I know of her, Lenn; the Kensrikan servant. I saw you meet her at the stairs, and the way you looked at her. I keep your secret. What if I needed neither your love nor your wealth, and simply wanted the enjoyment? It's not like you're married to her. You have no cause for guilt."

"Then I value your honesty about the matter, and your discretion," he conceded, "but my heart tells what is right for me even if the alternative would break no rule. Please don't take this personally, for there is nothing wrong with you."

Adina sighed. "Are you terribly certain you would rather have no other, not even for fun, in the name of someone whom you might never see again?"

He needed little time to contemplate his answer.

"I am terribly certain, yes. I know loneliness, Adina. And I'm convinced that if one thing makes me more uncomfortable than loneliness, in which I have made my home, it's being with someone I don't love. Let others do what they will, with others, as makes them happy, but not with me."

And if Monika was forced to make that choice for him, he doubted she would choose a court musician.

She let go of his hands and looked down for a moment as she considered this. Nothing he said was a harsh rebuke, nor was it the desired answer.

"Then I will continue to sing you songs, good Duke, and hope that through such sorcery I might one day convince you otherwise."

"You are always welcome to do that. I think my uncle still lives for the sound of your voice. Shall we walk each other back indoors? There may soon be a meal prepared."

She nodded but said nothing. They did not hook elbows.

WINTER WAS a spell of the coldest weather of the year which never lasted long in the capital, and the warmth of spring returned on helpful wings. It seemed to bring a certain redness back to the cheeks of King Julian, though in all other respects his health only worsened.

Unfortunately, from south of the mountains, frigid tidings would arrive.

The royal family was observing another private performance of the three court musicians, King Julian now resting on a light bed which servants could carry, when the news arrived.

"What word? Oh," Monika directed servants, "tell the musicians to depart for now."

Indeed, Julian could barely produce a sound audible to anyone who put their ear next to his lips. Even had the trio been privy to this news, they would overpower his voice no matter how softly they played.

Adina gave Lenn a quick and surreptitious look of concern before she, Judit, and Samuel were quickly ushered away. The look was not lost on Lenn. What was dire enough to justify taking the King's favourite music away? It did not bode well.

This was, however, a message solely addressed to King Julian, which he read into the ear of a servant, who would speak it aloud to his present family.

"To my... friend," Julian corrected the actual phrasing of the page, which suggested some more formal strategic relationship, "King Julian of Wancyrik. I write to properly inform you of why there will be visible movements of soldiers, not terribly far from your southern border. While sleepy Etrouk may not pay much attention to their beach, neither does this concern them terribly, I have heard tell of your unfortunate turn in health, have heard no further tidings, and must assume that having your scouts approach you with great alarm would be a dangerous and unwelcome idea."

Lenn tried not to give away that he perfectly anticipated the remainder of this letter, and that it filled him with great concern.

The message continued: "There is treachery in West Kensrik, and I am landing a force of soldiers to recapture the province. While I am sure you would have surmised that a force of such diminutive size posed no threat to your kingdom, once again, I thought it best to inform you. Yours in trust, King Jonnecht Kenderley."

Lenn could barely remain in his chair, so quickly did he want to move, but while neither his uncle nor his aunt could stop him from doing what he intended, he did not have the heart to argue with them. He knew that even if his uncle did not want to admit any alliance with Kensrik, for this would be impolitic, his uncle was still perfectly comfortable calling Jonnecht a friend.

Zinnia herself would not approve the plan he had in mind, but she was not in the room to argue with him. If her life would be in peril, then she was welcome to berate him after he rescued her.

Julian himself looked troubled.

"My, my. That man we met, Lord den Holt, what happened to him then? But Jonnecht said nothing of him; surely if he had been slain..." The servant spoke for him.

Monika patted her husband's hand.

"Please, these are unwelcome thoughts. This turn of events, though troubling to Jonnecht, is his problem. He did not ask for help, did he? So, he shall take care of his own matters, and we need only trouble ourselves with our own."

Lenn finally stood up. "Someone has to let the scouts know not to be alarmed. I can send word."

Neither his aunt nor his uncle stopped him, but he saw the look in her eyes; he should not go far, because she would soon expect him to maintain order, to hold the kingdom together himself.

It hurt him to have told that lie, however necessary.

18
DEPARTURES

The previous evening, Lenn informed Tibor of his true plan, and they argued about it all. The chain of command easily decided it, though not without Tibor voicing dissent and demanding to accompany his Duke for protection.

The next conversation would settle something different. Lenn met with the three musicians on a hill of the castle grounds which overlooked the walls of the innermost city. The sun always appeared to set early when one was looking toward mountains, even though with the approach of spring each day grew a bit longer.

"Look at that, all of you. Every day, when the clouds permit, the sun reminds us that even the ends of things can be so beautiful, not tragic," Lenn observed.

Samuel grunted. "At least you can count on the sun to come back the next day. If only many more of us were so lucky."

Lenn nodded and grinned at his friendly acquaintance. After becoming an official court musician, Samuel apparently wasted no time replacing his worn boots, trousers, and plain cotton shirt with only the finest fitted clothes money could buy. Samuel's vest and cap, once the statement pieces, might need an upgrade to stand out once again, unless he preferred the ensemble's new coherence.

Perhaps he would get an opportunity to do that where he eventually settled.

"In the spirit of that retort, perhaps despite it, I am making you aware of your options. These are uncertain times. We spend every day wondering whether Jarek will go back on his word. You know you are always welcome in the west."

"Is the west somehow to be untouched by vengeful Jarek?" Samuel asked.

"He may be a terrible person, but he is no fool. If he burns down the west, people of his land may find it vastly more difficult to eat." Lenn replied. "And should he be so foolish, the west is wide open and easy to flee in a few directions."

Adina bit her lip, then said: "We have, rather, received conflicting advice from Iris regarding where we should go, good Duke. She said to go south until we reach a great forest. Is there such a place south of the capital?"

Lenn smiled. "Once you're in Kensrik, yes. I should have expected her to warn you. Fair enough; that was the second option I would have related, but she cannot have told you that there's fresh turmoil that way. Fortunately for her, she planned to take the route along the outer ocean coast for the view. This goes through the west, along the outer ocean coast, and around the lowlands. You'll avoid all the things that could happen in the valley and its city, and she will be delighted to see you. She said she was going to establish an artistic community with some associates. Your talents would be valued."

The musicians looked to one another; the description of Iris' venture did not distract them from the nature of the news Lenn delivered, or from wondering how he knew about this fresh turmoil.

"You're attacking the City in the Valley?" Samuel guessed. "Is this the work of King Julian, gone mad in the throes of his final illness? Good Duke, please take control at once."

"No," Lenn said, "you cannot know the full story, and there are things I shall not tell you. What you don't know can't be compelled from you. I just want you to be safe."

Samuel blinked and crossed his arms. "In that case, we can't act on what we don't know. And as you say, the south is dangerous as well. Perhaps it's safest to stay here."

Lenn glanced mischievously at Samuel.

"I like you. It will be a shame if I never see you again. Very well, here's how convoluted it gets: King Jonnecht is attacking his former province, and I suspect he intends to raze it. Julian will do nothing."

The musicians muttered to themselves.

"Leaders with half the world between them, each cursed," Judit said.

Adina immediately recognized what this meant for Lenn.

"Julian may do nothing, but how about you?"

Lenn just looked at the sunset, which was on the verge of conclusion, and neither confirmed nor denied that this was the case.

She took his hand. "Oh, good Duke, let the madmen tear themselves apart, for what they do cannot stand, not without reason. Come with us, where you would let us go, if such places are safe enough for you to recommend."

"No, stay here and be King, you fool!" Samuel said. "The people will follow you. If anyone can repair this land, it's you."

Lenn glanced with furrowed brow at the hand which held his, then looked Adina in the eyes. She understood and let go.

"I will not perish in Kensrik, not if I can help it. I will return here, Samuel, and should I survive my ordeal, then I will deserve to rule this land. What moral authority would I have if, just like my ailing uncle, I obediently let Jonnecht slaughter his own people? Wancyek kings have never been in the thrall of House Kenderley, yet under Julian, this appears so."

"You and your moral convictions. Far be it for me to save you from them." Samuel said with resignation.

To Samuel, life was a special thing which seemed to be there once for a measure of time, and after this time elapsed, never again for that one instance, that person; what greater good could there be than to preserve such a precious and irreplaceable thing? If something else appeared to be more important than one's life, however, that was for the person to decide, and after all, Lenn had provided advice which would help Samuel's prerogatives. It would have been terribly inconvenient to venture directly south and get caught up in a different chaos.

Adina stepped away from Lenn.

"I'm not sure I can save you, either, because we both know what really drives you. But against Jonnecht, why, you would need a whole army! And if you take that army away from the capital, you're betting the whole kingdom that Jarek will keep his word."

"I could not pull the army away in its entirety if I wished," Lenn said. "I have men, riders who are loyal to me, and there may be soldiers whose loyalty is yet to be decided, who will come with us. But you must realize that when Jarek withdrew the portion of the forces loyal to him, he left drinking-cups of water waiting to put out a fire as large as a castle. If it was only my presence that kept him at bay, he would have struck after I returned to the west."

"And you would ride south, with even fewer men, to put out a fire as large as a city?" Samuel asked.

"After a point, does the magnitude matter? The men will be free to choose their fire just as I have. All I need you three to do is stay vigilant and know your escape route. Servants know the ins and outs of the castle grounds. The moment you get word that Jarek might lay siege, or if you've had enough for any other reason, flee by the route Iris chose." Lenn said.

Lenn produced a scroll and stuffed it into doubtful Samuel's upturned hand.

"This document entitles you three to the horses you'll require, and a substantial purse. Enough that you should never have to worry where you'll sleep."

Adina opened her mouth, then closed it. He had been paying attention...

"Consider it your severance pay in advance, drawn from my personal account."

Then he departed with haste, leaving the musicians to

glance at each other. Samuel sheepishly put the scroll in an inner vest pocket, where he was least likely to lose it.

"That was your grand offer, Adina?" Samuel observed. "Well, I don't know what happened between you two, but I suppose it makes as much sense as anything else that occurs in this castle."

"You had nothing better." Adina replied. "Talking with people as if your point is the obvious one, as if they must be foolish not to see it, compels nothing but spite in return."

"Yet when people never listen to me, what am I left with? There is nothing more, really, that we can do here. Let's not wait for Jarek to be at the gates, let's get out while the roads are safest. Try not to be too loud when you pack. I doubt the regents would be happy to find out."

Adina's eyes widened at a possibility.

"Maybe *they* can stop him, Sam. Perhaps they are the ones we should warn."

"Why would we want them to?" Judit asked. "Lenn gave us options; it would be disrespectful to take advantage of his information while rejecting his choices."

Samuel shook his head. "The only people to warn are people who can leave, Adina. The King and Queen have nowhere else to be, and you know, Duke Lenn is already leaving. Yes, I see it now; there's a chance he makes it through this ordeal he imposes on himself. I wish he understood how worthy he already was, but somebody must stand up to House Kenderley some time. Let him go."

"He could die down there." She protested.

"Let him go." Samuel repeated. "And let us go, so that we can live."

* * *

TIBOR MET Lenn outside of the stable where some of the others waited.

"A scout brought intriguing news while you were taking care of your private matter, good Duke: Jarek amassed the better part of his army and left the remainder to watch the border we share."

Lenn paused. "Jarek is moving? Where did he send that 'better part of his army'?"

"Over the Frontier Wall." Tibor said, sounding as mystified as Lenn felt.

Had Jarek lost his mind? But Lenn saw the opportunity this posed.

"We both know no route past the Frontier Wall loops around to this city, and it is such a big production to move a large force past it. He has committed to something over there, Tibor. And the soldiers in wagons drew their lots, as I instructed?"

Tibor gave one quick nod. "We already sent the allotted number to reinforce the Capital Guard."

"I think that combined force is the largest the capital has seen in decades. If whoever Jarek left behind gets any strange ideas, that number of guards should make them think twice." Lenn reasoned.

"Then are we bringing enough soldiers with us to stop the Kensrikans?" Tibor asked with quiet caution.

Lenn knew that tone well. "I think we have all we need, Tibor."

* * *

LENN AND TIBOR walked into the all too quiet stable, where he found all his companion riders and a greater number of foot soldiers.

"So, is this everyone?"

Tibor smiled. "We let a few of them volunteer for gate duty. They will keep that portcullis up; they will be the ones to let us out before they follow."

Lenn nodded. That made everything run smoothly.

The good Duke then put on his heroic speech face and addressed his companion riders.

"There are two roads past that city gate. One will take you west, and home to the plains. If you follow me, however, you will not take that road; you'll go south with me. I am going to war with House Kenderley for the horrible thing they are doing to people they claim as their own, this nearest group of whom had the sense to free themselves for as long as they could. I doubt the people I ride to assist have had time to assemble much of an army, and today, your King was sent a polite message from Jonnecht Kenderley himself, asking that we not be alarmed at the imminent landing of soldiers on the Etroukan beach. And politely asking us to stay out of their business."

Most of the soldiers frowned doubtfully at Jonnecht's request; they already had questions.

"We know the people being attacked are not Kensrikans, because we can fairly agree that they were never our people in that bygone time when we ruled them. I believe they should have a land of their own, and I expect you agree. But even if you question that, know this: Jonnecht's message stated that we would not have believed the number of soldiers being sent were enough to threaten us anyway, and our alarm would have ceased at this reasoning. If they send too few soldiers for us to even worry about a raid, I ask you, do they really intend to recapture that land? Or is it something more sinister?"

Many of those gathered nodded fervently at the question. Given House Kenderley's reputation, sinister was easy to believe. This was but an additional reason to ride with Lenn, whom they knew as sincere and trustworthy.

"We ride south to find out, and by the Winds, may we punish the Kenderley Army for their cruelty no matter what they are up to. I suspect this much: we are not so outnumbered as you imagine, and they have no reason to expect us.

"I ask you, who rides with me?" Lenn finished.

They gave a short cheer that rattled the walls of the stable. Then they moved quickly to prepare.

"Our fathers waited their whole lives for an excuse to battle House Kenderley again." One rider mused.

Lenn laughed bitterly. "I have done better than give you an excuse. You have reasons to act, compelling reasons. Round up your horses, prepare the wagons, and meet me at the gates."

19

THE BURNING VALLEY

When Kensrikans wanted to joke about Etrouk, they claimed it 'slumbered'. They would describe this kingdom as lazy, sleepy, uncaring about what went on outside the walls of their mountaintop capital; manufacturers and traders by necessity, but otherwise an inwardly looking culture.

All the opposite things were true. Etroukans wished they could get away with ignoring what other kingdoms were doing, but the survival of everything holy to them depended on paying attention. They constantly had eyes on their beach, and when two ships flying the flag of House Kenderley disembarked, scouts quickly related numbers of soldiers crossing the beach; it was alarming to think that this might finally be the moment Kensrik invaded, and all soldiers and guards were awoken to prepare for the capital's defense.

What followed was further confusion, for no more ships

were sighted immediately after the first two, and the invading soldiers continued back into Kensrik on foot.

"Ferruh, my son, what are you doing? You're not taking that field if this is, after all, war." The King of Etrouk said to his eldest.

Someone had informed him that Ferruh was suiting up, albeit lightly, with other riders near the armoury.

"I know, father. So far, it isn't war. Only two ships landing, in our full view, and they sailed off as their soldiers went back to their territory."

"So, we're both apprised of the situation. If it's *not* war, then why are you suiting up at all?"

Ferruh paused what he was doing to explain: "It's important to send out a light patrol, one that can survey lower down the mountain and ask questions if needed."

It was also important to send a blocking force now, to that same beach, in case any late straggling ships arrived, landing even more soldiers. Ferruh left this part out because it would reveal he could possibly involve himself in combat.

His father nodded. "And the transport wagons of archers you're preparing, are they also for a light patrol?"

Ferruh paused and smiled with some bitterness at having his motives be guessed. His father deserved credit: the King did not maintain his status or the affairs of state by being gullible.

"Two ships, father; two so far. And you know me well enough to trust that I am not going to try invading Kensrik with such a small force. No, the archers are for the beach, to discourage any further landings if they are attempted. My role is to lead the light cavalry as a survey, and if it becomes necessary, to speak for you. Horses can help me retreat to safety quickly if needed; the lightness of the armour helps me do that faster."

Before the King could voice any consent or refusal, a slender scout messenger who had spent some time asking around for the whereabouts of the King finally made it to the armoury and kneeled and said, "Urgent knowledge to convey."

"Then hurry up and rise and convey it," said the King, grumpily.

"Wancyeks riding south; they approach but have not passed us."

Upon hearing the scout's words, the King gave his son a look that suggested his outright disapproval of the survey mission, to be voiced pending completion of this message.

The scout messenger continued: "A small force, by estimation, fewer in number than the Kenderley Army soldiers who landed. Riders and a few soldier wagons."

The King's disapproval was then cast into doubt.

"Those two forces combined would fail to knock a single stone loose from our walls before we could slaughter them." Ferruh observed.

The King briefly stroked his beard. "It's the peculiarity of this that troubles me. Very well, son, you have a task I can personally sanction. There are no more sails sighted at the beach yet, so you should have time to take a route that brings you near the Wancyeks. If they are hostile, then let the archers do your fighting along with the other riders, but only if provoked. Once you have answers from the Wancyeks, let them know they are being watched and divert your course back toward the beach. And be most careful. Something foul is afoot; I just know not what."

Ferruh nodded. "Very well, father. It would be grand if the Wancyeks gave us some answers. They are wrong-headed pagans, but of the most honest type."

It was a humid day in the Valley. Most days were, but it was better that the air be warm and moist than cold and damp.

On the northeast side, people went to and from the elevated aqueduct with buckets, wheelbarrows, and anything they trusted to help them carry clean water to their homes or farms. It was from the elevated vantage of this structure that somebody first noticed columns of people approaching from farther east; the strangers must have disembarked on the beach, over the hills. The boulder-casters that they brought with them made it clear these were soldiers.

"Who do you expect me to call upon on such short notice?" Roc bellowed as he ran a hand through his own hair and grabbed a handful in his stress.

"Who else am I supposed to alert? You're the first council member I could find," argued the lookout.

"Then you'll have to settle for my solutions, and I'm thinking as fast as I can," Roc said.

"Hopefully faster than the fires in the east end can spread."

Roc scowled at him for that remark. "Then why stand here

looking at me? Raise alarm in the city. You're going to flee west as far as you can with the others. Take only what you can carry, get everyone out." Roc ordered, and most scouts left to do that.

Some remained.

"And what happens if the invaders simply follow everyone west, Roc?"

He took his hands out of his hair and gestured wildly. "I hardly have anything to fight back with, what are you expecting me to do? The best weapons are theirs. Get your spears and slings if you really think it will work. Get the couple of springbows left over from occupation times."

They took his cynical order in earnest. "Where do we gather?"

He realized that if his people's only advantage were numbers, and the best weapons were Kensrikan, they should take some weapons from the invading force if they could.

He thought of the fires spreading over swamp land that was parched and reclaimed after certain facilities were built to conduct that water.

"Fighters should meet me at the aqueduct. I know how we can buy the others some time."

THE BOY HAD TAKEN to standing and even some hesitant first steps impressively quick for his age, but Zinnia carried him anyway, wrapped in a cloak. He could struggle and wail in her ear until she went deaf; they needed to flee.

Part of her wanted to take him and make a break for it

right away, but all around her was confusion. There were fires coming in from the east and boulders crashing into roofs, and all that and the soldiers responsible were creeping closer, but no one immediately knew where they were meant to go and what they were meant to do about it.

One imagines the solution as simple, but one imagines in tranquility. Things get murky in panic.

"Go west! Everybody west! North if you must! These aren't Wancyeks!" Zinnia called out over the screams as she did the opposite; she walked east to tell the stragglers where to go.

In uncertain situations, some people see the good that others are doing and feel authorized to follow their example. The majority followed the advice to flee if they had not already been doing so, but others realized that Zinnia could only alert so many people. Soon, others spread out to different directions, heading as far east as they would dare to see who needed to hear the news, who needed to be warned another way if they could not hear, and who might need help leaving their homes.

There was no time to debate anyone who had been alerted but refused to leave. Those who insisted that walls of Kensrikan stone would protect them had chosen their fate.

Then the followers of Zinnia's example got to learn whether they were the fastest sprinters.

The springbow was a versatile weapon of war, deadly in close quarters, and capable of being fitted with longer bolts bearing thick oily ends for the purpose of setting wood and grass aflame. At the first sight of a bolt whistling wide of her, Zinnia turned and ran, still clutching her restless son and now pivoting him in front of her to shield him with herself. She barreled forward in as full a sprint as her burdened frame could, haunted by the approaching whistling sounds, alarmed by the crashing.

The sounds seemed to subside. She nevertheless kept running until she couldn't.

Once she was down to panting and pacing onward, she noticed the relative quiet; the whistling and crashing had not gained ground and was softer than her son's tired whimpering.

She realized the soldiers were in no hurry to catch her. She walked as quickly as she could, nonetheless, but these attackers seemed more intent on demolishing every building than killing every person—for what little the difference was worth.

And then, the thinnest trickle of water appeared underfoot.

Where was Helynn or Glyn? Hopefully warned and fleeing to safety.

Glancing at the water underfoot, she guessed exactly where Roc was, if he still lived. There was nothing she could do for him.

* * *

"AIM AGAIN AT THE PILLARS, the supports," Roc ordered a small group of helpers. "We get one more try at this. The other fighters can't hold them off for us forever."

They quickly gleaned how to work the boulder-caster they had captured, having witnessed Kensrikans using it.

Then they needed to work together and load the boulders. Aiming the thing was not as easy to pick up from observation, but they had no more time to learn. Kensrikans wanted their siege engine back and were quickly overpowering a dwindling number of defenders.

Roc hissed a prayer under his breath before the hefty boulder was launched. The projectile struck the target just enough to topple it. Now water emptied out of a huge gap where a section of the aqueduct used to be.

Then they hurriedly took a firesteel and scraped flint against it, lighting some of the long oil-bolts they had recovered, and they jammed these into the ropes and sinews of the boulder-caster. The water that spilled on to the land was some distance from the siege engine itself, and all the water would do was creep along the ground, making it more difficult for existing fires to spread in the city; the boulder-caster had struck a target for the last time.

They took out a small group of invaders, wrecked a siege engine, and bought their people some time. Roc grinned at the gushing and spreading water, and the growing flames consuming the siege engine. His last thoughts were of what they managed to do. Then a storm of bolts rained on him and his helpers.

DUKE LENN, his rider companions, and their wagons of soldiers rode toward the land that had been known as West Kensrik. They were neither inhibited nor assisted by the Etroukans. This was unfortunate but expected; Prince Ferruh had a solid future to protect and a stable kingdom he should not compromise with the threat of war. Lenn had only uncertainty behind him, and on the path ahead, skies darkening at midday from the conflagration.

"We really did choose our own fire, Tibor." Lenn said.

Tibor sighed sharply. "Well, on the bright side, this is more like proper war, is it not? Somewhat?"

"Look at that conflagration, Tibor. What's proper about it?" Lenn countered.

"We finally get to kill some Kenderley scum. It feels more heroic than fighting sixteen-year-olds in tunnels."

"We'll kill Kensrikans." Corrected Lenn. "By rights, I would find that monster Jonnecht on the field and toss him into one of his own fires. But Kenderleys are too crafty to let one of themselves stray in harm's way when they can get minions to do it for them."

Tibor conceded the point. "It must have tempted them, though. All these people with nothing but sticks and stones to protect themselves... why the slaughter and the burning? Is this some hideous ritual of theirs, a sacrifice for power?"

Lenn shook his head. This was no ritual or sorcery. "The same House Kenderley once sealed our drunken slumbering warriors into their barracks after a harvest festival and burned them; what you see is what *they* consider war. We are going to stop them and their masters in turn, Tibor." Lenn spoke louder after this so the men in the wagons could hear: "We fight men. Evil men, yet just as vulnerable to our steel. Shall they taste it?"

* * *

There are soldiers to the left and right, boots stepping through the thin film of water at street level before soldiers rush up remaining stairwells and attack Kensrikan spring-bows who have taken defensive positions at windows and rooftops.

None of the bodies in the street look like Zinnia, but Lenn doesn't have the time to inspect them all, nor to search every charred husk and collapsed roof in the east end. He thinks he might have time if they can eliminate this threat, but he eschews that consideration for the task at hand.

At the end of this street, most of the Kensrikans have retreated, dragged flimsy barricades of debris across the road, and prepared to make their stand.

Lenn has riders behind him. If he times this right, the focus of that springbow encampment will be split between the soldiers taking the buildings and the riders barreling directly at them, giving both Lenn's groups a chance. The Kensrikans must not be allowed to direct their focus.

He knows only one man has the responsibility to lead that charge. The same man who invited them into this peril. The same man who brought them here too late to stop this, but not too late to end it.

He pulls his horse in a tight turn; the war mount finally living up to the breeding, not just taking him toward the capital at a canter on a nice day.

None of the other riders were prepared for him to turn so soon and they rush to do the same. No one will catch up with him, but they will do their damnedest to try.

He knows they will follow exactly where he wants them to go, but once his serpentine course around falling Kensrikan soldiers straightens into a gallop, Lenn makes himself the rapidly approaching target.

Did you hate me when I left you, son?

Lenn mutters into his mask.

"You didn't leave. You were taken when you did what you had to do."

He hears the voice of his mother.

And now you do what you must.

Boots firmly in the stirrups, raising himself from the saddle, he begins a prolonged battle cry.

Duke Lenn dies too suddenly to feel pain from the bolt that strikes him. A moment later, his horse ploughs through the flimsy barricade and crushes his killer.

THEY HAD WITNESSED the end of a tradition on this worst of days. They found it difficult to believe they had prevented it from being worse. They lost few, but those few mattered so much.

Tibor, held up on one side by a companion rider, placed a hand on Zinnia's shoulder as if he really had the strength to support her. Perhaps she supported him.

He had been injured while scouting and was placed on a broken wagon far from the combat in the city while Lenn and the others took care of the rest. There, Tibor recognized this woman, and he explained everything to her. There, Tibor met the son that Lenn would never get to know.

They grieved together in sight of the duke's funeral pyre, close to the pyres of fallen others. She wore the necklace she had given to Lenn, one which she never wanted back. Not like this.

The surviving soldiers had cobbled together these arrangements with dashed wagons, charcoal, abandoned Kensrikan fire implements, the tools at hand. A hawk's discarded feather was found by chance; this was placed under Lenn's hands which were together atop his chest.

Tradition called for flowers braided at the stem to be laid around the fallen. Small blooms picked from shrubs at the edge of the city were the only ones to be found, so loose bouquets of these would have to do. A marigold remained undiscovered in Lenn's pocket.

They cut the shaft of the bolt that killed him, but they could not remove his helmet, nor did they see a purpose in doing so. They built the most intense fires they could manage for each of the fallen, hoping these would consume the bodies as thoroughly as was possible. Then they buried the remains near a heavy stone, carved into which was the same sacred symbol that Zinnia wore on her pendant.

The local populace had their own dead to grieve and to bury, but some of them witnessed this display, and Zinnia tearfully explained it as best she could; they already understood the gist. They hurried back to where the others laboured, to speak of Duke Lenn's intentions and demise, and to relate that Zinnia had survived but would not be joining them.

But she would not go to Wancyrik, for no such place existed anymore. A dead man would not keep the kingdom together. Whatever was left of the capital by the time they could return, they would never know. The survivors of Lenn's efforts would bring Zinnia and her son to Lenn's former dukedom.

There, they hoped to begin something new.

And gathered in the distance were a people who survived and would one day thrive again.

20

THE BURNING CAPITAL

A highland post between the capital province and Jarek's domain had become an unofficial border point. Everything behind it had been the frontier dukedom administered by Jarek, and everything past it was not claimed by him. Under law, the entire land should kneel to King Julian; out of respect for Lenn, Jarek would claim nothing beyond his traditional domain.

There, Jarek had left a detachment of his army to watch the border. Lenn might be an honourable man who spoke his terms, but Lenn answered to Julian who might have other ideas.

A rider scout shut the heavy door and saluted his commander.

The heavy-set commander looked up from his stew and ale.

"You can put your hand down, man. It's not such a formal

occasion, me eating my stew, unless the ale's run out," the commander said wearily.

Now at ease, the lean scout reported: "Fires in the capital, sir."

The commander frowned; his drinking partner straightened his posture as if finally paying attention and muttered: "Like signal fires, or what?"

The scout shook his head quickly. "Those would be smaller. These must be whole buildings set alight, to be so visible from such a distance."

Both the commander and his drinking partner set their mugs and spoons down carefully.

"Think carefully. Does it appear they're being sacked?" The commander asked the scout.

"An army would have torches of its own at this time of night. And we would have spotted the Kenderley Army moving in large numbers for such an occasion. No sign of that."

"Are they just falling apart down there? Do you think old Julian finally croaked? It seemed only a matter of time," the drinking partner mused.

"Round up everyone. Whoever would assume control, they'll not come after us, not yet. We need to saddle up and get pre-emptive. We circle slightly to the west and use that road as a back door; no matter who is left at their posts, nobody in the capital watches from that direction." The commander barked at the scout, who then hurried out the door.

The drinking partner looked doubtfully at his

commanding officer. "Aren't we sworn to leave them alone or something?"

"The way I see it is this," the commander said, stroking his beard once in thought, "Jarek swore an oath. He's not here in this room right now, is he?"

"That's a bit disingenuous; we answer to him so that oath should apply to us."

"The capital is on fire, you fool. We go in there, we restore order, we are in charge, and by extension Jarek is King. I don't know where Lenn is, but he's clearly not getting the job done if the place is on fire; that's his problem."

The drinking partner edged his chair away from the table to prepare for standing as he thought about such technicalities.

"Well, that could be the opportunity of a lifetime. But we're also completely unauthorized; would it not make sense to ask Jarek first?"

"No, because maybe you forgot he's out past the wall making war on a bandit king. By the time he comes back, the capital could be a settled affair. If Jarek is cross with us, we basically go, 'sorry we acted out of turn, by the way here are the keys to the entire bloody kingdom,' does that not sound like the type of apology he would enthusiastically accept?" The commander stood up, hoping he didn't have to explain further.

The drinking partner followed him to standing. "Very well, I guess you're already getting the group together. But if this goes sour, everything was your idea. You're the commanding officer."

"If you're going to claim you're just following orders, start now by shutting your mouth and following them!"

* * *

QUEEN MONIKA WAS LIVID.

Unbeknownst to her, it was the morning before Jonnecht's soldiers would attack the City in the Valley. All she understood was that neither her nephew nor any of his riding companions could be found when she woke up; all she could do was alert the capital guard to close ranks and close the gates of the castle wall.

Even the musicians had vanished. She would not be shocked if the servants did the same.

But Monika needed to hide that lividity, to appear to Julian that nothing was wrong, because she thought that the slightest ill tidings might end his life. She had no heart to do that for personal reasons, and it was also terribly impractical when the heir had disappeared.

"My beautiful wife, it's too quiet in here. I can hear the wind. Is something the matter?" Julian asked hoarsely into her ear.

His voice was a bit louder, but he laboured. His medicine was fast wearing off, so some of his alertness returned, but horrible pain followed close behind.

"Oh, it's just a quiet day, save for the winds." She replied. "A chill has pervaded the air, and it's for the best that you stay near this hearth today. You might be vulnerable to the reach of the ancestors."

He thought about this for a moment.

"Well, that might not be so bad anymore."

"Please, husband, never talk like that." She drew his comforter up his chest a little bit; it was going to ride back down because he was sitting up, but she thought to at least make the effort.

All the efforts today had been hers. She tended to the hearth's fire, the only one left in the castle at that time, and she stayed at Julian's side. Every day she wore the same lavender dress; she had never preferred the details of the piece, but she knew he loved it.

"It's probably better, yes, that I die here in the warmth of love," Julian said. "When I join the Winds, I will no longer have a body to feel the chill. I will find us a nice tall cloud and I will ready us a palace there, my love, grander than the Kenderley Palace. We shall have the best view of every sunrise."

She embraced him. "Julian, is it really so close? Can you feel it?"

His eyes seemed increasingly unfocused, as if he saw something far away. "Stay with me. I'm scared."

* * *

THE MESSENGER GUARD easily made it into the royal chambers because there was nobody at that bedroom door to stop him, nor at any door; all the other guards and soldiers were outside.

"My Lady..." He said before she glared him to silence; then he just shook his head.

The Market Square was a raging fire, and that fire was

spreading. It was not the only one. A frightful blaze would spring up, many capital guards would mobilize against it, but another blaze just like it would erupt elsewhere before they could contain the first. Able-bodied citizens had formed bucket brigades, but soon enough there were too many infernos.

After so many fires had begun, strange belligerents took to the streets, assaulting whoever stood against them. Soldiers were drawn into chasing and scuffles. Between this and fire-fighting, no one wanted to stand at the perimeter of the castle grounds; no one had dropped the portcullis in case they needed to return or let others flee at great haste. Opportunistic belligerents rushed this open entrance and raided the armoury; they captured boulder-casters. Heavy stones clumsily arced across the skies.

They had not yet dared invade the main section of the castle, but it seemed inevitable.

Now, having seen a dead King Julian, and the grieving Queen Monika next to him, this messenger understood it was no use. He glanced away for a moment, crestfallen.

Then he looked apologetically into her eyes. Each understood from the countenance of the other that it was the end of everything they knew. Down the hall, a boulder struck a window, and glass loudly shattered.

She waved him away. He might have some means of escape, but not in that room. He drew his dagger and fled.

Monika already knew the warmth remaining in that bed was her own, and Julian no longer breathed, nor would he ever again.

"Then make me a space in the clouds," she said to Julian, "I could be along shortly."

She tucked him in neatly and kissed his forehead. Then she found her sword.

As they prepared for this day, Ignacy had worried that they would draw too much attention to themselves with the sound of chiseling and scraping, the widening of the cellar drain. To his apparent fortune, so much went on around the castle and outside it that nobody noticed.

The three invaders lifted buckets with oil and implements of fire into the cellar before climbing out of the hole; they had carved themselves hand- and footholds up that drain long ago. They didn't have to widen or break any other part of the passage except for the drain; metal bars mortared into the masonry topped a passage that, like all others in the system, had always been wide enough to fit construction workers.

"Start dousing. If you find their stock of lamp oil, add it to the mix while you wait. Just make sure I come back before you light it, so we can all get out." Ignacy instructed his two minions, who were in their late twenties, not much younger than him; he wouldn't trust children on this mission.

Ignacy drew his short sword and left them to that task. He stalked up the spiraling staircase, one of a couple that ascended from the cellar, with the soft steps of a thief. He reached the entrance to the main level just in time to jump at the loud slamming of a door.

So, not every servant had left, or perhaps that was some messenger. He couldn't imagine the Queen running, especially not when her long-ailing husband lacked the strength to follow.

He swiftly checked the ground level: the waiting hall, the banquet room, the throne room. Not a soul to be found. Perfect; if he had been provided correct information about the castle, then there was one central stairwell leading to the bedrooms upstairs. His enemies must be trapped...

Still alone but cautious, he crept along searching for that stairwell, stopping only at the sound of pained shouts from somewhere below. The way echoes carried in those halls, he supposed someone had killed whoever he had heard slamming doors. Or maybe one of those oafs in the cellar tripped on something in painful fashion. It would probably not matter. Their job should be a quick one. Given the time this search was taking him, they should have nothing else to do now but wait for his return.

Then he found the central stairwell.

As he climbed it, Ignacy scraped the flat of his sword against the metal rail which protruded from the middle of these wide steps. Now that he believed he was alone up here with the King and Queen, he felt no more need for stealth.

"Come out and face me! There is no escape."

The only answer was the sound of a window smashing down the hall as another boulder struck the castle.

He reached the top of the stairs and looked down one quiet hall, then another.

"There are only two ways out of this, you decadent weaklings. My steel will taste your guts, or you can die in a fire after I leave. I give you to the count of ten!" Ignacy called.

Then he began to smell something burning. He turned to see Queen Monika, whose sword and best dress were equally blood-spattered. She grinned sardonically at the little man who caused so much trouble.

"I could say the same for you, Iggy. Perhaps neither of us leaves..."

His eyes widened. "You lit the fires? And you're still here? Has grief driven you mad?"

She stopped at the base of the steps.

"Your minions lit it, intending to leave without you. Don't worry, I made sure they couldn't get out. And the damned flames spread through the cellar." Monika scowled.

"But there are ways out behind you, fool! Will you not flee?"

Monika laughed wickedly. "Not if that means letting you out. We'll burn together."

Ignacy tried to cross over to one side of the staircase in wide-eyed panic; Monika would dart over to whichever side he tried to descend. He thought she must be bluffing. He waited for her to crack, but all she did was laugh with tearful eyes.

"I'm the only one left, Iggy. Don't you want to defeat us once and for all? Or are you scared?"

Then he dove off a higher step toward her, short sword poised, with the most pathetic whining rendition of a battle cry. She sidestepped his falling form and deflected the blade which he clumsily swung on his way down. He had no time to do anything before he felt her sword enter between his shoulder blades.

She planted her heel on his sword-hand's wrist as he

twitched through his death throes. She let go of her sword, leaving it lodged in him.

Monika felt the heat rise behind her as the flames crept up runners and wood panels and reached for the air that came in from smashed windows.

She stepped off the dead man's wrist and took a long look at the hallway entrance, tears beginning to spill from her eyes.

She didn't have to die in a fire, but there was no escaping the end of everything she knew.

Monika, destined not to be Queen of anything for much longer, turned and hurried for the kitchen. A trick wooden panel in the pantry revealed a tunnel that left the city altogether.

WHAT REMAINED of the capital guard, and of those soldiers from the west who did not accompany Lenn, abandoned all hope of dousing the fires. It was better to lead survivors out to safety through the widest streets and some of the abandoned rain tunnels.

The surviving guards dealt with a good share of weeping younger people who had failed to imagine what this would be like and who gave themselves up as prisoners, renouncing ever sneaking out of their homes to go with Ignacy; some of them were young enough to think it was all a game, or that all the grown-ups would be chased outside before any fires were set. They were bound at the hands for later consideration and watched closely but hurried to safety with all others. What would later be said about those who never paid attention to these youths, and never understood what was happening to them?

Most headed west. The land once ruled by the good Duke was known to be charitable to those in need, for there was plenty of everything. The survivors looked among themselves; was Lenn himself hiding in a cloak? What happened to him, after all...?

Some would head north toward Jarek. His domain always had a place for new people because they constantly tried and failed to expand past their frontier wall.

But whatever came after Wancyrik would not dare wear this name. The kingdom had failed at its very heart. The former capital would be avoided for generations, presumed to be haunted and cursed.

21
ENCOUNTER ON THE WESTERN ROAD

The approaching force had been set aside by Jarek to deter any attacks from the capital province; as such, he made sure it was of considerable size to put up heavy resistance, yet mobile enough that it could flee and regroup with the rest of his army against an insurmountable force.

It was mobilized for a different purpose. The commander, drinking partner to his right, rode on horseback just like the others. Riders on the sides of the formation carried torches, given what the time of day might be by the time they expected to do anything in the capital.

"This ride has taken a lot longer than expected; this route is deceptively roundabout," the commander remarked to his friend.

"Well, if it's all burned down by the time we get there, that will be terribly easy to capture, and not much of a prize for Jarek."

The commander grunted. "This turn being the half-way

mark on the map, it feels rather late to be having second thoughts. But yes, not much of a conquest..."

As they nosed their horses around the corner of the road carved through the hills, they immediately saw what they had not bothered to listen for over the sound of their own horses and light armour.

Battered capital guard members leaned on staves and stood watch as folks, many weeping, made their way up the road, toward the west, filing neatly from the direction of the capital.

An imposing man, former door guard of the Market Square, pushed a hefty cart of belongings; he glanced at the approaching riders and slowly shook his head before continuing down the path to safety.

The commander put a gloved hand up and the order was relayed behind him for all riders to halt, just as this sight had halted him.

"I say, guardsman: do you have any idea what happened in the capital? We... saw massive fires from our outpost. And we rode here in concern," lied the commander.

One of the Capital Guard stood straight, hand still on his stave, and shook his head slowly.

"You know, I'm not sure I care anymore whether you're lying. Ride down past the people and have a look for yourself. Perhaps by the time you get there, the flames will have nothing more to consume."

"Well, that's equal parts disturbing and unhelpful," noted the commander.

His drinking partner clapped his shoulder and pointed. "Sir, look straight ahead, across from us."

Another large group made their way up from the south. This one looked predominantly like soldiers, whether on horseback or in wagons. Any pattern or insignia to their leathers could not be made out from that distance and in that diminishing light.

But that group must have seen Jarek's men with their bright torches, because the main group slowed to let a horse-driven wagon get ahead of them. This brought a lone injured man.

Jarek's commander began. "You there! Are you willing to answer what exactly has happened? We saw massive fires from an outpost on Jarek's realm—"

"I am Tibor. I have a message you can bring to Jarek. I assume you speak the truth and did not come to harass these unfortunate folks. I'll trade this message for news of what's become of the capital, if you or anyone else knows," said the man in the wagon.

A capital guard turned around upon hearing the introduction. "Tibor? We thought you died in the flames, man! Did you escape south? Is Lenn among you?"

"What happened to the capital? What of the King and Queen?" Tibor asked aloud, puzzled that Jarek's soldiers equally sought such answers; he would have expected Jarek to have been behind it.

The capital guard blinked rapidly. "Most of the strange belligerents are believed slain. The youngest of them surrendered in tears, saying something about Ignacy ordering the fires; no idea who that is or what happened to him. The castle itself..." He shook his head.

Tibor knew that name. He almost yelled in frustration. So

much for trusting Captain Bruno to handle things; if only they had all listened to Samuel.

"Julian had little time, but I wished Monika would be safe." Tibor said.

"We saw neither die, sir, it's just that we haven't seen them at all," the guard corrected, "but I would have little hope for the great King knowing his condition."

The commander of Jarek's detachment, listening quietly, understood that the elder struck to the ground by his lord may have died in flames, or even of inner wounds from his master's attack. Though an opportunistic sort, the commander was a person. He could not look into the eyes of these people and think of capturing a tragically lost domain; not now.

But he was left with a question yet unanswered.

"Lord Jarek will ask after Duke Lenn," the commander interrupted sheepishly.

Tibor sighed painfully. "His spirit is given unto the Winds. Lenn perished a hero, leading us to victory against the forces of King Jonnecht."

His words cast a pall over everyone within earshot, and news quickly travelled to the back of the formation of Jarek's riders. It would take longer to travel in either direction of that queue of former capital dwellers.

The commander looked down the road from whence the refugees came. Then he looked down at the ground in shame.

"It's over, then, for House Wancyek. Over for the kingdom."

It was easy to resent Julian and to want to act against him. It was more difficult to hate Lenn for winning a fair fight against a man of similar age and in better physical shape, though the commander's loyalty to Jarek ran deep in unspoken ways.

Tibor replied: "If Jarek will hear my advice, stranger, he should understand that everyone who travels west looks to make a new and peaceful life. We have no desire for that cursed capital, no taste for war, and no conflict with your lord, for he is freed from his agreement; there is no throne to which he would surrender. He may wish to prepare himself in case the Kenderleys return with a vengeance. We would appeal to his martial sense of honour and decency.

"And if you'll hear my advice, stranger, turn around; tell him you rode to see what happened. Tell him you brought soldiers in case it was the Kenderleys, and you turned back the moment you heard all this news. Jarek was willing to keep his word out of respect to our fallen hero, and we know his temper. I would not wish a terrible fate upon you."

The commander considered this, nodded, and ordered his group to turn around.

Tibor then signalled for the rest of his group to overtake his wagon and join the refugees heading west. He thought of Zinnia and her child, who, like all others, merely sought peaceful lives.

It was, indeed, over for House Wancyek and for the kingdom.

But hope for the future still lived. It would dwell in the north, in the west, and in the hearts of a woman and her child.

EPILOGUE

"Mother?"

He looks in the bedroom, the kitchen, the front yard. Where has she gone this time?

"Mother?"

He checks the garden in the yard, then the barn. Finally, he remembers where else she could be, but it doesn't make him happy.

He runs to the edge of the property, the respectable farm-house and plot to which Zinnia and her son moved after the former Duke's Manor became the temporary seat of the Free Plains government. He scrambles over the sturdy livestock-fence and toward a grassy cliff.

There sits Zinnia, gazing at the distant water.

"Mother," he complains, "you know I dislike you sitting here. That stony beach is a long way down, and all it would take is for you to slip."

"Sit with me, then," Zinnia replies, "and make sure I don't fall."

He looks much like his father, but she can see some of herself in him.

Though a considerable amount of time has passed since they settled here, Zinnia has fared well for her age. It's the tiredness of her eyes that betrays her old soul.

With her thumb, she lightly taps the face of the pendant on the silver necklace she wears and observes the sun setting far to the west, as if falling into the ocean. Moments ago, a Longneck had reared out of the deep water, merely a thin moving sliver in the distance that quickly vanished. It takes patience for anybody to see one. That, and keen eyes.

She lets go of the pendant when he speaks again.

"They call me exemplary in my studies," he tells her. "They will allow me to end my schooling now if I wish."

"Do you know what you would do with your life?" She asks calmly, the sort of question he dislikes but eventually must answer.

He stares at the sunset. He takes the sight for granted, since he has no memory of a home other than this scenic property, but his mother frequently enjoys the colours.

"I wish I could ask my father. I think he would have something wise to say."

She places an arm around one of his shoulders.

"Now, what makes you think that?"

He accepts this embrace casually. He used to squirm a bit when she hugged or placed an arm on him, but it doesn't bother him so much now.

"They always have a quote from him at the study hall. It seems like he only ever said wise things."

She nods slowly. She understands the pressure. The more time that passes, the greater the mythology around Lenn seems to grow. Some expect his son to be this titan, this demigod, though the tragedy behind his name will keep the Council from offering him leadership; he works hard to do his best, but she fears he will resent the expectations. People sometimes need reminders to let her son be a person like any other, living a peaceful and meaningful life.

"Was he really like they say?" He asks. "A giant of tree's height, able to satisfy his hunger for days at a time with chest-nuts and raw acorns in the wilderness if need be?"

Zinnia laughs. "What, they say he was half squirrel?" She lets the humour drop, for she understands it's a serious matter to him. "Son, I hope you understand how they make a legend of him. He was a man, much like you have grown into."

"What kind of man was he, then?"

"Oh," she wants to say he was a good man, and leave it at that, but this is hardly informative, so she considers carefully what to say.

"He had a noble heart, a yearning to do what was right, but a mind capable of compromising even his heart for the sake of loyalty. When faced with an apparent choice, between a duty to the throne and a duty that made him feel he deserved that throne, he knew only one thing to do. He was sincere, cautious to love, but eternally giving to the ones he loved."

She removes her arm from its place across his shoulders. "If you stayed to study, son, I would want you to consider the tales that seem least exaggerated about him. The ones that show a living person; Tibor wrote earnestly of him, for example. I couldn't make you, though. This is your life. I think your father would tell you to consider the reasons all you like, but never forget the difference between what you see is right and what others demand of you. Or maybe I put words in his mouth."

A long pause ensues. He wants something simple to resolve the conversation, a summary. That's not what she does, so it's up to him.

"I guess he would have been happy to know that we lived. It's easy to assume he would have loved nothing more than to see us here."

"Especially you, all grown up and enjoying a sunset," Zinnia muses.

He nods. "Perhaps the rest is for us to decide."

They sit there for a moment. The sun is almost finished for the day, and the clouds reflect brilliant reddish orange hues. The moon will conquer the sky not long from then.

Zinnia silently agrees. They lead lives Lenn gladly gave his own to protect, not even knowing if his actions avenged their deaths instead. To survive, to live their lives in peace and to uphold a community that remembers what he stood for, is like a gift they give every day to his spirit.

A light wind whispers by, for a moment lifting strands of her hair, then letting them settle.

"Shall we go?" He breaks the silence.

"We can. First," Zinnia reaches back and carefully undoes the clasp of the fine necklace, "I think this better fits you than I."

"Yours...?" He's puzzled, but doesn't resist her putting it around his neck.

"I once gave that to your father. He wore it as a hero, and it returned to me. But it can belong to a good and dignified man. As you have become." She says, her voice faltering as tears emerge.

"Oh, mother." He helps her up. "Please don't cry. This has been a pleasant day, right? Come inside, and perhaps some tea will help you feel better."

The survivors carefully turn away from the cliff, climb the short but sturdy livestock-fence, and walk toward their house.

A hawk watches from above, wings outstretched, upheld by the winds that know him intimately.

THE END

ACKNOWLEDGMENTS

I would like to acknowledge the role of the *Advanced Seminar in Social and Political Thought: Postcoloniality and the Nation* course of the Fall/Winter 2006/2007 semester for how it shaped my treatment of empire, colonialism, and war in these six books. Through seminars, lectures, tutorials, and conversations, I encountered many different ideas in my time at York University, but this course stands out as one that inspired me to approach some fantasy fiction tropes differently.

Thank you, Dianna, for editorial advice.

Thank you, Brendan Perry and Lisa Gerrard, for the music you made together and as individuals that was there for me on a playlist nearly every first draft of this six-book series.

I would once again, and finally, like to acknowledge everyone who supported me through these six books. I have no set plan for what comes next, but I am happy enough with where we have gone so far.

ABOUT THE AUTHOR

Dylan Madeley is a Torontonian currently working out of a headquarters in Vaughan, Ontario. He is the copy editor of and a frequent contributor to Auxiliary Magazine, an alternative fashion and music zine.

His first novel, The Gift-Knight's Quest, was released May 28, 2015. He has appeared at The Word on the Street Festival in Toronto, Canada's largest book fair, and successfully debuted his second novel, The Crown Princess' Voyage, at the Ad Astra convention in May 2017.

He completed his trilogy with the official release of The

Masked Queen's Lament in July 2018. His fourth book, Alathea: Goddess and Empress, was released in the disastrous pandemic month of May 2020; his fifth, Prince Ewald the Brave, was released May 1, 2021. His latest, The Fate of Lenn, rounded out the series on September 14, 2021.

Manufactured by Amazon.ca
Bolton, ON

38178086R00177